Homicidal Humor

Street Stories, Statements, Confessions and Quotes

Sgt. Brian Foster

ISBN: 0983707308
ISBN-13: 978-0983707301

DEDICATION

I would like to dedicate this book to the memory of the man who was both my father and my friend. Early in my life he instilled in me his love of "hard sayings." Some of his favorites and mine appear in the chapter titled *Quotes from the Uncouth*.

CONTENTS

DISCLAIMER

Welcome to the world of urban police legend and lore. Although inspired by true life, this book is a work of fiction. The following fables that make up *Homicidal Humor* are either completely fictional, or based upon some rather mundane investigation that has been highly embellished or embroidered upon.

If I had firsthand knowledge of the events described herein, I would likely be hauled before both federal and state investigative grand juries. What I have actually done is record stories told to me by cops from all over this country. In some cases, stories are based on a single incident related to me several times, with the alleged city of origin varying by as many as three different cities.

These stories are set in areas along the Texas Gulf Coast and include historical facts and interesting tidbits about the city of Houston and its police department. All individuals, as well as locations alluded to, are fictitious. You might say the names have been changed to protect the imbeciles. Only the chapters regarding quotes, street terms, and Ronnie Beck are true. The rest were created for entertainment purposes only.

Have a good read.

WELCOME TO SODOM

A bit of history….

The city of Houston was founded on a pigeon drop land development scheme pulled off by two New Yorkers, John K. and Augustus Allen, commonly referred to as the Allen brothers. They founded what was to become the fourth largest city in the United States on the swampy Texas coastal plains, along the banks of Buffalo Bayou, where the town of Harrisburg once stood. Harrisburg was burned to the ground by the Mexican army following the battle of the Alamo. The town founded by the Allen brothers was renamed for Sam Houston, a hero of the Texas Revolution. Local legend says that the Allens determined the exact spot where Houston was to be founded (known as Allen's Landing) in one of two ways—either where they ran aground as they floated down Buffalo Bayou, or where they stopped so that one of them could change out his chew of tobacco.

This muddy bayou (a slow-moving stream) is not named for the noble cloven-hoofed animal followed by the Plains Indians. Instead, Buffalo Bayou is named for the oily trash fish that still inhabits its waters. This sluggish waterway is either green or brown in color, depending on whether there is runoff or an algae bloom, and it is always murky. Locals proclaim the waterway to be "too thick to drink and too wet to plow."

Houston was billed by the Allen brothers as having sea breezes and a tropical climate, yet most of their descriptions left out the details of hellish hot summers and high humidity. They also neglected to mention the hordes of mosquitoes that swarm the area and spread a multitude of diseases, which include, but are not limited to, malaria and several types of encephalitis. It should be noted that the Allen brothers bought and developed huge areas of farmland. They laid out a city with broad streets, sold off the lots, and became very wealthy by selling agricultural land at the market rate of one dollar per acre.

Houston very likely would have remained just a backwater town had it not been for corruption within the city of Galveston. Galveston was a natural deep-water port with several navigable rivers leading into it. As a city, Galveston had three things going for it: location, location and location. "The Island City" also came equipped with very well-established organized crime operations and ingrained local corruption problems. These problems gave the city of Houston proper incentive to dig a twenty-seven mile long ship channel, large enough for ocean-going ships to navigate, creating an inland port. Houston would later become the second largest port in the nation, and the seventh largest in the world. All this occurred just to get away from the problems encountered when dealing with the islanders.

The one thing about Houston that has never changed since its frontier days is its Old West orientation. The corny expression "God did not make all men equal, Samuel Colt did," still holds true today. To this day the hanging tree used when Houston was founded still stands. Originally located on the outskirts of town, it now sits, ironically, two blocks west of the United States Federal Courthouse. A historical marker notes the hanging tree's history at the corner of Bagby and Capital streets.

Old-time Texas logic dictated, "There are some men that really need killing, but there ain't no horses that really need stealing." Keep in mind that many of Houston's early inhabitants either arrived with very little looking for something, or they had been run out of everywhere else.

The political climate varies throughout the state of Texas, as do local rules regarding the state penal code and the way those laws are adjudicated. The way justice is meted out depends on where you live. For example, in the Rio Grande valley, along the Mexican border, all criminal convictions are open to a possible probated sentence. It doesn't matter if the criminal charges filed happen to be murder or possession of 100 pounds of marijuana; probation is always looked upon as a viable option.

Beware however, if you shoot someone while in the cosmopolitan city of Dallas. Even under the best of circumstances, the police are likely to try and build a case against you. Then the Dallas County District Attorney's Office will attempt to ruin your life, even if your actions were justified under state law. Just ask the first man with a concealed carry handgun permit in Texas to be involved in a fatal shooting. He was being brutally beaten by a truck driver and was unable to get away or defend himself. His attacker was a man half again his size, but the assault victim justly dispatched his attacker by shooting him with a .40-caliber Glock pistol.

Unfortunately, the real victim in that case—the man assaulted by the truck driver—was arrested and charged with murder, even though the shooting was justified under Texas law. The charges were not warranted, and a grand jury ultimately dismissed them a month or two later. Despite that, the Dallas County District Attorney's Office espoused that they still held life to be sacred, which was their basis for charging the assault victim with murder. The real victim (the shooter) was out the $10,000 to $20,000 it took to defend himself against the State of Texas. Justice is said to often jump the track east of the Trinity River, the line where Tarrant County (Fort Worth) ends and Dallas County begins.

Under a similar set of circumstances in Houston, the police will take your statement and tag your weapon in their firearms laboratory. Within two to three months, your case will be presented to a Harris County grand jury. If you are no-billed (cleared) by the grand jury, the police will gladly return your weapon to you. Both the police and the district attorney's office in Houston understand that "there are some folks out there that just need killing." These shootings are referred to locally by many investigators as either urban renewal or predator control cases.

In Texas, by statute, all violent death cases must be reviewed by a local grand jury. In Harris County, Texas (in justifiable fatal shooting, stabbing or beating cases), such cases are simply sent to the grand jury section of the district attorney's office for review. News releases in these types of cases will reflect that the case was referred to the district attorney's office without charges. These cases are bound and cataloged in a bundle of reports that include witness statements, suspect statements, photos and diagrams.

When statements are taken from a shooter, whether the shooting was justified or not, it is taken in the form of a confession. The shooter's legal warnings (Miranda warnings) are laid out in the format. This is a tricky prospect, for the real victim (the one who has just taken the life of some dirt bag) can potentially have his freedom denied if he signs a statement that has been wrongly worded. The investigator typing a statement can often pre-determine a grand jury's absolution or indictment, simply by the way he shades or words a statement. Here's how it goes: The citizen who was just forced to kill someone is in a state of shock. He or she will question very little and will sign almost any statement shoved in front of them that has the correct date, time and location listed. These folks are usually scared and will agree to many things if they feel like they have a friend in the room, namely a friendly and helpful detective seated right across from them. The attitude of the Houston Police Department's Homicide Division, 99.9 percent of the time, is to help out the good folks and piss on the crooks.

When it comes to urban renewal shootings, Fort Worth and Houston share a similar perspective. The good citizens of Tarrant County support their law enforcement to the hilt. If you're a crook and you mess up in Fort Worth, you will immediately become identified as being a Philistine. As such, the rules of engagement dictate that you will be smote hip and thigh, repeatedly. The good citizens of Cow Town want it that way. Flashlights and nightsticks have now taken the place of the jawbone of an ass.

A side note to this topic is that many rural counties in Texas literally do not have the necessary funds to prosecute cases. Their position (though they will never openly admit it) is that they do not want to pay for an autopsy, much less the investigation and prosecution of crimes committed against victims not from their jurisdiction. A capital murder case in Texas can cost taxpayers up to one million dollars from conviction through to the appeals process. An example of such a mindset comes from down near the Mexican border, where one Houston investigator's father was the foreman on a large south Texas gas pipeline project. In that region of Texas sat one particularly huge ranch where illegals frequently crossed to enter Texas from Mexico. This ranch had its own full-time security force, staffed by personnel—most of whom were former Army Rangers—who drove four-wheel drive vehicles to patrol the premises. Many of these security personnel were born on that land. Their roots often went back multiple generations on that particular ranch. Their parents and possibly their great-grandparents may have been buried in the ranch cemetery. Their culture was rooted in both Anglo and Mexican ways, and they even spoke a mixture of both languages, which some folks refer to as Spanglish or Tex-Mex.

During the pipeline construction project, human skeletal remains were discovered on an almost daily basis, and construction would have to stop. The sheriff's department and a justice of the peace were called out. The local authorities would walk around for a bit, kick a few rocks and proclaim the remains to be "old Indian bones." They would then gather up the bones in question and direct the construction operations to continue. One thing continued to strike the construction crew chief as odd, though. It bothered him that some of those old Indians were still wearing remnants of blue jeans and some had gold or silver fillings in their teeth. The sheriff's department in that particular county is highly acclaimed and supported by the local residents. Whenever a homeowner or rancher was forced to shoot someone, the deputies were known to be very community oriented. The County Mounties (as they are called) are so thoughtful that they will literally drag a body to any location you'd like prior to the taking of crime scene photographs.

The most human side of life is evident in homicide investigations, and if you don't get personally involved, it can be darned entertaining as well.

A LITTLE KNOWLEDGE

Kewanna Anderson (pronounced Anacin, like the aspirin) passed on to his untimely—and very likely his just—rewards following a cuss-fight with a neighbor named Dante Howard. The cause of Anderson's earthly departure was a .38-caliber bullet placed approximately two inches above his belly button.

'Wanna (Anderson) had recently taken up with Dante's former beloved, a Nubian princess named Syberia Cain, who was well known by most of the neighborhood folks, but only by her street name, Bay-Bay. According to witnesses, the killing occurred because Dante apparently took offense to being called "A needle-dicked punk mother-f**ker." The newly-sainted "Mister Anacin's" passing would have gone unnoticed, had it not been for the actions of some of his dim-witted (but good-intentioned) kin folks.

The dearly departed was center-punched with a 158-grain lead hollow-point bullet. He reportedly died just moments after fire department paramedics arrived. They had no sooner hooked him up to their machines when he was noted to be unresponsive, and had no vital signs. They unplugged their equipment and told the first uniformed police unit that arrived, "This guy is as dead as a hammer, and we're out of here." The blue suits held the scene until Homicide showed up, which was about an hour later.

Refuse and disorder in this neighborhood is the norm. The detectives made their notes, spoke with witnesses and gave the scene an overview for what they deemed might be evidence. It is often hard to determine just what relates to your scene investigation and what is simply filth or trash left behind by the losers that infest a neighborhood such as that one. The cops then promptly got the hell out of the 'hood before tempers flared.

You see, it really doesn't matter who actually killed Homey—in this case Mr. Anderson—you had just better not leave him lying out in the middle of the street too long. If you do, friends and family will get hostile and want to fight with the police. In the ghetto, family and friends get caught up in what the academics call an emotional transference of hostility. The killer is usually not available, so loved ones parley their grief into hostility and channel it toward the closest available authority figures. Who can figure out the logic in such a situation? In the lower quarters, when the outdoor air temperature gets close to that of body temperature, the hostility level of area residents increases rapidly. As soon as you pick up a body, the show is over. Crowds then disperse, and the hostile attitudes drop off markedly. A statement heard frequently at shooting scenes is, "Just get me two Polaroid photos of this scene (so the detective can describe it later in his report) and let's get that body loaded." If you don't, the likelihood of another killing in a close time period increases markedly.

When the girlfriend of the late Mr. Anderson gave her sworn statement in the Homicide Division that evening, Kewanna's passing became immortalized into a favorite story throughout that unit. His name has been long forgotten, but the antics of his kinfolks will be long remembered—and all because of the following statement.

STATE OF TEXAS
DATE: 8-17-02
COUNTY OF HARRIS
TIME: 7:55 PM

Statement of Syberia Cain

My name is Syberia Cain and I live at XXXX Dumfort in apartment XXXX. My home phone number is 713-XXX-XXXX. I am currently unemployed. I can also be reached by my pager at 281-XXX-XXXX. My Texas Driver's License number is XXXXXXXX.

My Social Security number is unknown. An alternative address I can be reached through is XXX Alicion in Houston, and the phone number there is 713-XXX-XXXX.

I spent last night over at my boyfriend Kewanna Anderson's house on Mayflower Street. He lives down the street from my ex-boyfriend Dante Howard. This morning after breakfast, about ten o'clock, Kewanna went outside to get something out of his car. A few minutes later I heard some screaming and yelling. I went outside to see what was going on. When I walked outside I saw that Kewanna and my former boyfriend Dante were arguing there. A crowd was gathering, and it included Dante's sister Julie. When I came out of the door, Julie pointed at me and shouted, "Here come your monkey." Dante laughed, and I heard Kewanna say, "The reason she dumped you (meaning Dante) was 'cause you ain't nuthin' but a needle-dicked punk mother-f**ker." Everybody laughed, and Dante pulled out a pistol and shot Kewanna in the belly for "dissing," or disrespecting, him. Kewanna was not bleeding much, but you could tell he was hurting bad. Dante ran off before the police or ambulance arrived. While in the Homicide office, I have been shown a photo of the man I know as Dante Howard, and who I saw shoot Kewanna Anderson. Just after the shooting, Kewanna's cousin Bobby and his uncle Ralph Comeaux got an extension cord and pulled it real tight around Kewanna's lower chest. They put the cord between the bullet hole and his heart as a tourniquet hoping to stop the bleeding, until the ambulance arrived. It didn't work, and he passed.

_____

Signature of person making statement

Sworn before me, the undersigned Authority this 17th day of August 2002, in Houston, Harris County Texas.

_____

Notary Public in and for the State of Texas

AIN'T MANY OLD FOOLS

Fifteen Edward Thirty, *see the complainant, a disturbance in progress. Shots fired. The 911 phone clerk reports she heard gunshots in the background— XXXX Martin Luther King—at Lester's Washateria. Any unit clear and close to check by with* **Fifteen Edward Thirty.**

Paul "Pops" Mouton was sixty-three years old, having retired from the Southern Pacific Railroad at age sixty. After six months of retirement he'd come to the conclusion that "Sex and fishin' is two things you can get behind on, and caught up on in a hurry." He then began to actively seek out some way to occupy himself. Pops wound up at Lester's Washateria, working five days a week. He would show up at three in the afternoon and shut the doors to the public six hours later. He could run his errands in the morning, work at the washateria, and be home in time for the ten o'clock news. Better yet, he got paid in cash and he and the old lady "Got along one hell of a lot better."

Paul now lived and worked in the neighborhood where he had grown up. It is known as Sunnyside, and has been rough and crime-ridden as long as anyone could remember. Paul knew the full name of well over half the people that walked through the washateria doors on any given day. On the afternoon of the night in question, he chanced to speak to a third cousin named Zelda Miller.

Zelda's youngest child, Zachary (also called either Junior or June Bug) had recently been paroled from prison. Mouton had seen him two days in a row, running with some really bad-news neighborhood thugs. Pops told Cousin Zelda as much, knowing that she would not want to see her baby go back to the joint. Zelda left the washateria as if her tail feathers were on fire, and hit the street at a dead run. She went to cold-trailing young Zachary like a prize-winning Red Bone hound.

Unbeknownst to Paul Mouton, Zelda caught up with her wayward boy-child thirty minutes after she'd left Lester's. She jumped Zachary in front of his hard-case friends and embarrassed the heck out of him. In the course of her lambasting him, it came out that Cousin Paul (Mouton) was the one who snitched him off. Zachary's pride caused him to storm off as his new friends stood around laughing at him. Junior then bought a bottle and proceeded to try and drown his troubles. Feeling better, he helped himself to a nine-shot .22-caliber revolver from the glove box of his brother's pickup truck. His plan was, in order to reclaim his manhood, to seek out the snitch and put him in his place.

At eight p.m., Paul Mouton shut off the washing machines so that the ladies' social circle would finish up by closing time. Fifty-three minutes later, Junior showed up. He, by now, was feeling no pain and was well armed. The drunk with wounded pride stood in the parking lot outside the washateria's front doors. Zachary began firing his pistol and yelling for Paul to come outside and atone for "puttin' my bidness out on da' street." Mouton locked himself inside the business, got behind a brick wall, and called 911. The responding one-man unit pulled up to the side of the building with headlights off. Officer Raymond Marx was exiting his marked patrol car just as Junior chose to round that corner of the building. June Bug's last mistake on earth was to point his gun at the wrong man. There is an old homicide saying that goes, "And tomorrow morning there'll be a newly-surprised face in Hell." June Bug was likely no exception.

"Who, me?" "Naw, man, you got it all wrong. I don't belong here. You can call and axe my Momma. She'll tell ya straight up how it is. My Momma don't lie."

Homicide made the scene, and Paul was interviewed and sent downtown for a sworn statement. The investigator he spoke with was trying to put the facts down on paper so the armchair quarterbacks could later understand just how everything happened. The investigator was trying to pinpoint that Junior was acting in a manner that made him dangerous and put Paul in fear of his life. The detective asked Mouton if he saw Zachary with a gun, and he said he did. Paul described locking the doors, calling the police and hearing approaching sirens. The sirens stopped, and about ninety seconds later, he heard one loud gunshot. Paul was asked if he looked outside when he heard the sirens or the loud gunshot. Paul answered "No, Sir." When asked, "Why not?" Paul tried to explain by saying, "Mister, it's like this here. There's a good reason there ain't many old fools in that neighborhood."

AIRPORT NARCS

One of the least publicized sectors of major metropolitan police work involves airport detail. Not only do these officers handle security for huge numbers of people, but where they work, smugglers and drug runners abound. The Narcotics Divisions, in particular, heavily staff airports. They use profiling and drug detection dogs as two primary tools. Ramey James and Juan Castrillon were narcotics officers assigned to Houston's Intercontinental Airport. Ramey was a transplant from Lake Charles, Louisiana and Juan (Johnny) hailed from Corpus Christi, Texas.

The Houston Police Department had recruited both men while they were still in the military. Former military personnel tend to do well in police work, because they've already lived a disciplined lifestyle, and know how to work both within, and around, a system. Ramey was tall, slim, dark-headed and male model pretty. Juan was a squat and powerful, flat-faced Mexican that sported a Poncho Villa quality mustache. Ramey often described Juan as looking like a Mayan fireplug. Juan could easily pick out and profile drug and money transporters. Ramey, on the other hand, typically struck out when trying to spot drug runners. Juan laughingly claimed that even the drug dogs lied to Ramey.

One red flag that narcotics officers always looked for was a turnaround trip being made by a single passenger. On one occasion, Ramey ran a daily manifest and got a hit on such a person named Otis Hart, who was returning to Houston from the lower Rio Grande Valley. The manifest indicated Hart left Houston at eight a.m. and was returning at five thirty p.m., with no checked luggage. Hart had one prior arrest in Houston for a misdemeanor marijuana possession, so, armed with a mug shot photo and a line of bullsh**, Ramey and Juan waited for their man.

Hart's plane arrived on time and the suspect in question was one of the first to deplane. He was both a portly and somewhat effeminate looking fellow. What's more, Hart was carrying a gym bag when he was stopped. The narcotics officers pulled Hart off to one side of the gangway, into an empty seating area, to conduct their interview. Ramey did the talking, and advised Hart they were narcotics officers and had reason to believe he was transporting contraband. The suspect denied the allegations, and balked when he was asked for permission to search his carry-on bag. When pressed, the man relented and agreed to the search. Ramey continued to interview while Juan knelt on the floor and went through the man's luggage.

Juan pulled a cloth Crown Royal whiskey bag out of the gym bag. He pulled the drawstrings open and peered inside. He then looked at Ramey and nodded his head. Ramey grinned and grabbed the bag from Juan. He reached inside it and triumphantly said, "No drugs huh? Then what do you call this?" as he pulled his hand from the bag, only to find he was holding a greasy dildo. Ramey James was speechless. Otis Hart just kept repeating the words, "Oh my, oh my," over and over again. Juan Castrillon could not talk, as he was too busy rolling around on the floor holding his sides and laughing.

Ramey scrubbed his hands until they were raw. He would later say that he would have microwaved his hands if he could have gotten the oven's door to shut. Juan made sure everyone in the Narcotics Division heard about his partner's big drug-profiling bust. The very first thing the next morning, Ramey went to a downtown adult bookstore that catered to a gay clientele. He then took out subscriptions to several homosexual magazines in Juan's name. For several years the magazines in question were delivered on a monthly basis to Juan Castrillon's listed address, the

Narcotics Division at the Central Police Station. In the words of the infamous Joseph Stalin, "Revenge is a meal best served cold."

BARRIO STREET JUSTICE
OR
WATCH WHAT YOU SAY

A uniformed unit responded to a call for service regarding an aggravated assault at the corner of Perry and Quitman. The reputed victim alleged he had been standing on a street corner visiting with a group of other young Hispanic males. An attractive young lady was said to have walked past and the victim passed judgment on her by saying, "Man, would I ever love to eat the crotch out of her panties." The complainant (alleged victim) said he thought it was odd that no one laughed at what he thought was an exceptionally hilarious statement. He said that talk of baseball and cars resumed, and one of the young men present simply walked off. That gentleman returned in five minutes with a pair of panties in one hand and a cocked .45 automatic pistol in the other, reportedly telling the victim, "That was my sister, you son-of-a-bitch. Now, start eating!" The victim seemed terribly offended when he was asked by one of the officers if he had been forced to ingest cotton or nylon.

HE WAS BIT SHOT

Tony Felder was dispatched to a shooting-ambulance call at XXXX Lyons Avenue, in front of Burke's Discount Liquor Store. Felder arrived to find a middle-aged black male shooting victim being loaded into an ambulance. The injured man was unconscious. Felder noted the ambulance number (for his hospital follow-up) and began trying to work the crowd of onlookers for information. Tony first called out, "Does anyone here know this man?" He got no response, other than a few heads being shaken from side to side. His next inquiry was, "Does anyone know what happened out here today?" A small, skinny little kid at the front of the crowd (who looked about eight years old) called out, "I do. Da Bit shot him." Tony knelt down and asked the youngster if he'd seen the shooting when it happened, to which the street urchin responded, "No, I dent. I seen da man just come 'round da corner of dat building. He took a couple steps and den he yelled out, 'The Bit shot me.' Den he fell down an' he dent say nuttin' else."

THE FREEZER GRANNY

Sara Lee Stannard was a frail old widow woman who lived in a downstairs efficiency apartment in northwest Houston. She had one child, a worthless ex-con lesbian daughter named Cynthia Ruth. Sara's only offspring would make most professional male wrestlers appear feminine by comparison. Though Cynthia did not have the words Love and Hate tattooed across her knuckles, they would not have detracted from her overall appearance. Sara Stannard's charitable behavior toward her substance-abusing Bull Dyke offspring was likely her only character flaw. As Cleopatra learned only too well, if you take a viper to your breast, you're gonna get bit. So it came to pass.

Miss Sara had lived in the same apartment for more than fifteen years. She visited with the office staff regularly and knew almost everyone in the complex by name. The office staff and most everyone else in the complex knew that her daughter was allowed to come and visit, but was not allowed to either spend the night or use Miss Sara's car. "Cindy's had some troubles in her past, you know," one resident commented. When the grieving daughter showed up at the complex, telling residents of her mother's sudden death, suspicions were immediately raised. The story told was that Miss Sara had been visiting relatives in Kansas and died of a massive heart attack. The tale continued that her mother's wishes were to be cremated and her ashes scattered about the old family homestead. The drug-addict daughter appeared to either not know about, or to have forgotten about, the pre-paid funeral plot beside Cynthia's late father.

The apartment manager, Iris Crutcher, was immediately suspicious. Miss Sara once told Iris (several years before) about buying a pre-paid funeral policy so that she would not burden anyone.

Following Miss Sara's untimely death, Cindy held a cash-and-carry estate sale and sold off all her mother's possessions, except for a chest freezer. The apartment manager noted the grieving daughter told everyone who walked into the apartment that the freezer was not for sale. Iris also keyed in on the fact that the freezer's top was sealed with multiple wraps of duct tape. At the end of the sale, Cindy told Iris that she would be back in two days with a truck, to pick up the freezer. Iris's brother also lived in the complex. He was retired from the Homicide Division of the San Antonio Police Department and now worked part-time at the complex as a handyman.

The story laid down by the retired cop at trial time was that he had been trying to run down an electrical problem plaguing several of the apartments the day after Cindy's estate sale. He testified that he had tested electrical circuits in two adjoining apartments before entering the apartment of the late Sara Stannard. Once inside, he tested several circuits, and then lifted the lid on the chest freezer to see if it was still running. Therein he found the frozen remains of Sara Lee Stannard. He was steadfast in his statement of facts. He also testified that there had been no duct tape around the lid of the freezer, and that the freezer's door had been unlocked. He did not testify to the fact that he was also trained as a locksmith, nor was he asked.

Haskell and Jenkins were the pair of detectives next up on the rotation when the "Frozen Granny in the Freezer" case came in. Knowing that everyone and his dog would read their report and armchair quarterback it at some later date, they obtained a search warrant to process the scene. The scene investigation was limited to photos and fingerprinting of the chest freezer. The apartment was clean and cleared of any trash or refuse. Cindy had seen to that, as she had need of her mother's security deposit.

Haskell and Jenkins were called Heckle and Jeckle by their co-workers (after the cartoon characters), and the nicknames were well-deserved. The investigators gave a somber statement to the news cameras that had gathered about the scene like blowflies on a dead cow. When Sara Stannard's body was rolled out of the apartment to the awaiting meat wagon (morgue transport vehicle), Heckle and Jeckle walked behind the gurney singing, "Everybody doesn't like something, but nobody doesn't like Sara Lee." The chief investigator at the county morgue would later report that Jenkins called him from the scene asking how to defrost a ninety-pound turkey.

Big breaks in murder cases often come about from what is sometimes called a "magic phone call." They occur more often than many investigators would like to admit. Such was the case in the clearance of the murder of Miss Sara. The Frozen Granny case got a lot of play from the television people, and that exposure brought out a witness. Early in the morning following the discovery of the body, Galveston Police detectives were calling Houston Homicide with information. A local street bum type in Galveston had supposedly made an admission to a group of bar patrons that he had been present when Miss Sara was strangled. The fact that she had been strangled had not yet been released to anyone. The supposed witness was a transient type who was well-known to the street officers, and was called "E.T." by everyone.

The Galveston cops said that they were quite sure they could find E.T. without any real difficulty, and they were positive he would become civic-minded and "volunteer" to come in for an interview. The Houston detectives headed south, and in an hour and a half were interviewing Eugene T. Wilson, a.k.a. E.T. Eugene was truthful and admitted to knowing the suspect in this case. He went on to say that he had been present when the victim was strangled with a bath towel. A phone call to the Harris County District Attorney's office provided a material witness warrant so E.T. could be detained for a polygraph examination and a sworn affidavit. He passed his lie detector test and his statement proved to be factual and entertaining as well.

Cynthia Ruth Stannard was subsequently arrested and charged with her mother's murder. E.T. got to live in a hotel for five days at the county's expense during the trial. He never wavered in his testimony. When the defense tried to discredit him based on his past, he flatly stated, "I'm a drunk, and an ex-con. A liar I'm not." Eugene did five years for the only felony he was ever arrested for. All of his other arrests were for minor infractions like drunkenness or disorderly conduct.

Two rather startling things came out during the testimony of a doctor named Ted Roberts, the medical examiner who performed the autopsy upon the remains. The first was that Sara was not dead when she was put into the freezer. The second was that someone had come back after the body was frozen and snapped off the ring finger from Miss Sara's left hand. Cynthia Ruth was found to have pawned her mother's wedding rings two days before the estate sale. The dead woman's initials and wedding date were engraved inside the wedding band, making them easy to identify. The jury had no difficulty sending Miss Sara's baby girl down the river for a very long stay.

The attached two-page affidavit is from the star witness in this case. E.T. Wilson, with his unique and interesting insights into the crime in question, saved the day.

Witness Statement

STATE OF TEXAS
COUNTY OF HARRIS
June 21, 2000
Time 3:15 PM

Before me, the undersigned authority, appears Eugene T. Wilson, a person known to me and who has sworn to or affirmed that the information contained in this instrument is true and correct to the best of his knowledge.

My name is Eugene T. Wilson, but everybody just calls me "E.T.", after the movie. I live above the A&G Lounge in Galveston, Texas. I do odd jobs and pick up cans to support myself. I basically kind of take life one day at a time. I've lived on the waterfront all of my life, and I tend to mind to my own affairs, and keep out of other people's business. The only time I've ever been in serious trouble was in 1985 when I caught my late wife in bed with my best friend. I marched her down to the East Jetties and made her jump in the ocean at gunpoint. I knew she couldn't swim, and she drown. I did five years for that.

I met Cindy Stannard when she worked at Rooster Miller's Bait Shop. It must have been about ten years ago. She left Galveston four or five years ago, and when she did, she took off with Bear, the best dog I

ever had. I was in the A&M lounge about a week ago and this woman sitting next to me up and asks me, "Well, are we gonna get married or what?" I had to look at her for a full minute before I realized I was looking at the bitch that had stolen my dog. She was with a big guy who she said she'd supplied transportation for him on some deal. I didn't ask any particulars. We drank several beers, and the guy she was with left with some Mexican looking fella. She asked me if I wanted to ride with her back to Houston. She had beer in the car, so I went with her.

We went to some little old lady's apartment in Houston. The old woman turned out to be Cindy's mother. I just sat around and watched TV and drank several cold ones. Cindy and the old lady went into the other room and got into an argument. I heard some yelling and some thumping against the wall. I walked into the other room and saw the old lady lying face down on the floor and Cindy sitting on the old woman's back. Cindy was all red in the face had a towel wrapped around the old woman's throat. Cindy looked up when I walked into the room and said "She won't die, she just won't die!" That was too heavy for me to handle, so I just kinda cruised back into the living room and finished off my beer. I heard some more thumps and bumps and then Cindy came back into the room. She asked me if I wanted to go back to Galveston, and I said I did. I was pretty well drunk by this time and didn't pay too much attention as to where we were headed. Instead of taking me to Galveston, Cindy drove me durn near half way to Louisiana and dropped me off in Winnie. It took me two days to hitch a ride back to Galveston. Several days later, I saw the deal on TV about an old lady being found froze stiff as a carp inside a freezer in Houston. When I saw the apartment complex on TV, I knew that it was Cindy's mom's place. I told some people at the bar about having been there when the killing happened. The next night after running my head, I was in the Houston City Jail. I am giving this statement because of what Cindy did. Croaking old people just ain't right. This is all that I know about the deal. I don't know about anything else that happened to the old woman. Cindy didn't say and I didn't ask.

_____

Signature of person making Statement

_____

Sworn before me this 21st day of June 2000. B.J. Bork a Notary Public in and for the state of Texas. My commission expires 1-15-2003.

KAREN

Karen Odom was born and raised on Houston's shallow north side. She was both a tomboy and an only child, and was raised as her father's only son. *Dear Old Dad* had been a Golden Gloves boxer in his youth and during World War II had been an army commando. He saw to it that on top of ballet and dance classes, his daughter knew Judo throws, kicks and the proper strike zones. "Always hit 'em where they live, girl. Remember, if a man's down, kick him. If he survives it, he can live to rise above it." Daddy always had a speed bag on his back porch. Both he and she religiously worked out on it for five minutes a day. Karen was raised hearing "Timing is everything in life, you know."

Karen attended John Reagan High School, whose alumni for several decades now have been reputed to either go into the penitentiary system as inmates or into law enforcement. More than one north side Casanova got his butt kicked trying to get too familiar with Karen. One wannabe bad-ass was shamed so badly that he quit school over the ribbing he got. It seems he was knocked out colder than a wedge at the Junior Prom by that little red-headed girl. Daddy was right; an upper cut isn't called a sucker punch for nothing.

Following two years of college, Karen joined the Houston Police Department. Upon graduation she was assigned to the Jail Division for a year. This was her first exposure to street whores, dope addicts, and Bull Dykes—the people Dad taught her to defend herself against. The rules in Jail Division were simple and straightforward: Come this way and do as you are told. If the prisoners tried to raise a hand or resist, they thought they were surrounded by red-headed banshees or a female version of Bruce Lee.

After a one-year hitch (and several allegations of brutality) Karen was transferred to the Sex Crimes Unit of the Juvenile Division. She soon was recognized for doing quality work and for aggressively working her cases. After six months in Juvenile she was drafted for a special assignment doing stakeout duty with the Robbery Division. The stakeouts were called for, following a series of armed robberies that occurred over a one-year period. The suspected robber always struck following open-air concerts at Herman Park's Miller Theater. The white male *jacker* blended in with the crowd and would rob well-dressed couples as they made their way to their parked cars. He pulled his robberies in a sporadic manner—maybe skipping between one and three concerts between heists.

The suspect's description varied enough that it was thought he might be using disguises. Robbery detectives had gone out in pairs to do surveillances at Miller Theater, but always came up empty. The suspect never struck while they were out there. A plan was formulated calling for male Robbery detectives to be paired up with female officers to hopefully identify and arrest the suspect. Detectives theorized that two men together on a stakeout had been unsuccessful, because they had stuck out like a star on a goat's butt. It was the detectives' hope that coed surveillance teams would blend into the crowd, hopefully as well as the suspect had. Her second night on this assignment, Karen was involved in what would be her first police shooting.

Stupid (the robber) picked the wrong couple to hijack that night. It is known that Karen hit the suspect with nine of the eleven 9mm rounds she fired. Her partner connected with only one from the three cartridges he got off. Karen drove herself to Homicide, typed her own statement and then had her pistol test fired in the firearms lab. After getting off that night she knocked down a couple of beers with her best friend, her dad. She would have gone straight home, but Dad had heard the shooting go down on the police scanner. He'd called her while she was still up in Homicide. She came to regret giving him that scanner more than once. The next day, Poppa Odom went out and bought his beloved daughter a .45-caliber pistol in the form of a lightweight Colt Combat Commander model. He knew from personal experience, that with the right gun she would need fewer rounds to put the trash where it belonged—below ground.

Two years and ten months after her graduation from the academy, Karen was promoted to the rank of detective and assigned to the Sex Crimes Unit of the Homicide Division. Detective Odom became renowned for her dedication to her job and her exceptional ability to mentally disarm sexual predators, and for getting many confessions from them. Reportedly, particularly when dealing with exceptionally brutal suspects, her strategy began by bringing an already-handcuffed prisoner into an interrogation room. Without so much as saying a word she would first drop kick him in the cojones, and then proceeded to whip the snot out of him with a phone book. She never raised her voice to him and would continue the whipping until he was groveling and became submissive.

The effectiveness of this program was once likened to the beating a vicious fear-biting German shepherd dog with a rolled-up newspaper. Suspects would enter the interrogation room with the attitude of a pack-leading alpha male street dog.

It's hard to be assertive if you're whimpering or have just pissed in your pants. Domination and degradation are two-way streets. The suspect used them on his rape victims. Karen used them on her serial or brutal suspects, which led to obtaining many confessions. Those confessions paved the way to a lot of long prison sentences. Of the cases where she was able to make identifications and arrests, her conviction rate was extremely high.

One of the funniest sides of Karen came out when her cases went to trial. She would testify in what she called her "Little Old Lady Outfits." She would appear in court looking like a rather dowdy grade school librarian. Detective Odom always showed up in a too-large and frumpy dress, wearing gloves and carrying a little old lady purse. She also typically wore a pillbox hat with some sort of tiered veils down across her forehead. She would sit on the witness stand clutching her purse with both hands. It was as if she were afraid that the evil defendant on trial would jump up and attempt to steal her pocket book at any moment.

The best of her trial testimony came when some defense attorney would inevitably ask this 120-pound person if she had beaten their client until he confessed to a crime he did not commit. She would answer in her best indignant grandmotherly voice with, "Did I whaaat?" Juries loved her—and so did the many victims whose cases she worked on so diligently.

JAILHOUSE MENTALITY

In some segments of our society, county jail or penitentiary time is just a part of life and holds no negative social stigma. Among the avowed criminal element, doing time is just the cost of doing business. Some idiots seriously hold to the belief that "You really can't be trusted until you've done time." Police officers learn early on that street trash expects to be cycled through the criminal justice system regularly. When you arrest and shake down the vermin on the street, you often find a wash cloth in the front of their pants to soak up the drips from their latest case of gonorrhea. Instead of going to the free health clinic for treatment, these dumbards will wait until their next rotation through the county jail system to see the "Jail Doc." Sometimes a crook will tell you that he won't mind copping to a one- or two-year sentence, because the last time he was in the joint the dentist didn't finish with all of his dental work before he was released.

When you try and explain to middle America how the thought processes of these idiots work, they either don't, or can't, comprehend such things and lifestyles exist. After a while you no longer attempt to explain such things to free world people. The other side of this coin may be seen in an expression used by prison system employees: "When you get to the point that you understand either convict orientation or humor—then it may be time to resign from the agency."

THEY ALWAYS LAND ON THEIR FEET

Bob Kroll and Jimmy Costa were partners in the Burglary and Theft Division for fifteen years. They were complete opposites in both personality and appearance. When it came to their work product they were completely focused and could have gotten a conviction on Mother Teresa for stealing from the poor. Kroll was slim with a fair complexion. He was a clotheshorse, and his temper was as quick as his right jab. His roots were in the shallow north side of Houston in an area called The Heights. The neighborhood he grew up in produced either cops or crooks, and very little in between. Costa was a hulking Galveston Island Italian who grew up in the construction trades. One of the pair's supervisors likened their partnership to a Rat Terrier and a Rottweiler being paired up. Kroll was nervous and extroverted, while Costa was very single-minded and everything about him exuded strength.

It was once said about Kroll that he was not happy unless he was flirting with either getting a divorce or a felony indictment. Kroll once joked that Costa had all the perfect attributes of a construction worker: a size five hat and a size 58 coat. Costa was a mother hen type, always looking out for the high-strung and trouble-prone Kroll. The two men had grown up in rough-and-tumble lifestyles, and enjoyed going after tough characters. They also worked a plain-clothes off-duty security job together at a trouble prone downtown department store. There they were regularly able to get into fistfights with shoplifters and street people. They looked upon the ability to get into fights as a job benefit, sort of like an employee discount.

Kroll and Costa were the kind of troops that supervisors call upon to work on problem or politically-charged cases. They knew how to take care of business, and crooks went to jail. Their reports read like a training manual, and you didn't ask too many questions about just how everything fell together so well. A large majority of their suspects gave confessions and seemed happy enough to be transferred to the county jail, just to get away from their captors. The pair was assigned to stop a rash of car burglaries at a posh downtown hotel frequented by high rollers and politicians.

The second night of the stakeout, they bagged an eighteen-year-old mother's son named Michael "Mickey" Nichols as he broke into a district court judge's Lincoln Continental. After the required body slam and handcuffing, Kroll told Nichols it was now time to confess the sins of his past. Mickey put on his best tough guy routine and suggested Kroll commit an anatomically impossible act upon himself. Following this soon-to-be-regretted suggestion, young Michael somehow fell off the second story of the parking garage. Kroll then ran downstairs and visited with him until he gladly confessed all. Big Jimmy Kroll stood by and took notes so that they could clear the cases Nichols was owning up to. Their offense report reflected that as soon as the suspect was handcuffed, and as they were trying to walk him to their police car, he escaped. Nichols was said to have stomped on Detective Kroll's foot, and then he broke from his grasp and ran off. The suspect was then alleged to have jumped over a three-foot high wall and to have fallen to the parking lot below in an attempt to complete his escape.

Mickey Nichols would, later in his criminal career, become a big time crook in and around the city of Houston. He first got notoriety as a cat burglar, and later became heavily involved in upper level narcotics deals. At the time of his arrest by Kroll and Costa, Mickey was on two years' probation for a tire store burglary. He'd been put on probation just weeks before he was nabbed. The detectives appeared for court as subpoenaed on Mickey's new *burglary of a motor vehicle* charge. Costa noted that Mickey was so afraid of Kroll that he actually shook when Bob was in the same courtroom with him.

Their suspect pled guilty and was sent off to prison for his first time. Nichols filed an internal affairs complaint and lawsuit from prison, alleging he had been thrown off a parking garage roof and denied medical attention until he confessed to multiple crimes. The abuse complaint was not sustained against the detectives, and the lawsuit was ultimately dismissed. Mickey served one year and was paroled. Kroll retired from the department six months after Nichols was discharged after his maiden voyage to prison.

True to form, Mickey could not stay out of trouble too long. Within a year he was arrested by night shift uniformed officers with a truckload of stolen goods. He was brought into Burglary and Theft so that the brand new duty Lieutenant, Jimmy Costa, could review the case before he was put in jail. Nichols was asked if he wanted to put his side of the story down on paper and he declined. The Lieutenant just smiled and told him "That's okay, Bubba, we'll just hold you over so Detective Kroll can get a chance to visit with you in the morning." Nichols immediately confessed and was subsequently sent back to prison. In fact, this scam was run on Nichols twice, sending him back to prison long after Kroll had retired to sunny Florida

CHOCOLATE

In the ghetto, stories get better with each telling. After a story gets told a couple of times, it becomes gospel. There was a stabbing at a huge government housing complex in the less-than-scenic portion of southeast Houston known as "The Village." An estranged common-law husband stabbed his beloved in front of the dearly departed's best friend. The best friend was known throughout "The Hood" as Chocolate. As a matter of fact, when you called the home phone number of the best friend/witness and asked for her by her given name, the standard response was "Who?" When you qualified your inquiry as wanting to speak with Chocolate, she would immediately be called to the phone.

Chocolate knew both the *stabber* and the *stabee* very well. She gave the homicide investigators a sworn affidavit as to what transpired. The suspect fled the scene prior to the arrival of the blue suits, but turned himself in later that night and confessed his sins. He was charged with murder and the case was set for trial. The *stabber*, upon sober reflection, did not want to do a bunch of hard time, as he had been to prison before. When offered twenty years for a plea of guilty, he gave the ex-con's often used line of, "I ain't takin' nuthin', you're gonna have to give it to me."

Chocolate showed up when subpoenaed for trial. She took the stand and stated the facts as she saw them. What the prosecution was not ready for was the parts she had been adding to her story since the murder. She testified that she and the victim had been seated on the side of the bed and were visiting and laughing while looking at old photo albums. The suspect reportedly walked into the room, and without saying a word, pulled out a knife and stabbed the victim once in the stomach. The star witness then added, "Then he looked straight at me and his eyes turned blood red, and then *hones* (translates as *horns*) popped straight outta his mudda-f**kin' head." This story had gone over very well in The Hood. The prosecuting attorney, however, had little kittens all over the courtroom floor as soon as he heard it from the witness stand. He called for an immediate recess and pulled the star witness into a side room, screaming and yelling at her. Chocolate stuck to her story and would not come off of it. The prosecuting district attorney, at a later date, said that it was his honest opinion that Chocolate had told the story so many times that she had come to believe it as the gospel truth.

The story spread throughout the courthouse like a wind-whipped grass fire. The victim and suspect in this case were of no real interest to society, yet the courtroom was full to capacity for the case's closing arguments. All parties present in the courtroom were hoping to see how the state was going to try and recover from the bombshell that had been dropped on them. The attorney representing the state closed his case presentation with the statement: "This act was so violent and vicious that the defendant took on a demonic glow." The jury must have bought it, because the suspect was quickly found guilty and was given a forty-five-year sentence.

ALWAYS THE LADY

Officers Payton and Ruiz rode *Ten Henry Twenty One*, a late side unit on the evening shift (three p.m. to eleven p.m.). Their beat was located in a slum area south and east of downtown known as the Third Ward. Many of the residents of their beat called the neighborhood they lived in "Da' Turd Ward." Everybody in a patrol car in that district pretty well agreed with their assessment. The two officers in question were forty-five and twenty-two years of age, with Payton being the elder. They were often referred as "The Father and Son" by the other officers on their shift.

Despite the difference in their ages the men worked well together, with Payton almost acting as a father figure as he taught Ruiz the job. Ruiz obviously looked up to Payton (as his mentor) and was more loyal to him than any dog could have been. Like so many police partners, the men were opposites in very many ways. That alone kept life interesting. Ruiz was straight out of the Marine Corps and was a jock by nature. He looked sharp enough to be on a recruiting poster and took good care of himself. Running and gym workouts were required five times weekly, with no exceptions. Payton, on the other hand, always had a cigar butt stuck in the corner of his mouth and his uniform could best be described as looking like an unmade bed. Regarding physical fitness training, Payton claimed to under his doctor's orders to never pick up anything heavier than the hem of a nightgown.

These two officers responded to a *family fight-disturbance* call at XXXX Delano, just minutes after coming on duty. They were met at the front door by a black female named Nancy Clarke, who was holding an ice pack to the left side of her sixty-five-year-old battered face. The old woman's face was already badly swollen, and she was obviously in a lot of pain. She told the officers that her drug abusing "Baby," who she called Butch, "hit me all up in my face" following an argument. Mrs. Clark told the officers that she just wanted Butch to leave her property and to never come back. Ray Ruiz responded by telling the victim "I think we can do a little better than that Ma'am." Texas law allows for warrantless arrests and prosecution in family violence cases, even if the victim does not wish to press charges. Causing bodily injury to an elderly person is a felony in Texas. What was more, the officers were elated to find Butch on the back porch and oblivious to their presence.

When the cops walked out onto the back porch, they found a short and squat Butch sitting in a rocking chair, clad in a jumpsuit, stocking cap and brogan shoes. They pounced on Butch, and after a short struggle, Miss Nancy's baby was cuffed, searched for weapons, and stuffed into the back seat of their patrol car. Ruiz stayed with the prisoner at the car while Payton went back to finish up with the on-scene investigation.

Payton took 35mm photos of the victim's injuries and got all of the information needed to complete the offense report and file criminal charges. When the senior of the two officers got back into the squad car he started chewing out the suspect. "Now listen up, you worthless son-of-a-bitch. The great state of Texas is filing charges against you for assault, not your mother. However, you need to know something else—you are not welcome here. I am also documenting that you are being given a trespass warning. If you ever show up on her property again, we or any other cop called out here will put your goat smelling ass in jail. Now do you understand what I just said?"

The handcuffed suspect in the back seat acknowledged the information. Payton went on. "Good, I'm glad you understand, 'cuz now I'm gonna give you my unofficial warning. First off, nobody should ever hit a woman like that—no matter what her age. Secondly, if I ever catch you over at that old lady's house again I'm gonna kick the shit out of you when I get here. Do you understand me, you dumb son-of-a-bitch?" Butch was silent for a few seconds and answered "Yeah, I hear ya', but they's somethin' you needs to know. I'z a lady too." Both cops responded in unison with, "You're a whaaat?" To which Butch repeated her statement of, "I'z a lady too." Ruiz was speechless, and all Payton could get out was, "No way in Hell."

The prisoner's information was obtained and she was transported to the Southeast jail. There, a female jailer was assigned to take the prisoner and make a visual determination of the gender of the suspect. Verification as to female status was determined and both men were aghast. They finished their booking paperwork and then washed their hands and handcuffs repeatedly. They laughed at each other about having to put hands on "that beast" when they'd arrested and searched Butch for weapons. After completing their offense report and filing charges with the district attorney's office the men returned to duty.

As they pulled back out on the street, Payton belched and scratched his belly before saying, "Hell kid, do you know what my old man woulda said in a situation like this? He woulda said one of two things. Either 'You could tell she was a lady just by the way she held her cigar' or 'Sometimes you've gotta sex 'em like a chicken before you can really be sure of what the hell you've just gotten ahold of.'"

CONFESSIONS

The Catholic Church contends that confession is good for the soul, and it may well be. It also is good for the prosecutor, and many times is good for some serious prison time as well. At times it can also be good for some exceptionally good entertainment. In the criminal justice system a suspect's written or tape recorded confession can be presented into evidence against him. Before either of these types of confessions can get put into evidence they must include a presentation of the suspect's legal rights. Further, the suspect in question needs to acknowledge that he understands his rights, and that if he gives a statement he is giving up those rights. If he really understood his rights, he damned well would not give you a confession and sign it before witnesses. Fortunately for the good citizens of America, there are enough dumb crooks out there that can be conned into giving statements and signing their lives away on the dotted line.

Crooks are first arrested and brought into the police station. Many give confessions after just a few minutes of simply visiting with them. Those individuals are typically distraught, strung out, or just miserable excuses for human beings who want someone to talk to. One of the things that astounds investigators is finding that crooks just have to lie about something. There is just something in their makeup that the whole truth is not in them. A suspect may be confessing to murdering a group of nuns and to drinking their blood as an afterthought. He will, however, have to lie about some minor detail that is of little or no consequence. You don't try and correct these lies or confront him about them, no matter how blatant or outlandish they are. What you want to get on paper is your suspect admitting to being at the scene and to having had the weapon in his hand.

Sometimes an interrogator will try and get a confession by trying to give the suspect an out. This is an excuse for the act that makes it not the suspect's fault. "Did you just happen to have the knife in your hand, and the dude that got cut simply turned into the knife?" A question like this gives your crook an out, so he thinks he can explain away the whole matter as an accident. That (by his admission) also puts him at the scene with the murder weapon in his hand. When a jury sees the confession saying it was just an accident, and the victim had three stab wounds to the back, the defendant is a goner.

The more outlandish his lie is, the better it will be for the prosecution. Juries will hang bald-faced liars the highest. Besides, once he signs a confession, you can always come back and try and get him to give you a second and more complete confession. You do so only after the first one is safely put away. He will lie in that confession too, but about something different. At least you know what to expect out of him. Consistency in life is often all you can ask from it. Another thing that shocks new detectives when dealing with low-life individuals is that so many of them are simply functional illiterates. He or she may be pretty articulate. They may know every verse to all the hit songs, but they can't read or write. To quote one learned jurist, "Life is but a pile of road apples, and our only decision is whether we should use our salad or dinner fork."

Mexican Interrogations

Americans often vacation down in sunny Mexico. However, when they screw up down there they find out that they have no civil rights. Furthermore, abuse is administered by the local constabulary at will. According to the laws down there, if you are arrested, you are guilty until proven innocent. Suspects always sign their confessions in Mexico, and usually they don't show any outward signs of abuse.

A much-favored interrogation tool in Mexico is a six-pack of Coca-Cola. This is the beverage of choice because it comes in six-ounce bottles. A suspect to be interrogated is strapped into a chair, and his head tilted back. The interrogator opens the bottle of Coca-Cola and puts his thumb over its top and shakes it up. In this manner, the interrogator is able to squirt the carbonated drink up the suspect's nose. The six- ounce bottle is reported to be the perfect size to fit a hand, and facilitate the best results. It's said that it does not require more than even two or three bottles to make even the toughest of suspects very civic-minded.

In the most notorious cases, after the confessions are signed, the suspects are paraded before the news media. They are made to pull up their shirts and show that they have not been beaten in order to get them to confess. The suspects are not made to take off their shoes, however, because another effective method used is to strap them to a table and beat on the soles of their shoes with a nightstick. Bruising to the bottom of the feet is not obvious. The methods routinely employed in Mexico reflect their interest in effective case clearance practices. Another very productive method used to extract the truth in Mexico involves the use of a pair of pliers. Determination of the truth is said to be almost immediate. You simply stick a pair of pliers up someone's nose and apply a fair amount of pressure. Then shake the subjects head back and forth for a minute or so. Psalm singers are said to be made out of even the most reluctant of men in short order.

When you are arrested in Mexico, you go to a federal prison to await the adjudication of your case. The authorities in the land of mañana favor the use of cattle prods in their prisons. Former inmates of Mexican prisons report weekly torture with a bucket of water and electric shock treatments.

When you are stripped naked and soaking wet, electricity is conducted so much better. The lighting up of your life continues until the guards either tire of it, or you mark your laundry. In the macho prison society you want to be able to come back from a cattle prod session and say, "They tried, but they couldn't make me shit."

If that's not odd enough, try this one. The authorities down there round up the known local homosexual residents every Saturday night and throw them in with the prison population. The stated logic here is that it relieves tensions and deters gang rapes among the inmate population. The Gay Caballeros are let out Sunday morning so that they may attend church, should they desire to do so. Something for everyone, as they say.

Mutt and Jeff

Cops throughout America use this interrogation technique, which is effective and yields results. Another name for it is good cop-bad cop. The first cop is a real butt-head. He is likely to offend you almost immediately. He will scream and yell at you, and maybe push you around. He will then storm off, leaving his partner behind. The guy left behind is nice and friendly. He apologizes for the butt-head's actions. He is easy to relate to. The bond to conduct a proper interrogation of this type is established.

Homosexual suspects always seem to want to talk and to develop rapport. They will ask you if you are gay or have a family member who is. These suspects are trying to develop some commonality with the interviewer. If you want a confession from a homosexual suspect, you lie to them and tell them you have a queer nephew, and they begin to talk. This method is used by investigators upon crooks, and against cops when they are under scrutiny. The technique is hard to resist, even when you know it is being used against you. This program has as many variations and angles as there are police minds to plot and scheme.

Very likely the most unusual application of the Mutt and Jeff system ever concocted was by detectives in the city of New Orleans, Louisiana. Their scenario would play out with the first cop entering the interview room dressed in a bunny suit, fully equipped with both floppy ears and a powder puff tail. He would hop into the room carrying a huge rubber carrot about two and a half feet long. He would never say a word, and would proceed to beat the prisoner thoroughly with his carrot. Without ever saying a word, Mister Bunny Rabbit would simply turn and hop out of the room. The nice guy would then come in and interview the prisoner (after he had been softened up). This method was used for a good while with exceptional results. The cops felt that nobody would ever complain, because nobody would ever believe some story about a cop in a bunny rabbit suit.

Mister Bunny Rabbit simply vanished, however, after three different prison inmates filed separate and unrelated civil rights violation complaints in federal court. Each inmate had been arrested and convicted in non-related cases over a three-year period. All alleged the same pattern of abuse, which led to each of them giving confessions. One of the inmates, in his handwritten jailhouse writ, claimed that "The Big Easy's" police department had a bunny rabbit-clad cop on staff that the other cops called "The Big Bopper."

The Drowning Man aka Water Boarding

This method of extracting the truth from prisoners got a sheriff named "Humpy" from an unnamed east Texas county sent to federal prison. This manner of questioning got exceptional results, and never left a bruise. The subject was strapped into a straight-backed wooden armchair. His ankles were also strapped to the legs of the chair, and his wrists were affixed to the arms of the chair. He was finally trussed up by buckling a strap around his chest, pinning him to the chair's back. A large cotton towel was then wrapped completely around the suspect's head from behind. It was pulled tight and gathered at the base of his skull.

The participants in this questioning method either kept several buckets of water available or a garden hose handy to get the desired results. The goal here was to keep the towel completely saturated, thereby cutting off the subject's air supply. The suspect was said to feel like he is drowning and reportedly will become amenable to talking with the authorities about any topic they chose. The process reported has the extra bonus that it leaves no obvious marks or injuries, along with obtaining very high rates of confessions and subsequent convictions.

Humpy was only too happy to share his methods and demonstrate its effectiveness to neighboring lawmen. Two men, it is said, are able to keep a secret when one of them is dead. This turned out to be true, but unfortunate for Humpy. Federal prosecutors put pressure on his brother officers, and they testified against him. Humpy was brought out of the piney woods of east Texas, and convicted of civil rights violations at the federal courthouse in Houston. He died in custody after being subjected to eighteen months of an unofficial and undocumented punishment program called "Diesel Therapy." This program is practiced by your federal government and will be discussed in detail later in this publication under the heading of Diesel Therapy.

The Chicano Squad 1970s through early 1980s

The massive influx of Mexicans and South Americans into Houston began in the 1970s. The Hispanic murder rate soared, so in order to adequately investigate the glut of Spanish-speaking-only cases, a new squad was formed within the Homicide Division. It was composed of Spanish-speaking officers. Prior to the formation of this new squad, one would have to have been promoted to the rank of Detective before getting to work in the Homicide Division. Members of the new squad were handpicked and all were street-wise cops. They worked under the premise that most of their witnesses and all of their suspects would lie to you until you hurt them. Only then, the truth might come out. The exceptions there being if the persons being interviewed were victims and were very scared.

The man who picked the troops and who acted as the unit's first line supervisor for many years had himself been born in Mexico. He understood the Hispanic culture, and its values. He also understood the value to an uppercut or a good shot to the kidneys. Besides, at this time in history, no Mexican or Latin male with any self-respect would ever admit that another man was capable of whipping his ass. This squad also enjoyed a clearance rate that bested any of the other murder squads by ten to twenty percent.

The Cold Water Treatment

This process works only in times of cold weather. It is a method that was used by detectives when dealing with either uncooperative and hostile witnesses or suspects. The goal of the investigators was prosecution of guilty parties by obtaining witness statements, getting confessions, or the recovery of evidence.

The object of the detective's attention would be in shirtsleeves and his hands would be handcuffed behind his back. Both detectives would be wearing their topcoats and stocking caps. Just prior to leaving the station, one of the detectives holding a full glass of water, accidentally trips and spills it all over the handcuffed and uncooperative person. The three of them then get into the detectives' car, and the suspect is seat-belted into the backseat. The detectives pull onto a nearby freeway and roll down the car's front windows. The party in the back seat becomes civic-minded and cooperative in short order. Once his teeth stop chattering and the blue color leaves his lips he becomes a whole lot easier to understand.

Lie Detectors and Other Scams

Crooks lie to cops, and cops lie to crooks. Confessions are sometimes obtained as the result of some deception on the part of the interrogator. The confession, if not unnecessarily tainted, is generally admissible. If you lie to a crook, telling him you have an eyewitness that has made a positive identification of him (even though you really don't) and he makes a confession—Hurray for our side. One of the most novel confession-getting scams to date is the fabrication of a polygraph unit from a large photocopy machine. A huge copy machine had just been delivered to the Homicide Division. It had lights that flashed, and it buzzed and clanked when it printed images.

A suspect had been arrested and was professing his innocence. He was asked if he would take a polygraph exam to prove his innocence. He agreed. The first detective left the interrogation room and set up the exam. This occurred at ten o'clock at night, many hours after the polygraph examiners had gone home. The detective took a marking pen and wrote the words YOU LIED in bold print on a sheet of paper. That paper was placed face down on the copy machine. The suspect was brought out and was directed to place his right hand upon the outside of the document cover on the machine. The suspect was asked, "Did you kill Benny Ray Childers?" and he answered, "No sir." The copy button was pushed and lights flashed and the machine rumbled and it spit out a piece of paper bearing the words "YOU LIED." The suspect hung his head. Immediately upon returning to the interview room he gave a full confession.

The Snake Man

Perhaps the most persuasive of all interrogation methods ever used in the Lone Star State was a method employed by a policeman named Jesse Upton, who also happened to be an amateur herpetologist (snake fancier). He was a single man (for obvious reasons) and his first love was catching and collecting venomous snakes. Jesse particularly loved the pit vipers, and rattlesnakes were his very favorite of all the species. He even went as far as defanging rattlesnakes himself, if he was going to keep them around the house as part of his private collection. His apartment was on Memorial Drive close to the central police station. It was not that unusual for him to go home and bring one of his pets back to the office. Jesse's little scaled friends were sometimes used to successfully break down communication barriers with even the most reluctant of suspects.

The suspects to be interrogated in this manner were first shackled both hand and foot to a heavy oak chair. Once they were properly restrained, "The Snake Man" would come into the room to visit with them. Some men cried, some became catatonic, while others simply wet themselves or worse. Luckily nobody ever had a heart attack. This can likely be attributed to the fact that the bulk of the suspects dealt with by his division were usually healthy young males between the ages of seventeen and twenty-five. Though this rather coercive methodology might be deemed both cruel and unusual, it was terribly effective. The program was reportedly at its very best when a freshly caught, or "hot," snake was used. The buzzing rattles of a highly agitated and freshly defanged reptile was said to add remarkably to the desire of a suspect to become cooperative.

Prior to joining the police department, Jesse had been in a military police unit as a Second Lieutenant. His last assignment was to a stockade at Fort Hood, Texas. The detainees in this unit were all serious problem children and almost all of them were African-American. The inmate population detained there was the source of an almost unending stream of both problems and paperwork. Every officer previously assigned there had hated this duty assignment. Upton, however, thought Fort Hood was as close to Heaven that had ever been put on earth. In his off duty time he was able to scour the military reservation searching out the pit vipers he loved so dearly. Jesse discovered that if he occasionally brought one of his pets to work with him (and was seen carrying it by the detainees) his problem children rapidly mended their ways.

On his first day as the compound's "yard boss," Upton unbuttoned his uniform shirt and reached inside it, withdrawing a buzzing rattlesnake. The snake wrapped itself around his forearm as Jesse used its head as a pointer. He then directed the detainees to another portion of the yard that he thought needed policing (picking up trash). The prisoner population acted in a far more civilized manner from then on. Interestingly enough, the amount of paperwork required to run the stockade dropped off dramatically also.

The Mister Rogers Interview Technique

This is a variation of the Mutt and Jeff method. The first man comes in and alienates himself from the interrogation subject before he leaves the room. He does so by mocking the subject while doing an imitation of the late Fred Rogers who was the star of the children's series, Mister Roger's Neighborhood.

The following is an example of the Mister Rogers method.

"Hello, drug addict Negro person. How are you today? It's a lovely day in the neighborhood. Are you my friend? I knew you were."

"Can you say new felony charges and revocation of probation? Can you say serious hard time? I knew you could. Are you my friend?"

"Would you like to be some three-hundred-pound animal's bitch? Can you say don't drop the soap in the shower, bitch? I knew you could. Are you my friend? I knew you were."

In closing, most confession situations are unremarkable. Some of the aforementioned methods are not only beyond rare, but are also outlandish and bizarre. Generally, the suspect feels some remorse and simply opts to give up information in his case. Many crooks, astoundingly, really get into the program (particularly in recorded confessions) and want to make statements to the court. Some want to change verbiage in their written confessions, because their original statements may make them look too vicious or bad. Whatever their real motivation might be, they help the state and help to send themselves down the river. Again, I would caution you that this book is a work of fiction, and the stories herein are such.

Many of the street corner rabble or gang types have no concept of what is legal or what is illegal. To them "to disrespect" someone in front of his peers (even if they too are low life illiterate drug dealers or users) is justifiable homicide. Gang trash often gives confessions to that effect and they don't understand how they could possibly get charged with a criminal offense. "But he called me a punk mother-f**ker in front of my homies! I couldn't just stand there and let him try and take my manhood from me."

The truth is, and always has been, stranger than fiction.

COUNTY HOSPITAL

One of the least favorite assignments for a patrol officer is to ride the beat car in a beat where a charity or county hospital is located. The reason for this is that you are subject to multiple report calls that will originate from that hospital.

Fifteen Edward Thirty—*Check the beating victim at Ben Taub Hospital. Victim is a Juanita Jones, a black female, age 25, came in from XXXX England by private auto.*

Not only do you have to crank out a lot of paperwork in these cases, but after speaking to the patrons of those establishments, you feel you should go home and take a bath with kerosene and a wire brush. What's more, you get to visit with some of the world's most accomplished liars. In some sectors of society, lying is looked upon as almost being an art form and is very highly revered. The following is a very often-spoken lie told by wounded burglary or armed robbery suspects regarding the events that led up to their getting shot. "I was standing on the corner of ------- and ------- mindin' my own bidness (business) when three dudes in a dark caw (car) pulled up and one of 'um shot me."

Of course our alleged victim could not see any of the suspects well enough to even describe them. Neither can he tell you anything about the model or color of the car his assailants were in. Very often these truth-challenged gentlemen are shot by decent citizens trying to protect either themselves or their property. Herein validates for the need for a well-run Civilian Marksmanship Training Program.

"Shoot for the center of body mass, concentrate on the front sight

—squeeze the trigger."

Street cops can tell you something about the seasonal changes in the mortality rates of cutting and shooting victims. The death rates in emergency rooms are highest in the late spring through about early September. This is when the newly-graduated Baby Doctors get to practice on the survivors sent to them by the Knife and Gun Club. By the fall of the year, these doctors have had enough practice that they kill far fewer of their patients.

Things Cops Know About Hospitals:

1. If you have to get hurt, do so between fall and early spring.
2. Baby Doctors have to practice on lower forms of life. That way, when they grow up they can work on real humans.
3. Doctors get to bury their mistakes.

Cops sometimes have to take their injured prisoners to county hospitals prior to booking them into either a city or county jail. Should you have to strum (repeatedly strike) someone's head in the course of affecting his arrest—to the county hospital you must go. The jail booking office will not take prisoners if they are bloody or battered. You and your prisoner must wait for a lull in the action so that they can sew or bandage up your non-emergency scum-sucking dirt bag.

It normally takes only one such Saturday night for officers to learn where to and where not to strike with their batons. The drunken low-life whose head you cracked will be completely sober by the time they get around to stitching him up. After three or four hours of hearing the life story of some subterranean cretin, you are far less likely to get into a blood-letting situation at some future date.

The Old Timers will tell you "If he's worth fighting, he's generally worth shooting." With luck the jerk will have the decency to die if you shoot him. Cops also often marvel at how hard it is to kill a "street turd." They will again tell you "To kill a Turd, you've got to first cut his head off, shoot it full of holes, and then kick it up and down the street for a while. Then and only then do you have a decent chance of killing the bastard."

Tasers and chemical sprays like CS, or pepper spray, have cut down the need to thump and bump as many idiots. There again, nothing is perfect 100 percent of the time and chemical sprays do not tend to work on mental cases. Also consider that if you are working with a lame-brained cop as a partner or backup he or she may hose you down with pepper spray along with the idiot you are fighting with. You still have to wrestle with suspects in order to get them handcuffed and stuffed into a patrol car. You can never totally eliminate cuts and injuries when trying to arrest uncooperative prisoners.

WHORE COURT

Not so long ago, before a change in the penal code, prostitution in the state of Texas could be prosecuted as a Class C Misdemeanor. The criminal sanctions for practicing what has been dubbed the oldest profession in the world were the same as a speeding ticket. The penal code has been changed and those cases are now filed in county court. A conviction can now mean a fine and jail time, or probation. Previously, the offense carried a maximum of a two hundred dollar fine.

To make a case for the offense of Soliciting of Prostitution, a suspect could be charged after naming both the act and the price he or she requires for the services to be rendered. A suspect is arrested and placed on hold for the Vice Division. A hold means that someone's detention was authorized by a specific division that would be processing that prisoner's paperwork. The processing of that person includes the time needed to fingerprint them and get their bond situated. With prostitutes, holds were generally released sometime after four or five in the morning. By then it is too late for them to go out and ply their trade. Their pimps would also be shorted that much more money from one less night of *ho'ing*. Known prostitutes are routinely arrested by both vice and patrol officers for just standing around in public. Their alleged crime is *hitchhiking*, meaning that the suspect is alleged to be flagging traffic and attempting to peddle her assets.

Before the penal code change, all prostitution and prostitution-hitchhiking charges in Houston were set in Municipal Court Number 3 at three thirty every Thursday afternoon. All other municipal court dockets were set for eight in the morning. It was the opinion of all persons involved in the system that the mid-afternoon court docket was set up as a professional courtesy. That way, the Sporting Women would not have to get up too early in the morning, following a hard night of hustling. This court docket was known throughout the municipal courthouse and the police department as Whore Court.

The persons who showed up for Whore Court were not strictly the working girls whose cases were on the docket. Often, up to twenty additional hookers would show up to see if there were any new faces on the Vice Squad to look out for. The attitude in this courtroom at times was somewhat festive. When cases were tried before the judge it was not uncommon for onlookers in the gallery to whoop and laugh out loud. These cases were handled somewhat casually, with both sides able to have their say, putting down the facts as they saw them, or wished they really might have been. Many times the Pavement Princesses came to court hoping that their arresting officer would not show up, and then she might get her bond money back.

In the case of The State of Texas v. Carol Denise, the arresting officer alleging Solicitation of Prostitution was one Adam "Hooter" Stephens. Hooter was raised on a shrimp boat in Matagorda Bay and he looked and acted like anything but a cop. Hooter was so named because, during the course of making whore cases, he regularly asked the lady involved for a look at her hooters. He'd tell the working girls that he wanted to play Show and Tell so he'd know if he really wanted to sample her wares. Hooter's partner was certain that Stephens was not bottle-fed as a child but had to have been a titty-baby.

Carol's case was presented before the judge and Hooter testified that he spoke to the defendant and that she offered him a sexual date for thirty-five dollars, with the breakdown being twenty-five dollars for the girl and ten for the room. Carol was a very cautious working girl who had not been snagged by "The Vice" very many times. Carol acted as her own defense counsel, and caused quite an uproar when she inquired of the court, "Judge, do it make any difference, you know, if he take it out and shake it at you?"

In another case, Sheena Archie had a solicitation case filed upon her by an officer named John Wills. Wills was the street-wise son of a northside

Houston grifter and pool hustler. Sheena, one Thursday afternoon, brought with her to court an attorney named Wendy Malone. Officer Wills testified that Sheena approached him outside a Ship Channel area bar and solicited him for a *French date* for the cost of twenty-five dollars. After her statement as to act and price, she was then arrested. The defense attorney inquired of Officer Wills as to just what a French date was. Wills answered that the term meant oral sex. The defense inquired, "Did she use the term French date, and if so, how do you know that she didn't want to go eat French pastry somewhere?" John answered, "No Ma'am, those were not her exact words." The defense counsel demanded to know her client's exact words. His response was, "Your client told me, and I quote, 'White Bread, for twenty-five dollars I'll suck your dick 'til the eyes pop outta your mother-f**kin' head!'"

It took the bailiff three to five minutes to calm the gallery down and for the whoops and catcalls to stop. During Wills' statement, the defendant had her head down on the defense table and was pounding on the table top with both fists. A side note to this case: Upon leaving the courthouse that day, Wills claimed he saw the same defendant drive off in a car that bore a bumper sticker reading "A HARD MAN IS GOOD TO FIND."

Over time, the Vice cops began noticing that the hookers would leave the courthouse and there were always several taxicabs lined up to pick them up. The cops also noted that the hack drivers never threw the meter arm for the working girls. If there were not enough cabs for all the ladies, it was noted that the ladies began randomly walking up to cars and talking to the male occupants. After a little investigating, it was determined that the two-legged vending machines were using the barter system to procure transportation, trading out sex for rides to and from the courthouse. Upon learning that, the Vice cops set up a sting, borrowing cabs from different companies and putting drafted street cops behind the wheels. By doing so they made a bunch of new whore cases, and sure pissed off a bunch of cab drivers and soiled doves.

DAD

Albert Harmon was a crusty old Sergeant assigned to Homicide's four p.m. to midnight shift. He was an equal opportunity grouch, snapping and snarling at everyone he encountered. The younger investigators all loved to pick at him. Their goal was always to attempt to set off an artillery barrage of colorful profanity. Harmon could say the most horrid things to people, and never be taken seriously. Anyone else would have been shot to death for committing half the atrocities. Albert's wife once commented that someday she fully expected a car to pull up in front of their house and dump her beloved's dead and battered body out into the yard.

Coworkers were generally addressed as either "you stupid bastard" or worse. Nobody else could have addressed the female clerks as he did so regularly, and not face either firing or a civil suit for harassment. It was not uncommon to hear pages over the public address system of "Suzy, you got a cash customer on line three." The clerks would just laugh and jab back at him. A common statement heard directed at the women in the office was "I'd kill you for saying such a thing, but I don't own an elephant gun." The Hispanic clerks all called Albert "Señor." This followed a particularly windy tale spun by him about when he rode uniformed patrol in Houston's predominately Hispanic East End. He claimed that all of the Latin ladies out there called him "Señor Lotta Incha" out of admiration.

Albert was forever known as Dad to the young detectives following a verbal exchange between Albert and a young crime scene officer named Kirk. Officer Kirk had been raised in Houston. He knew that he had been born in San Antonio and had been adopted at the age of three days. One evening after a masterful cursing by Albert, Kirk responded indignantly by saying "Hey, you shouldn't talk to me like that. For all you know, I could be your son." Albert was silent for about ten seconds then answered, "Yeah, ya know—that could be the case. I had me some two dollar whores a time or two in San Antonio." Everybody in the squad room got real quiet. Kirk then stood up and threw out his arms and yelled "Dad!" Albert responded with a cry of "Son!" and the two men embraced.

For the rest of his career, Albert Harmon was called Dad by all the young officers on the squad. If they were black, white, yellow or brown it made no difference. He was called Dad, and they were all called Son.

DEATH BY CELLULITE
OR
AN OVERDOSE OF CRACK

Harold Walker is a man of few external emotions and even fewer feelings for his fellow man. His mother died when he was in grammar school in northern Louisiana. His father was a construction worker who came to the Houston area in the late 1960s, during its boomtown growth. Harold's dad remarried and died five years later from a massive heart attack. Harold and his stepmother tolerated one another while his dad was alive, but when his father died they were at each other's throats.

Harold and his dad always shared a passion for fishing. They often fished in Galveston Bay with a Pasadena police detective name Socks Bradford. Socks owned partial interest in a mom-and-pop funeral home in a working class section of northeast Harris County.

At age seventeen, Harold left the rent house he had called home for five years and moved into the back room of the Memorial Funeral Chapel located in blue collar Channelview, Texas. Harold worked evenings at the funeral home and finished high school. Socks came by every evening after work and checked on the kid and took him out to dinner four or five nights a week. Bradford was a widower and he and Harold still averaged at least one fishing trip a month. He stayed on Harold's case to finish school and to make decent grades.

This part of the Houston metropolitan area was made up of petrochemical workers with a mentality that was best summed up as "Four on the floor and a fifth on the seat." Harold's new father figure (Socks) was often heard to say, "When I walk into most of our funeral services, the number of teeth in the room normally doubles." Many of the residents of this part of the Gulf Coast hail from the eastern part of Texas. The term "Redneck" applies to many of the working class folks from east Texas due to their ancestors. They come from the Scotch-Irish stock and their skin does not tan well. They tend to work outdoors and the backs of their necks sunburns and stays red, hence the term "Redneck."

The east Texas Redneck knows that all people go through life with three sets of teeth. These consist of baby teeth, adult teeth and store-bought teeth. The cops that deal with Crackers know that in a confrontation with a Redneck, when the Redneck pulls his false teeth out and puts them in his front pants pocket, the fight is on. This is a hard-working, hard-drinking crowd and many of its members age early and have a wrinkled or haggard look about them. They are, at times, described by their clansmen as "having a face that looks like it wore out two bodies." This condition often afflicts the female of the species early on. A subset of the males of this sub-species can be identified easily: The end of their noses, their chins and their Adam's Apples are all on the same line.

Harold finished high school and joined the Army in time to become a participant in some police actions in a couple of third world countries. These garden spots he felt would be no worse for the wear due to the military actions, as "they already looked like they had been decorated by vandals." After his three years of military service he made his way back to Houston. Socks had married a rich widow, sold his part of the funeral home and moved to Arkansas.

At the time of Harold's discharge from the Army, the Houston Police Department offered him something nobody else did—a job. He functioned well in a regimented organization, given his closed-mouthed way of doing things. He made an easy transition from soldier to police cadet, and finally to street patrolman. Harold, by choice, rode the late evening shift from three p.m. to eleven p.m. He habitually carried his own print kit and his own 35mm camera. Young Harold Walker dusted for prints on most burglary calls and took photos of battered wives or cadavers on his dead man calls. He turned them into the photo lab dutifully. What his supervisors took as wanting to do a good job was actually boiled down to the fact that Harold was not afraid of dead bodies, and he enjoyed catching crooks through their fingerprints. He felt that any person dumb enough to leave fingerprint evidence behind had prison time coming. Harold also usually rode alone, as he knew who he could trust that way. He learned in combat that if you are the only friendly out there, you don't have to worry about friendly fire. Two points that stuck in his mind from infantry training were "Friendly fire isn't" and "After the pin is pulled Mister Hand Grenade is no longer your friend." Harold thought that these two statements were applicable to many things he encountered in life.

What others did not know about young Harold was the pleasure he got out of seeing and documenting just how well people could screw up. The milk of human kindness had curdled in the young man's soul early in life. His superiors also did not know that Harold shot two rolls of film at many of the scenes he was called to. The first was for the photographic services lab. The second roll went to Harold's private collection to be enjoyed at leisure. Walker became an investigator unit, so aside from running patrol calls he was now called out to take photographs on many major scenes and on all natural deaths and suicides.

Something not known outside of police circles is how irreverent police and medical examiner's office body car operators are toward those who have chosen to commit suicide. This is odd, given the frequency of suicides of police officers. At one time, the act a police officer fatally shooting themselves was called "The Police Disease." When some suicide victim has come to the end of his rope (sometimes literally) or has sought to pacify his mind with a bullet, what is said about him outside the hearing of family members is cold-blooded, to say the least. When a man or woman kills himself or herself over a spouse or some meaningful other, the standard comment of cops or the morgue investigators is "Well, he sure showed her." This is a defense mechanism, because if you internalize what you see and take it personally, it will eat you alive. There are some police officers that do internalize what they see. Those that do are the ones prone to age very rapidly, crawling up inside a bottle, or getting into dope. Harold did not internalize anything that he saw in the course of his duties. He looked upon victims, cadavers and crooks as being put on this earth for his entertainment.

Harold hung names on cases and people. Some of the names he shared with coworkers, but most he kept to himself. He dubbed most Hispanic shootings as "A hole in Juan" or sometimes "Two holes in Juan and one in Juanita." If there were two Hispanic victims or suspects they were designated as "Hose A and Hose B." Harold was aware of the climate of political correctness that the administration wanted the line officers to adhere to, yet he refused to comply. Harold had picked up on Sock's off-beat sense of humor, and always referred to dead people as "The Dearly Departed," although he did not tell his coworkers the reason behind the phrase. The expression went, "They wuz dearly, and they's now departed".

Harold particularly liked to make black death scenes because of all the screaming and yelling that went on. He coined the reactions of the black females as either "Oh Lauding" or "Oh Jesusing." When overweight women would throw themselves onto the ground and "commence catching fits" Harold would make a mental note. Would the shaking of the earth register 4.5 or greater on the Richter scale? Harold once made a remark in front of witnesses that came back to haunt him, though. He said that he judged his scenes as exceptional if he had two large black women thrashing around on the ground and squalling. He only wished they could synchronize their rolling and flailing of limbs, like the 1940s movies where synchronized swimming was ever so much the rage.

When that story was told at a choir practice (after-work beer party) the word got back to Harold's supervisors. Harold was brought in and raked over by Lt. J.B. Simon (aka John the Baptist). John the Baptist warmed up with the poor taste lecture and moved up to the "Are you a bigot?" questions. The Come-to-Jesus-Meeting (as they are called) closed with a veiled threat. Simon hinted of a forced review from the Psychological Services Unit to see if Walker was unfit for duty. Harold would no longer hang out with his squad and knock down a few beers with the boys after work. What's more, John the Baptist had made an enemy for life.

John the Baptist joined the ranks of countless others who had incurred the wrath of young Officer Walker's throw-down program. This was a program that Harold shared with none of his coworkers. Rather, it was a program he reserved for irate traffic violators. Harold particularly liked the program when the violators were both white and affluent. In police terminology, a throw-down is a gun or knife that can't be traced. The story goes that some officers carry such a weapon in case one of them was involved in a bad (not justified) shooting. The gun can be thrown down beside the body, making all things right. In other jurisdictions these may be called throwaways. The term can apply to dope also. Dope dealers will drop or throw their dope down as the police approach and they will run off. This dope can allegedly be gathered up and saved so it can be put on some deserving crook at some future day and time.

In Harold's case, he would never falsely charge someone with a crime, nor had he seen anyone ever plant throw-down guns or dope. Instead, young Harold chose to employ the throw-down program to cause problems with the home life of butt- heads he encountered on the street. When Harold would stop traffic violators after dark and the violator would begin ranting and raving, the throw-down program would kick in.

The program worked best when the traffic violator was alone in the car, and it worked on either men or women. The necessary information for the citation would be gathered and Harold would step back to his patrol car. He kept his briefcase on the front passenger's seat, as he habitually rode alone. Under such circumstances he would open the briefcase and from it extract one cheap prophylactic and a bottle of hand lotion. After unrolling the rubber and squirting one shot of hand lotion inside it, the throw-down was ready for deployment. The throw-down was then palmed and held in his right hand under the traffic ticket clip board. When the citation clip board was handed to the irate violator his eyes immediately went to the offending document. He did not see Harold throw the unrolled rubber onto his backseat. Though the final results of these gifts would never be known, Harold always felt better just for having donated. The anonymous donor program continued over the years he worked either evening or night shift.

The one thing Officer Harold Walker never wanted to do was to draw attention to himself. He was a good employee, showed up on time, and did his job. He was quiet and reserved, and did not plan on becoming legend material. He got along well with the Homicide Division investigators, as they had outlooks on life similar to his. He'd processed scenes for many of them on the evening shift and as a result, had spent many hours warming a bench while waiting to testify at criminal trails.

One July evening, Harold was called to a death in custody scene in Houston's less-than-scenic southeast side. Patrol officers were called out to a family disturbance regarding a possible mental case. This was a home known to many of the district officers. The home was lower-middle income and well-kept. It was occupied by a single mother and her twenty-year-old mental case daughter. The daughter was equipped with a bath water temperature IQ and a personality prone to violence when she became frustrated or angered. The mother and her sister had been in the master bedroom preparing for a church social. The daughter was upset because she was unable to get financial aid to attend a local junior college. The college financial aid office advised her she did not qualify for a student loan due to her failing grades the previous semester.

The daughter and the aunt got into an argument and first tried to eye one another down. The aunt would later describe this by saying, "She was standing there—just pissing at me through her eyes." That session reportedly broke up, and five minutes later the daughter came into the bedroom and tried to punch out the offending aunt. The portly sisters were no strangers to a friendly brawl. They body-slammed the wannabe student, and both sat on top of her while Momma called the neighborhood 24-hour family counselors (the Houston Police Department). Before proceeding any further into this story, some information about the parties involved needs to be shared. Each of the participants in this family brawl could be described as being two axe handles wide. In Houston, women of the aforementioned stature are commonly referred to as Wart Hogs. Men that are stout and scrappers are often called Tush Hogs. It would be safe to say that none of the lovelies involved in this root-hog-or-die family get-together would have field dressed at under 220 pounds.

The first unit to arrive at the fight scene call was a one-man unit, and he was a veteran of family disturbances at this address. He'd arrested the enraged daughter in the past and knew of her combative nature. When Officer Melvin Johnson entered the master bedroom, the 20-year-old was being held down by a minimum of 550 pounds of pressed ham. He put one handcuff on the immobilized brawler. Then Momma and her dainty sister got up and he cuffed the other wrist. He spoke to the prisoner and got no response. The two other females in the room were calling out to him to be careful: "She's tricky. Watch out Officer, she's playin' possum." Johnson found a pulse but no respiration. He immediately began CPR.

Paramedics transported the daughter, Natasha, to Ben Taub Hospital where she was dead upon arrival. With the placing of a handcuff on a wrist of the dearly departed (she was dearly and she's now departed) she became considered to have been in custody. With the in-custody status bestowed upon her death, a full-blown investigation began. That brought out the Homicide Division and the District Attorney's Office Civil Rights unit. A review by a county grand jury always follows, with a final overview by the Texas State Attorney General's Office. A death in custody investigation is every bit as much trouble as a fatal shooting. The medical examiner's office has to make a ruling as to the cause of death. Because the death of one party came about as result of two others seated upon her back, Natasha's death was ruled a homicide.

The local media monitors all police and fire emergency channels around the clock. They knew that Homicide and a Crime Scene Unit had been called out, so the TV cameras and newspaper and radio reporters showed up shortly. What they all want from a scene is a summary of facts and some short statement from the police that they can put in print or on the air. The term that radio and TV stations use for these recorded statements is a sound bite. This is what came back and bit Harold Walker and also made him famous.

Harold assisted at the scene with the photos and the gathering of evidence. He stood back beside his patrol car while the interview with the scene investigator took place. Sgt. Gustav I-never-met-a-camera-I-didn't-like Alvarez gave a short and somber statement as to the victim's passing. After the camera lights were turned off, Harold walked up and spoke to Alvarez. What he did not know was that a radio reporter present still had his recorder running.

With the recording of a short statement, fame was bestowed upon Officer Walker. To Sgt. Alvarez, Harold matter-of-factly said, "Hell Sarg, this case is nothing to get excited about. This is obviously either a case of death by cellulite, or just an overdose of crack." This, unfortunately, was recorded on a slow news night. The radio station first played the somber Alvarez version, followed by a "reading from the book of Walker." The local civil rights activists got excited, and the Mayor's office got a nose bleed. John the Baptist started his period.

Harold took it all in stride. He figured that with recorded evidence he should admit to it and scare them to death. Harold became known for his recorded statement, and he told John the Baptist (in front of witnesses) "This was still America, and I am of the opinion that private conversations between consenting adults are still legal." The bystanders laughed out loud. The holier-than-thou Sergeant became further enraged and stormed back into his office to review his rules manual. John the Baptist vowed never again to call a subordinate down in front of witnesses, and not be caught off guard in the future. Both statements were linked to Harold Walker for the rest of his career.

NO GATO

Nineteen Edward Thirty—*See the woman regarding a disturbance at XXXX Troulon*—*Advise on backup.*

John Mata, riding the day shift out of the Southwest Station responded to the call for service, and met the irate caller named Karen Andrews. Ms. Andrews was found to be a rather loud and rather pushy woman. The lady would later be described as being a "double-wide kind of woman that lacked only mud flaps and turn indicators." She was clad in a tent-looking lime green dress. She demanded that Officer Mata arrest a member of a non-English-speaking work crew who were engaged in clearing tree limbs from the neighborhood's power lines. The workers were cutting tree limbs along a power right-of-way. They would then run the limbs through a huge wood chipping machine. Ms. Andrews advised Officer Mata that she had been talking with the alleged suspect (later identified as Francisco Avila) asking if he would like to adopt a stray kitten. She said that without provocation, the suspect grabbed the animal and threw it into the limb chipping machine, immediately shredding "Poor Kitty."

In the course of the investigation, it was determined that Ms. Andrews approached the alleged suspect while he was operating the large limb chipping machine in front of her home. He spoke little to no English, but she was not deterred by this problem. She appeared to John Mata to be the kind of woman that refused to accept the word "No" for an answer. She reportedly had the half-grown Tabby cat in her arms, and kept trying to hand it to Mr. Avila. She spoke to him only in English as she inquired if he was interested in the kitten.

The complainant said that the suspect would only repeat the phrase

"No gato, no gato" to her, while holding both hands up with his palms towards her. She would simply not take "no" for an answer, and asked if he didn't have a child at home that would just love to adopt this lovely kitten. The only response she kept getting was, "No gato, no gato." The complainant just kept up her hard-sell program. She knew from past experience that she could break this man's resolve if she just kept at it. Ms. Andrews admitted that just before he committed the horrid act, the suspect simply shrugged his shoulders. He then reached out and took "Poor Kitty" and threw him into the running limb chipper.

Ms. Andrews became further distraught when Officer Mata doubled over with laughter upon hearing the complete version of the alleged criminal episode. She later filed an Internal Affairs complaint against Officer Mata for the "insensitive and unprofessional manner" in which he handled himself during the investigation of this matter.

POINTS OF VIEW

May 27th—1835 Hours—Northeast Patrol Channel Dispatcher:

Nine Zebra Sixty-Three *(Z denotes an accident unit)—Make the auto-house major accident at XXXX Zarzanna—Multiple victims—All victims transported from the scene to L.B.J. Hospital*

Officer Bert (Swede) Lawson, riding unit Nine Zebra Sixty-Three, arrived at the scene to find a wood-framed shotgun shack that had been impaled by an eight-year-old white Pony-Ack (Pontiac) car. The car was embedded so deeply into the building that its tail lights were level with the structure's front wall. The vehicle was roughly centered where the front door had once been. There was enough crash debris in the front yard that it looked like at least one stick of dynamite had been detonated in close proximity to what had once been the front porch steps. There was also a pretty fair amount of medical-related debris left behind by paramedics that attended to the injured.

From the mass of humanity milling about the front yard (gawking and scratching), Larson picked out a gentleman he thought might have some live brain cells left. He inquired of the man, "Can you tell me who was driving that car at the time of the accident?" The genius in question pointed to a skinny nine- or ten-year-old kid who was standing off to one side of the property and who was crying silently. Officer Larson walked up to the boy and asked, "Can I talk with you for a minute?" The kid responded with, "Am I going to jail?" After the young man, Junior Burns, was assured that it was only an accident and that nobody intended to harm anyone, did the events begin to unfolded.

Junior's mother's house was the gathering place for his extended family on every Friday evening of the world. Their front porch ran the complete width of the house. Some of the tribe were "slapping dominos" when Junior's Momma told him to go and get the family car and pull it into the driveway. She didn't want to leave the car out on the street because it was Friday evening. Following sundown on weekends and holidays, drunks regularly customize parked cars throughout the neighborhood. The Burns' driveway crossed a drainage ditch (that parallels the street) by means of a concrete culvert.

As Junior pulled the car into the drive, the driver's side rear wheel slipped off of the culvert. The left rear quadrant of the car began listing and slowly sliding into the ditch. Junior became scared as the car leaned and crept into the ditch. He had a death grip on the steering wheel, and in his fright, he shoved down on the gas pedal. The rear wheel that was hanging out into open air was the car's single drive wheel. It spun furiously as the car's engine roared. The car kept slowly sliding until it was leaning at about a forty-five degree angle. Suddenly, the drive wheel touched solid ground and the car caught traction. The family sedan then rocketed out of the ditch—and homed in on the front of the house.

Junior's Momma had been hot-footing it towards the high-centered car from the front porch just as the Pontiac transformed itself into a rocket sled. Momma (carrying her thirteen-month-old niece) sought refuge behind a clothesline pole, but the 4x4 pole proved no match for one of Detroit's finer creations. Momma, Baby Elizabeth and the clothesline pole were swept aside by the seemingly demonic Pontiac as it progressed toward the house. First came the front steps, followed by the front porch, and finally the three-foot high wooden spool that served as the domino table. All three became kindling as the car continued on with enough velocity to burrow itself into the house.

Junior and his Uncle Bobby both gave enlightening renditions as to what transpired on that fateful day. Junior explained the events from his child's orientation. "Momma told me to pull the car into the driveway. I've done it lots of times before, without ever havin' no troubles. Today when I did, one of the tires slid offa the driveway pipe (concrete culvert). I guess the car musta got nervous 'cuz it first kinda slid sideways and the all of a sudden it just jumped outta the ditch."

Junior's Uncle Bobby related a similar set of circumstances, but with a slightly different twist. He went on to say that his sister and niece were both hit solidly, and thrown clear of the car. When asked about the other three people that had been loaded into ambulances, he replied honestly. "They wuz all on the porch, true enough. But ya see, they all went to the hospital just in case my sister had some good insurance on that Pontiac of hers." All parties transported by ambulance in this matter were treated and released from the hospital that very evening.

THE ENCHANTED FOREST

Police department management groups, like many in big businesses and school districts, are unable to stick to the basics. If your program works and has proven to be effective, it needs to be reviewed by an expert from some consulting firm. An expert is someone who has to travel over 200 miles to get to your location, and gets paid big bucks for his time. He studies your operation, leaves, and sends you a bound and written report. It is filled with charts and graphs, and it comes equipped with catchy phrases or buzzwords.

If your operation was too simple and straightforward it needs to be modified. The K.I.S.S. method (Keep It Simple Stupid) program works well, but it hardly ever gets implemented. With the K.I.S.S. method, you simply determine your goal and work toward its completion. In police work, it's simple: You are cops, and they are crooks. If you put crooks in jail, there are fewer crooks on the street. This equates to there being less crime. One chief of police in Houston realized this and he opted to pay overtime to his officers during peak crime time. He did not need to hire extra cops. The cops knew they had to produce to continue to get paid overtime. They put scads of crooks in jail. Crime rates dropped markedly in a matter of months. One Harris County Emergency Management director characterized the management style of the Houston Police Department as "When in danger, when in doubt, run in circles, scream and shout." The command staff restates this concept by putting out statements like, "The matter is being investigated" or "A task force has been formed to study the situation and make recommendations." Direct translation from street cops: Bovine Fecal Matter.

You may drive down the true crime rates, but your name will not appear in textbooks. Neither will you get acknowledged by The Old Boys Club (The International Association of Chiefs of Police). These are the academic types who brought you programs like open school classrooms where students can't hear their teacher and the rejection of phonics so that little Johnny can no longer read. In police circles, similar programs exist. One such brain fart was called Neighborhood Oriented Policing. It gets great play in textbooks and police managers' periodicals. This concept appeared on a limited basis in Houston, and it failed under the name of the D.A.R.T. Program.

D.A.R.T. stood for Direct Area Response Team. This program, had it been successful, would have been added to the resume of the then chief of police and would have been written about some textbook. The D.A.R.T. program was supposed to bring back the neighborhood cop. This was a Utopian setting where Officer O'Malley knew all the children, as well as all the good guys and the bad guys in their neighborhood. All the criminal investigations and case follow-ups were to come from detectives assigned to the substation serving only that specific neighborhood. One particular neighborhood was located directly south and east of downtown and its population was lower to lower middle-income blacks. The new police substation this program began in was formerly an elementary school. The South-Central Station was born.

To staff this station, two adjoining police stations were each tapped to send a specific number of uniformed officers for reassignment. The officers to be transferred were picked by their immediate supervisors. Naturally, the new station was staffed with blue suits that were the culls and problem children from the Central and Southeast stations. The patrol supervisors drafted to work this station openly called their line officer subordinates "The Boat People" or "The Clones." These troops appeared either to be from some foreign country, or worse yet, another planet. They could not quite read or write English well, nor did they seem to understand the system they worked in.

The Investigations section was made up of detectives from all divisions except Homicide and Auto Theft. Homicide and Auto Theft remained centralized for their needed area of expertise. The Armed

Robbery, Burglary and Theft, and Forgery Divisions supplied the needed investigators from a pool of volunteers. The detectives would work day shift and had most weekends and holidays off. The other drawing card to attract detectives was paid overtime. This was used in an attempt to guarantee the success of this program. The goal was to show a higher clearance rate through neighborhood oriented policing. Its success would further prove just how bright and talented the then chief of police was.

Wesley Lewis, a third-generation Italian-American, was one of the detectives who transferred into the grade school turned police station. His grandfather immigrated to America, and upon arrival at the Port of Galveston, was given the last name of Lewis. The given family name proved too hard for the Immigration Service clerks to spell, so they Americanized it. Lewis came to the D.A.R.T. program from the Robbery Division. He was assigned as an investigator in the combat zone neighborhood known as the Third Ward. The program's crime clearance statistics were padded and manipulated so that it was obvious that the program was going to be a great success. Management had again proven that they were brilliant, and they wanted to further expand the program. Crimes against persons and property were no longer enough. The time had come to move against drugs and vice-related problems that have plagued the area for decades. The chief soon abolished the rank of Detective and made Wesley and his cohorts into Sergeants. With the title change, Wesley opted to become a leader of men and put in for a supervisor position in the newly-formed Narcotics and Vice Unit.

The political sectors of Houston now called precincts were once called wards. Each ward had its own city councilman. For fifty years now, the ward system has ceased to designate political boundaries. The term "ward" is now used by all races in Houston to designate low-rent and crime-ridden areas inhabited by blacks or Hispanics. Middle and upper-class blacks will tell you, "He didn't look like he was from around here. He looked like somebody out of the Ward."

The Third Ward neighborhood that Wesley transferred into was once an upper and upper middle class white section of Houston. The highest rent district was on its southern boundary. The southern boundary was

Braes Bayou and it was bordered by stately boulevards with mansions lining either bayou bank. In post-WWII, Houston's Third Ward was where people moved that had made it in life. They were the hard-working people who lived the American dream. The houses were well-built and a tribute to the industry of the people living there. In the late 1950s, blacks moved into the area. Anglos with cash supplied by the NAACP bought the houses for them. These blacks were called "blockbusters" and several families of blacks would move into one house. The area residents fled, selling their houses at great losses. The mansions along North and South Macgregor, with their tennis courts and horse stables, sold for pennies on the dollar. Houston's Third Ward quickly transformed from a showcase into a septic tank.

Wesley and another Sergeant had squads of six officers and were charged with running the street vermin back into their holes. Two out of the twelve street-level plainclothes officers were black, and had been assigned to uniformed duty in the area for several years. Dope was easy to buy from street vendors. The drug crime arrest statistics were always easy to keep up. In short order, however, the street whores knew who the new Vice boys were, and the hours that they worked. After four months, the station Captain was putting heat on the D.A.R.T. Sergeants to put higher Vice statistics back into the mix. Statistics can be the cause of many things rolling downhill, some of which will not pass for roses. Wesley's squad was pretty well known in the small geographic area, and solicitation of prostitution cases were falling off markedly. Necessity is said to be the mother of invention, and if nothing else, Wesley was creative. Wesley had lived part of his childhood on a hardscrabble dirt farm in Giddings, Texas. He understood how to poach and trespass in order to survive.

Houston's Memorial Park is a wooded 5,000-acre expanse just west of downtown. The land was donated to the city as a park by the Hogg Foundation, set up by former Texas Governor Jim Hogg. The park can only be used as a public park, or it reverts back to the foundation. The park has a golf course, running tracks, a huge softball complex and an area set aside for bike riding. Houston cops know the reputation of the park as being a meeting place for homosexuals. However, everyone has always fought shy of morals enforcement out there because they didn't want to have to mess with "The Queers."

AIDS-infected street whores are one thing, but your Momma and Daddy told you to stay away from faggots. Dwindling statistics drive men to extreme measures. The "Happy Guy" squad was formed. The then-mayor of the fourth largest city in the nation had strong ties with the gay community. Therefore, the troops were given the "It is not what you do, it is what you say, that will come back to haunt you." lecture. The hunt was officially on. Wesley and his troops converged upon Memorial Park with a paddy wagon, a minivan, and a couple of unmarked cars. The uniformed officers assigned to park patrol duties told Wesley's squad where to find the highest concentrations of unattached men who were looking to become attached.

The goal was set, and the crime stats needed a boost in the Vice department. Who cared if the arrested parties were male or female? Full speed ahead, and don't get damned by arrest statistics. Wesley designed a tactical program, whereby fruits and nuts could be nabbed and officer safety insured. There was no reason for anyone to get hurt trying to arrest some sissy who wanted to "bump wienies." Lewis devised a plan to have his troops on the ground in groups of three.

According to his plan, one officer was the "bait" (called the queer bait, or the mullet) and he was to be followed by a pair of officers who covered him. The bait, or mullet, would stroll along ahead of his cover team, and when solicited for sex, he would give a pre-designated bust signal. This would tell the backup officers to move up and that an arrest could be made. Cops typically do some act to bring on the bust-team, like taking off their sunglasses or removing a baseball cap. (Wesley swore that if he was a drug dealer and a prospective buyer came up wearing sunglasses and a cap he would run like hell.) The backup or bust-team carried portable radios in a backpack. A fourth officer sat nearby in a minivan and monitored the radio. His job was to be available if a foot chase began, and to pick up the prisoners. A Sergeant was to be nearby in an unmarked car if he needed to get involved in a foot pursuit or to as backup. Due to the political climate in Houston, the plan always called for supervision on scene at all times during any "Pansy Patrol."

The men's bathrooms were productive places for indecent exposure cases. The Weenie Wavers were referred to by a variety of terms. Some were said to be "men just doing their own thing." Others were dubbed "fellows just trying to get a head in life." After the initial grumblings about not wanting to deal with fruits and nuts, the troops began to go out and try and find the best hunting grounds. The trails running through the woods were the spots the officers found they were solicited most often. The key was simply walking alone.

What shocked this group of hardened street cops was the sheer number of cases they were making. During their first month working the park they tripled the highest monthly number of prostitution solicitation cases the regular Vice Squad had ever produced. The other shocker was the fact that their suspects were from all over Texas. Johns came to Memorial Park like Muslims flock to the holy city of Mecca. Originally the troops began to call Memorial Park "Pickle Park." After a short time, however, it was dubbed "The Enchanted Forest." It was so named because it was full of fairies and trolls, all of whom were in search of Prince Valiant.

The Happy Guy Squad found they had three classes of crooks to catch. Primarily, they were street hustlers and the Johns, but there was also another group drawn to the park. These were men seeking similarly-oriented men who wanted to play "escaped convict and the warden's wife." Some came to just to play, others didn't mind paying. The street hustlers were obviously just a bunch of down-and-outers. When you spoke to them and asked the price of their wares they were up front about it. When arrested, they were quick to tell you they were not members of the indefinite sex. "Just because I take money to let some guy suck my dick don't make me no queer."

The other group of suspects was from the other side of the spectrum. They came from middle or upper crust America. Many were often professionals and fairly high-profile people from small towns. The Pansy Posse was snagging bank presidents, preachers, and school board members from all over Texas. It seems that the small town boys did not want to get caught short on their own turf, so they came to the big city to commit "Assault with a Friendly Weapon."

There were so many people to arrest out there that the posse often had more prisoners than squad members. At times they had to shut down a sweep early, just so they could get off on time. Fridays got so crazy in the park that either both squads went out to handle the wealth of prisoners, or nobody went out. As the roundups of the happy guys went on, competitions began between the squads. They would come up with pots, putting in a few dollars each, like you would on a charter fishing boat. There were different categories you could participate in. There were cash prizes for the oldest suspect, the youngest suspect, the most fruits you could arrest in a thirty-minute time period, and the most unusual act that you were solicited for. The competitions between the squads became fierce. Fridays were always the day of choice for completions in the Enchanted Forest. There were just so many more suspects to hit on you, and you could pick and choose if you were trying to win a specific fruit pot. The jokes between officers got funnier as the competitions went on. "Is it entrapment if you strolled through the park with your trouser fly down?" or "If you introduce yourself as Tom Trick from Trick City, Texas, will you improve your chance of scoring?"

One officer in Wesley's squad, Gene Smith, was a body builder. He would show up on competition days in a pair of skimpy shorts and a fish net tank top. Smith would roll up one gym sock and stuff it in the front of his shorts before trolling the Forest. He invariably won the contest for the most suspects arrested in a thirty-minute period. One time, a bidding war broke out between two aging queens that happened to fall in lust with Gene at the same time. In a downtown police bar after a couple of beers, Gene once lamented, "I can hear my mother now. Eugene, we tried to raise you right. We took you to church, sent you to college, and just see what you've become. Just look at you, twenty-eight years old, college-educated and queer bait. I just want you to know one thing Eugene—it makes your mother proud!"

After one harrowing experience, Gene quit wearing his tank tops and short-shorts. He also no longer competed in the most-suspects-in-thirty-minutes category. He was "strolling through the park one day" in his best-producing attire and was literally mobbed by gay blades. They came crashing through the underbrush that ran along the trail he was on. Gene said he now understood how a bitch dog in heat felt as she was being chased down the street by a pack of horny street dogs.

All good things must come to an end it is said, and so it was with the operations in the Enchanted Forest. The Direct Area Response Team was set up to work a specific part of town. The sector designated was east of downtown. The Enchanted Forest was, unfortunately, located west of downtown. On an otherwise dull afternoon, a high-profile senior official from a federal law enforcement agency was arrested at the park bathrooms. Like the old country and western song says, he was "lookin' for love in all the wrong places."

He put up one hell of a fight, and after he was "cuffed and stuffed" his identity was learned. The troops had been forced to put hands on the man and he sustained some knots on his head. When that happens, even if you are Mother Teresa, you're going to jail. No professional courtesy would be shown. After all, "he showed his ass, and got what he had coming." City cops don't have a lot of use for "The Feds" anyway. If the Feds need help or information, you're a long-lost relative, found at last. If you need something, you get treated like a bastard stepchild with AIDS. An old police expression goes, "The Feds will use you like a rubber and then throw you away."

When the media determined that a high-placed federal law enforcement agent was arrested it became front-page news. It also was the lead story on the evening TV news. The moral to this story is, don't get in trouble on a slow news night. The official in question made bond and subsequently retired from his agency. The arrest report was read by most of the command staff and it was duly noted that the arrest took place two police districts west of the response team's sector. Wesley and the other Sergeant present were dressed down and written up for their poaching activities. Wesley's Pansy Posse was now barred from working any cases west of the downtown area.

It didn't matter that nobody else had ever tried to clean up the cesspool before. The D.A.R.T. group made hundreds of misdemeanor sex solicitation cases and many felony drug cases. Two child molestation cases had been encountered. The suspects were caught in the act, arrested and charged. Many other investigations were made where possible Chicken Hawks (child molesters) were checked out. When men and young children were encountered, the squad would interview them, and when no relationship could be determined, the child's family would be contacted and potential abuse situation headed off.

There was no denying it—the posse had been trespassing and poaching. They carried on in a manner that was contrary to the rules of the game. The D.A.R.T. program continued for another year and was disbanded just like other neighborhood-oriented policing programs had been in other cities. The regular Vice squad will occasionally respond to complaints from City Council or the Mayor's Office regarding homosexual conduct in the park. They will, at times, set up a short-term sting operation. The fairies and the trolls still inhabit the forest, but the posse led by Marshall Dillon and Festus were forced to return to Dodge City. The days of full-scale roundups of odd-wads, weirdos and whackos on the open range are over.

EVABODY KNOW

Ohganizm: Pronounced *oh-gah-izm*; translates in English as orgasm.

Murder cases in Houston are normally assigned to a pair of investigators and on a rotation system. When you get an assignment, you go to the end of a rather short list. Your hope is that you can finish your investigation before you come up for the next murder scene. Homicide is centralized downtown rather than spread out into the various quadrants of the city. In each sector of the city there are command stations that would be called precinct houses elsewhere. The command stations have small branch offices with burglary and armed robbery investigators working out of them, but the uniformed officers make up the bulk of the command station staff. In Houston, the command staff will tell you that "Patrol is the backbone of the police department." The blue suits will tell you that they are located somewhere just south of the backbone. Homicide is looked upon as a plum assignment, but for the most part, burglaries may be harder to solve and prosecute. There again, burglary victims don't lie around under bed sheets for the TV cameras to film.

Jim Easterling and Jon Benson were assigned to the murder of a white male found shot to death in a motel room off South Main Street. The motel was located between the Astrodome and the Medical Center. This was not a run-down, hot sheet, no-tell motel, but rather was a high-dollar Marriott. Its very location brings in clients with a multitude of interests ranging from sporting events and conventions to the world-famous Medical Center. Oddly enough, the Harris County Morgue is located between this motel and the hospital district. Hotel maids found the year's latest statistic lying on the floor beside his bed with a surprised look on his face and powder burns and a bullet hole in his shirt front.

The dead man's pockets had been turned inside-out and he had no jewelry on his person. He was from San Antonio and was a salesman for a wholesale hospital supply company. He had come to the Sodom of the South on business. There were two glasses on the bedside table and an unopened package of condoms there too. One of the glasses had lipstick on it. There is, and always has been, a large amount of prostitution going on in the South Main area. The scene overview did not look like any business transaction had been consummated between some Pavement Princess and the dead man. The bedspreads looked like they'd been sat upon, but little else. There were no soft drink cans, nor whiskey bottle present. It was surmised that the glasses came from the hotel bar and were brought there by the victim and some unknown female.

The scene was processed, photographed and the two glasses in question taken to the fingerprint lab. The prints picked up on the glass with the lipstick were run through the AFIS fingerprint computer. It spit out four possible names, one of which became a positive identification on a known prostitute named Pebbles Hanna. Pebbles was a South Main prostitute on occasion, but most of her arrests had been in northeast Houston on Jensen Drive. The hit on fingerprints on a working girl was what every Homicide investigator is looking for. "It's better to be lucky than good" goes the expression. There again, many times you have to make your own luck. The gods of luck further smiled on investigators, because Pebbles also had an open warrant for a violation of probation regarding a cocaine conviction. The drug arrest offense report in question reflected that she had a purse over her shoulder when arrested and that there were two vials of powdered cocaine in it.

That arresting officer's report indicated that Pebbles made an immediate outcry statement of "That's not my stuff Officer, I'm just holding it for my mother." Benson and Easterling now had a suspect with an open felony warrant. If they could find her, they could arrest and detain her without having to procure a warrant in this case. An open arrest warrant is nice, but fingerprints alone would not prove murder.

She was also flagged with the county jail system, so that the detectives would be contacted immediately if Pebbles came through there. Street trash is in and out of the county jail system so often that it is just a way of life with them.

Benson had come to the Homicide Division from the Northeast Patrol Station. There he had worked uniformed patrol in the high crime area known as the Fifth Ward. The beat he worked was known for its volatile inhabitants and high levels of drug and alcohol abuse. Benson was tall, had a fair complexion and eyes so pale that they looked like those of a Siberian Husky. The street animals called him "Blue Eyes." Jon Benson knew the suspect, Pebbles Hanna, as she had been a regular Ho Lady (street whore) working Jensen drive. She was a junkie and her lifestyle was quickly pulling her down.

What the out-of-town business man types or convention-goers do not grasp is that the drug addict street whore often comes off the street corner, takes a bath, puts on a clean dress, and works the high dollar hotels for bigger money. She may also have hooked up with a pimp that wants her to put her assets to work in a higher rent district. She can be working a twenty-five-and-five motel (twenty-five dollars for the girl, five dollars for the room) on the waterfront one week, and the next week she is working a posh hotel bar. The oversexed out-of-towner thinks he's found a Nubian princess, and in reality, had encountered a microbiologist's nightmare. Jon Benson was working days, and he contacted his old patrol partner, a street cop named Todd Fincher. Fincher was called "Scattergun" by many Fifth Ward residents. Fincher treated his 12-gauge Remington pump shotgun like an American Express card: "Don't leave home without it." Benson felt Fincher very likely slept with his shotgun. Scattergun (Fincher) worked the three p.m. to eleven p.m. shift and said that he would keep an eye out for Pebbles. He was admonished not to ask around about her specifically because she would hear about it and run to Louisiana. Everybody and his dog living in the Fifth Ward has relatives and extended family in Louisiana. When they hear the cops are looking for them, they regularly run east. The crooks generally will return within a few weeks to a month, because they could not function outside of their little world. Jon always tried not to complicate matters when he didn't have to. The plan settled upon was for Benson and Easterling to try and locate their suspect from mid-morning to early afternoon. Fincher took the second shift.

Easterling and Benson started dragging the locations that Benson thought Pebbles would frequent. They started about ten each morning. Easterling did not know that much about this part of town, and experienced a sort of culture shock. From there out, he often referred to Benson as the Mayor of the Fifth Ward. Dopers are going to wake up and need their first dope of the day, or their "wake-up medicine." The detectives drove through the known dope motels and stopped at a couple of clubs that would cater to the dope users. Along the way, Blue Eyes would stop and visit with working girls with street names like Lovie, Ruby Jewel and Big Titty Marilyn. He would ask about one girl and then another, and then yet another, so as not to let on who he was looking for.

The last northeast Houston sperm bank they spoke to the day after the killings was a tall and skinny female called Red. Now, Red looked like she had to be between twelve and fifteen months' pregnant and was as plain as homemade soap. She was later described by Easterling as looking like a blue-black praying mantis with a goiter. In the course of asking about the different working girls, one of the two investigators asked Red how business was. She said it was real good "cuz black mens likes having sex with pregnant womens, it's good luck, ya know." Blue Eyes tried to keep the conversation going by asking when the baby was due. Not to be outdone, Easterling inquired of Red if she knew who the baby's father was.

Red piped up right away: "Oh 'das Billy Roy's baby." Both men sat in the car totally dumfounded. At the same time, they asked her how she knew that to be the case. She put her hands on her hips and answered the inquiry with a pearl of unsurpassed ghetto street logic. "Evabody know that to get pregnant you gots to have you an ohganizum (which is pronounced oh-gah-nizm) and Billy Roy's the onlyist one I had me an ohganizm within the last two years." Easterling was speechless. Blue Eyes was able to get out the words "That's nice." Neither man looked at the other for fear of breaking out laughing. Benson drove off slowly and the interior of their Ford sounded like a pack of hyenas were being hauled off. Benson's vision blurred so badly from his tears of laughter that he jumped a curb and hit a garbage can about the time he yelled out, "Somebody's got to, but it ain't you, bitch."

Pebbles got busted by Fincher in a couple of days and she confessed to being part of a robbery deal with an old time pimp named Dancing Billy. Pebbles and Dancing Billy went to the joint and are long forgotten. A Momma in San Antonio had to tell her kids that the Houston Police got it all wrong about their daddy going with a prostitute. For the two investigators of this case, however, the phrase "evabody know" will never again be the same.

FLUFFY

Steven Rowan rode the night shift out of the Northeast Station. He was a tall, slim product of a northeastern Texas hand-to-mouth upbringing. Rowan came to the Gulf Coast following a four-year hitch in the Army, and now only returned to the land of his birth for two holidays yearly and for funerals. He'd been heard to say that he did not care much for pine trees or the people that lived under them. The only other thing that he was really ever known to dislike in life was house cats.

Growing up, Rowan had personally killed at least half of the meat that he'd eaten off of his mother's table. His ability regarding the use of firearms was so uncanny that he had perfected his shots (on game animals) so he did the least amount of damage to the meat. Whenever possible, he chose to shoot squirrels through the throat with his .22 rifle. Both his hillbilly uncle and grandfather relished the eating of squirrel brains. During his military service, Steve Rowan had been through Army sniper training school. He had not only been able to shoot with extreme accuracy but he also possessed the very mentality they were looking for: "It's not the kill that matters so much—it's the shot placement that counts."

About one night a week, when it got quiet out on patrol, Steve would hunt housecats. He returned to the weapon of his youth, a .22 rifle. This one, however, was honed to perfection and babied by its owner. He chose for his ammunition a short-range .22 rim-fire cartridge called a CB cap. This round, when shot from a long-barreled .22 rifle, was every bit as quiet as a pellet gun. The projectile, however, hits with a whole lot more authority. Coupled with a one-inch diameter scope with lighted crosshairs, this made a wonderful night-hunting companion.

Head shots out to twenty-five or thirty yards were the norm. The bullets generally would enter but would not exit the bodies. The sniper's mantra is B.R.A.S.—Breath, Aim, Relax, and Squeeze. "Let it be a surprise when the gun goes off."

The last known kitty-sniper shooting by the feline serial killer of Northeast Houston took place while attempting to execute a headshot. The animal was perched on a residential window ledge. Steve unfortunately misjudged the shot. The big yellow cat he had fixed upon was later determined to have been sitting upon the *interior* rather than the *exterior* window ledge. His aim still held true, and Fluffy the cat caught it between the running lights. The homeowner heard the commotion and found poor Fluffy DOA on the living room floor, just lying there attempting to assume room temperature. Steve Rowan and his partner were dispatched to the shooting call. The two patrolmen did their best to be conciliatory toward the owner of the late Saint Fluffy.

"Yes ma'am, that is a terrible shame. No ma'am, I can't imagine what sort of person could ever do such a thing."

Steve had seen both crooks and officers push their luck too far, and they had always paid the price. His pet rifle was taken home, cleaned and put back into the gun vault. "The man who thinks he's smarter than everyone else invariably gets sloppy and steps on his own tail, or worse— his dingus. The fella who knows he's nothing special, he knows that if he pushes his luck too far it's all over. He'll get bitten on the butt for sure."

GOAL ORIENTATION

Jeff Wald came from a family with extensive pine timber holdings in the Lake Fork region of northeastern Texas and northern Louisiana. At the age of twenty-two, and upon the completion of a college degree, he joined the Houston Police Department. After the police academy he was assigned to the night shift out of the Central Station. His training took place in 15 District, a high-crime area known locally as the Third Ward. At that specific point in time, each officer in that district (as well as their immediate supervisor) had been involved in at least one fatal on-duty shooting.

In his off-duty time (at least once, if not twice, weekly) Jeff would go to a private gun range and fire between fifty and 150 rounds through his duty weapon. He would then drive home and clean his weapon. He was eleven months out of the police academy when he exchanged shots with a mentally unstable individual. The mental case missed, but Jeff Wald did not. His second shooting involved the dispatching of an armed robbery suspect who was exiting the front doors of an Asian-operated "Stop-N-Rob" type convenience store. The late hijacker went to Glory with a gun in his hand and several solid hits to his central nervous system. The robber obtained seventy-five dollars from the cash register just moments before he was centered in a swarm of 00 buckshot pellets.

The Crime Scene Units and the Homicide detectives marveled at how tight the buckshot pattern was in the chest cavity of the very dead suspect. It was not until they examined Jeff's 870 Remington riot gun that they determined just why. The shotgun had been customized by adding a modified screw-in choke system and a glow-in-the-dark front sight. The dearly departed would never be able to report that the last sounds he heard before his eyes clouded over were a shotgun blast, followed by a shout of, "Halt-Police!" A black area newspaper's headlines billed the shooting with, "Police Kill Youth for $75." A grand jury reviewed the matter and justified the killing as nothing more than a case of urban predator control.

Following his second no-bill from a Harris County grand jury in only nine months, Officer Wald submitted his resignation to the Houston Police Department. It read as follows:

Jeff Wald left the Houston-Harris County area to attend law school in Dallas. Upon becoming a lawyer, he returned to northeastern Texas small town life and became a respected member of the community.

August 12,XXXX

To whom it may concern,

I, City of Houston Police Officer Jeffery D. Wald, Employee Number XXXXX, do as of this date, hereby tender my resignation from the Houston Police Department. I have enjoyed my tenure as a Houston Police Officer, and have fulfilled the goals that I set out to accomplish for myself.

Jeffery D. Wald

HANGIN' WITH FRANKY

Halloween is a big event in the homosexual community. The occasion becomes quite festive and people are able to play dress-up and role-play their fantasies for at least one night a year. Southern Belles in hoop skirts and Ninjas in black pajamas abound. In Houston the costumed gays traditionally bar hop and stroll between the 100 and 1200 blocks of Westheimer Street. The neighborhood they covet is called Montrose. On this particular night of the year both gay and non-gay drivers always snarl the sector's vehicular traffic. They slowly drive through the area to gawk and take in the freak show. The area nightclubs run at full blast with a Mardi Gras-like atmosphere.

Marty Stuben was a gay dwarf living in the lower Westheimer district. Herr Stuben was a regular at the leather bars and wore his hair in a flattop which he bleached a stark white. He was prone to outlandish behavior and described himself as being a "Montrose Muppet." Marty chose to live out his life's greatest fantasy for Halloween of 2002. He was going to be tall, and the most frightening and famous monster of all time. A trip to Houston's premier theatrical supply house provided him everything he needed to become the best Frankenstein to ever grace the Texas Gulf Coast. Marty first bought a pair of sheetrock hanger's stilts and had extensions added to his pants legs. Now, for once in his life, he could tower above the rest of humanity.

The eight-foot-tall Frankenstein was the Belle of the Ball. He stalked back and forth across the dance floor of the Brushy Bottoms Club, growling and clawing at the air with his hands. A hangman's noose hung from the monster's neck, with the rope's loose end dangling and almost touching the floor. All of the club's patrons were so very much impressed with the green-tinted Frankenstein. It seemed that everyone wanted to either buy Marty a drink, or to have their picture taken with him. The end result of it all was that Marty became so drunk that he couldn't have hit his butt with both hands—even if he'd had the benefit of a radar tracking device.

Always loving to draw attention to himself, Marty continued to put on a show as he staggered around the dance floor on his stilts. At one point, Marty threw the loose end of the rope trailing behind him over an exposed beam. He pulled back on the rope, grabbing his throat and growling as if he were strangling. The crowd loved his antics. This continued for about twenty seconds, until due to his drunken state, Marty tripped and fell. The rope hung on the beam it had been thrown over and the slip knot tightened easily, just as it had been designed to do. His audience roared as Frankenstein thrashed and writhed on the floor and clawed at his neck. Then he became quite still.

A two-man uniformed police unit was dispatched and arrived before the paramedics. Raul Martinez had seen some odd sights in the two years he'd ridden the night shift in the Montrose district. What he encountered that night truly caught him off guard. Frankenstein lay dead on the dance floor with his face terribly contorted. Franky's head was in Dolly Parton's lap and Little Bo Peep and a pumpkin sat on the floor on either side of the cadaver. They sat there holding his hands and crying their little eyes out. Martinez got his first Internal Affairs complaint generated that night for his alleged improper attitude and demeanor. When he initially viewed the scene, Raul burst into an uncontrollable fit of laughter. The IAD investigators reviewed the death scene photographs and fell prey to the very same reaction. The unofficial ruling regarding the complaint was either: *occurred and was justified, or some people get their feelings hurt too easily.*

THAT BIG

Albert Harmon and Bobby Forrest were partners working the four p.m. to midnight shift out of Homicide. They were ten years apart in age, and the only real values they shared were their complete and total contempt for all of mankind. They laughed and made fun throughout every homicide scene they encountered, except those where children or old people were victims. Those were the only cases where horseplay and irreverence were taboo. When there was nobody else close at hand to harass or annoy, they chose to pick on one another just to keep in practice.

Harmon was a first-generation American whose parents had emigrated from Germany. Forrest was a Houstonian by birth, and his mother was Jewish. Harmon, upon determining his partner's ethnicity, only called him "J.B." (short for Jew Boy). Hearing Forrest called J.B. all the time, the rest of the squad picked up on the nickname. Forrest was, at times, heard to tell Harmon that he was so ignorant that he would have not even made a decent oven-tender at a Nazi death camp. To cutting remarks, Harmon typically responded, "You can't hurt my feelings, I been married twice ya' know" or "Hell, I've been married to meaner and uglier bitches than you." Harmon appeared to take great pride in only one thing, and that was his German heritage. He would tell people that he was raised to never discriminate against any group. Where he had grown up in the Texas Hill Country there were only two groups of people: Germans, and all others. Forrest keyed in on the heritage angle and began calling all fat women German-American Princesses, or GAP's for short. All blacks were always referred to as Black Forest Germans. Harmon was forever finding newspaper articles left on his desk regarding impotence treatments, or penal enlargement operations. The sources were always anonymous.

On the opening day of deer season, "Punkin' Joe" Carter was shot and killed on Houston's shallow north side. Harmon handled the witnesses. Forrest did the scene description and coordinated with the crime scene unit, as to what evidence needed collecting, and what just needed to be photographed. Both men preferred to work in this manner. Harmon did not like to testify, and in fact, prosecutors did not like to use him very often. Juries did not relate well to Harmon. Harmon did, in fact, look like he could have been a Hitler youth director. He wore his hair in a flat top and had coffee cup handles for ears. Forrest would describe him to people in one of two ways, saying either "You can't miss him—with those ears, he looks just like a wing nut" or "He's the guy they modeled the Mr. Yuck poison safety stickers after." Harmon's third chin always sat atop the knot on his tie, just to enhance his striking good looks. If that wasn't enough, his lower lip hung down like he was carrying half a can of snuff in it, even when it wasn't. Forrest liked the way he and his partner split up the scene investigation duties. He didn't like dealing with distraught people, and he wasn't intimidated by lawyers or testifying in court. Forrest also had an almost ghoulish interest in both firearms and terminal ballistics. One of his favorite lines was "Dead people won't lie to you, and neither will blood spatter."

Part of any scene investigation includes going to the morgue and filing an autopsy request. While there the investigators will chart the obvious wounds on the body. In their report, investigators will note locations of bullet or stab wounds in approximate distances. This is so his report and the autopsy report don't differ as to as to exact measurements. When the body arrives at the Harris County Morgue it is brought into the rear, or receiving section. The subject then has a toe tag wired in place with his vital information written in. His or her clothing is also removed and put into a plastic bag. The bag is then placed on the tray that sits below the one the cadaver lies upon.

While Forrest was going about his routine of locating wounds and making notes, Bubba (one of the night shift ghouls called morgue attendants) called out to the detectives, "Hey come over here guys, you gotta see this one." The two men walked over to the other end of the receiving area. Bubba pulled back the sheet covering a middle-aged man and pointed to the cadaver's crotch. The dead man's flaccid appendage that Bubba pointed to was approximately eighteen inches in length.

Bubba marveled, exclaiming "Have you ever seen anything like that in your life?"

Harmon snorted and responded with a sneer, "Hell, I've had one like that for years."

Bubba was astounded and gasped "That big?" Harmon flatly answered, "No, that dead."

HOMOSEXUAL KILLINGS

Ask any experienced Homicide investigator and he will tell you that you can spot a homosexual killing as soon as you walk into the room. No it's not from seeing pink frilly dust ruffles on all the furniture, but from the extreme amount of overkill involved. Often you may read in the newspaper of a man being found in his home, dead from between twenty-eight to thirty stab wounds. In those cases, there is a damned good chance that either the dearly departed or the suspect (usually both) were light in the loafers.

Another thing a detective will most likely determine at the murder scene is that the dead Sweetie's car, electronic equipment and microwave oven will all likely be missing. Just why microwave ovens are fixated upon by suspects in queer killing cases remains uncertain. The common thread running through these cases, however, seems to be that the suspects were very often picked up by their victims from gay bars. The suspects go home with Dear John where they consummate the act. The victims very often tend to be found naked and either on a bed or on the floor beside it. The crooks appear to fold, spindle and mutilate his host just after copulation.

Their method of killing is so similar that you could have multiple homosexual serial killers working all over the country simultaneously and never know it. Stabbing the victim is the most common method, sometimes accompanied by a brutal beating. Knives are very often the weapon of choice in these killings. The killer is generally a short term "friend" and extreme overkill is almost always present. Even when they kill someone who may or may not be their lover, the same level of excessive violence is often present. When the killers are caught, it's generally either through finding the victim's car, fingerprints found at the scene, or stolen credit cards are used. Yet another method that the killings are regularly cleared through is that the killer tells someone about it. Many times the killer will talk about the deed to his buddies. When his buddy gets into trouble, that party often wants to play Monte Hall—"It's time to play let's make a deal." In some murder investigations you clear cases where you have no clues, and in others you can't buy luck even when you know who did it and why.

There was one suspect in Houston that was ultimately tied to three homosexual monogramming (stabbing murders). He was caught in one case through his fingerprints. He simply volunteered the information about killing the other two Johns, strictly because he got along with the investigator who took his confession. Due to the frenzied sexual lifestyle of the homosexual male, it's a wonder there are not even more of these types of murder investigations.

Many times a street hustler (male prostitute) will go home with a wealthy John and set him up for a home invasion or a burglary. The hustler may spend a day or two with the victim, doing drugs and playing escaped convict and the warden's wife. While there, he scopes the place out for valuables. He may let his buddies into the house while he's still there, or shortly after he leaves, the Mongol hordes will descend upon Sweetie's (the victim's) lavish abode. Sweetie is beaten and bound and his valuables are carried off into the night.

During one such home invasion in southwest Houston, a silent burglar alarm saved the day. The alarm was set off as the suspects kicked in the leaded glass front doors. The three black male suspects brutally beat the two aging Sweethearts living there. The robbery victims were both bound with duct tape and left on the living room floor. A uniformed patrol unit was dispatched to the silent alarm call. The suspects were carrying out the loot as the responding officers arrived. One suspect was carrying out a shotgun belonging to the victims. He was shot in the arm by one of the responding officers. It was now an *officer involved shooting*, and Homicide investigators were called out. The lead investigator, Fred Harmon, called the Homicide desk to advise the Duty Lieutenant about the scene. When asked what led up to the shooting, Harmon flatly answered, "It's sort of like bein' in a poker game out here. Three spades beats two queens."

Soon thereafter, Harmon and a brand new rookie detective named Douglas Baker were assigned a homosexual killing scene in north central Houston. The victim was found lying nude in bed, dead from multiple stab wounds. Silly's penis and testicles had also been cut off (post-mortem) and were now unaccounted for. In the course of the investigation (and as the scene was being processed) a wad of tin foil was noted to be laying on the bedroom floor. The home was a wreck and the foil was not really a high priority. The foil had, in fact, been kicked out of the way a time or two as photographs were taken and diagrams were being made. After being there for an hour or so, Baker, out of curiosity, picked up the foil and unwrapped it. Therein he found the victim's missing private parts. He threw them into the air with a resounding "Oh, shit." For the rest of his police career, Douglas Baker was known as "Dick" Baker.

ROSA'S CANTINA

Investigators Forrest and Sosa were assigned to a double shooting DOA call. It came in as an apparent murder with an attempt at suicide on the part of the suspect. The DOA victim was a female Hispanic who owned the bar in which the killing took place. The suspect, Hector Mares, had been the murder victim's boyfriend. The day before he killed her, she had broken up with him, or as they say on the street, "She gave him his walking papers." By all accounts he had not taken it well. Hector responded poorly to being jilted. He walked into her bar and put multiple rounds from a 9mm handgun into her torso. He then turned the weapon upon himself, sustaining an apparent self-inflicted gunshot wound to his head. Doctors at Ben Taub Hospital said the killer was not expected to live. This was only one of many such cases that the two investigators had made over the years.

The shooting took place inside a cantina bar on Houston's East End. The neighborhood is almost exclusively Spanish-speaking. Shootings and cuttings in the clubs in this area are frequent. When they occur, the Texas Alcoholic Beverage Commission may choose to shut the club down for three working days for a "cooling off period." This law is called "The Cantina Law" because of the frequency of the murders and deadly weapon assault cases that occur in barrio clubs. Many times a shooting or cutting call will drop, and it will be alleged that the crime occurred next door to, or outside, a cantina. The police and fire department will respond. They will find a victim either dead or wounded upon the ground or in the street. The sidewalk in front of the beer joint often will be wet from having just been washed down. The bar in question may or may not be open. If the bar is open, the responding police will be told by persons therein that nothing happened inside. The other thing the officers will note is that there will be one large freshly-mopped spot on the floor. They will also see a freshly-mopped trail leading from the large spot to the front door. The bar location which Forrest and Sosa responded to that particular night was a place of this sort.

The victim was dead at the scene. The doctors at Ben Taub Hospital told the detectives that it was not a matter of if, but rather a question of just when the shooter was going to die. There were several witnesses to the killing and they all gave sworn affidavits. The murder victim was well-known and liked by the neighborhood drinking crowd. The scene was processed and a suicide note written in Spanish was found on the dash of the suspect's car. The county morgue was given the suspect's name and hospital chart number so that when he died the cause of death information would be immediately available. Neither investigator could read Spanish, so they submitted the note for translation by a dayshift clerk. The report was completed and cleared by means of the death of the suspect.

Four weeks after the shooting (with the case already filed away in the archives), a hospital charge nurse called Homicide inquiring as to what the department wanted to do with the suspect. He was now ready to be discharged. A uniformed unit was quickly dispatched and Mares was taken into custody. The somewhat startled scene detectives filed charges later that day. The suspect was observed to be both functional and mobile. Forrest advised Sosa that the suspect's recovery reflected one of two things: Either a brain shot was not a fatal wound to a Mexican, or the Hispanic brain is too small to be an easy target.

Miraculous recoveries by poor people coming from impoverished countries are quite common. Many have never been treated with antibiotics. They are the products of selective breeding. Where they come from only the strongest children survive, and infant mortality rates are extremely high.

The following is the translation of the suspect's intended handwritten suicide note.

I, Hector Mares,

In plain state of mind without the effects of any kind of drugs, I want to write this letter. I will only drink some beers so that I get the courage for what I am going to do. I am going to kill a person that I love most in this world besides God and my mother. But I want to tell you the following so that it will serve as an example to other men like me that have gone through the same thing. I am originally from Monterrey N.L., Mexico. I arrived in this city with hopes to progress economically and find a woman of my life and form a family and do the best to achieve this goal. Some years ago I lived with a woman. I don't want to mention her name for reasons that I prefer not to say, OK. She played me wrong, I gave her money and all the goodness that I could to live happily but it did not work. Only God knows why we separated and it hurt me a lot. I tried to continue living my life struggling and working hard as I always have since I arrived in this country.

I sentimentally and economically recovered, I sent money to my mother in Mexico—she is in need and I accomplished to save some money in the bank. Thinking of my future I tried to establish a welfare fund for a family that I planned to form. Unfortunately I met Rosa Castro and again the routine of my life changed. She promised me love and I confided in her because I loved her. I will continue loving her until now that I am writing this letter. She is the owner of a nightclub that is not functioning well because of lack of money. She let me know this. Me, with a kind heart—not thinking what would happen later, helped her economically. I gave her everything that I had, including my savings. Now I don't have anything except my hands that I can continue working, she says for me to leave. She says she doesn't love me anymore and doesn't need me. She thinks she wants to continue her life without me. The money does not matter, but she has destroyed my heart for the second time.

I can't handle this, it is too much for me. The only thing I own is a Ford Bronco truck, and it needs a little repair due to an accident I had before. Well I'll sell it for the best price so that I can get some money for the funeral. They can send my body to my beloved land, with my family that I should never left. Over there I was poor but I had my family which I loved and missed a lot, and who I ask for forgiveness for what I am going to do.

I know by words from those I consider friends, that this woman has done the same to two or three men in the past, that which she has done to me. She has made fools of them. Don't worry because she is not going to be hurting anyone. To kind-hearted persons and noble people like I consider myself. I am going to kill her. So that they don't blame someone else, after that I am going to kill myself. I don't expect God's forgiveness, but only he knows that what I am writing is the truth. Together with this letter I am leaving the keys to this truck that I am selling. Inside the truck are the documents. By law documents and original title can be picked up at XXXX Oak in Pasadena. You can ask for it at this address. They were supposed to send the title to that address. In case they don't want to turn it over for any reason, I am dead. I don't care anymore. They can do what they want with my corpse, I don't want to be a burden on anyone. A depressed person says goodbye to this world. Not from this world or life, but from a bad woman.

Hector Mares

The investigators that made this scene were somewhat surprised by the letter of their suspect. He turned out to be more than just some mindless day laborer whose macho got the best of him, which is usually the case. The criminal justice system was not impressed and his writings didn't keep him from going to prison for his actions.

QUOTES FROM THE UNCOUTH

Warning: These assaults upon the English language were committed by professionally crass and/or illiterate individuals. Do not attempt to use these statements at home. For a complete appreciation of what has been recorded here, the reading of these statements aloud at times may be beneficial.

From a conversation regarding a coworker's perpetual use of obscene language: "You've got to keep this point in mind—we're talking about Russell, not some normal human being. Profanity is an integral part of the man's vocabulary. If he couldn't use the words shit, goddamn, and motherf**ker, he'd either stutter or just stand there silently working his lips like a goldfish."

Unorthodox Miranda Warning: "You have the right to remain silent. We really wish you'd exercise your right to remain silent. Let me translate that into plain English. We're tired of your mouth and you need to shut the f**k up before someone slaps the shit out of you."

From a locked-and-cocked Colt 1911 automatic pistol fan: "The double action automatic pistol is the answer to a problem that doesn't exist."

"Count yourself—You ain't so many."

"The only difference between my ex-wife and a rabid pit bulldog is about twenty-five pounds and the overpowering odor of Chanel Number 5 perfume."

"That boy is interested in only one thing—money. It's just as well that he wasn't born a good lookin' woman, least-wise his Momma would have to deal with there being a whore (pronounced hoe-er) in the family."

"Take note of that young lady over there. She is nothing more than a coin-operated machine. She is sitting on a gold mine, and she damned well knows it. When she smiles at a man, you can almost hear the cha-ching sound of an old timey cash register ringing up."

Regarding a promise from city hall regarding a pay raise: "You just can't trust what they tell ya' about nothin'. The terms politician and pile of shit are really close in both sound and practicality."

"That old bastard is so vulgar that he thinks Peter Pan is a wash basin in a cathouse."

Statement made by a Good ol' Boy-Bubba type describing a fellow he held in very high regard: "Well I'd say he's just about as fine a fella as ever pulled a dick out of a mule's ass."

Statement of a fugitive from Huntsville, Alabama regarding women in general (it should be noted that this Cracker pronounced his home-town's name as Hauntsvul): "You know, Boss, if it weren't for the fact you can screw them, there'd be a bounty on 'em for sure—just like coyotes."

"Keep this in mind young man, there is a direct link between ovaries and insanity. The trick is to find a woman whose level of insanity you can live with. When you say, 'For better or for worse,' you'd better realize it may not get any better. Rest assured it sure as hell can get a lot worse."

Statement of an old Homicide investigator to the chief investigator of the Harris County Medical Examiner's Office: "If you see me come through this place, all I'm asking for is a clean tray. I don't want to be lying around in some other dead bastard's body fluids and pubic hairs."

"That girl's personality is such that her bridal registry will have to be through the American Kennel Club."

"In East Texas, women don't have beauty marks on their faces. Those are called ticks."

"There's no accounting for taste—some people eat buggars, you know."

"You gotta treat a Colt .45 automatic and a pump shotgun like you would a Mexican wife. If you treat them nice and gentle, they don't work right. But if you rack the hell out of 'em, then they will function flawlessly."

Describing weather conditions: "It's as cold as a whore's heart out there."

From a range officer, addressing an all-male group of officers at a Narcotics Division Survival Training School. These schools are put on regularly for training and safety reasons. This session followed a series of accidental discharges from both Glock and Colt 1911 pistols. Some of these discharges resulted in injuries, while others simply caused either constipation or loose bowel syndrome among those present at the shooting scenes. There had been enough of these incidents in a short time frame that the department was considering banning those specific types of weapons. "Think of it this way gentlemen—an accidental discharge is sort of like a premature ejaculation. There's no taking it back or doing it over again. What's done is done, and you're stuck with the final outcome forever. The one hard and fast rule is, keep your finger outside of the trigger guard until such time as you've decided to destroy something that is in front of you."

"You, sir, are living proof that you cannot shine shit."

"No good deed goes unpunished."

"What good is it being a Shithead, if you can't act likes one?"

A Latin homosexual is also known as a Gay Caballero.

"It was obviously a natural death—you're just naturally gonna die if somebody shoots you that many times."

"A virgin in this neighborhood is a nine-year-old girl that can outrun both her father and her brothers." (Statement by an old patrol officer in northeast Houston regarding a predominantly Hispanic sector of town known as Denver Harbor.)

"The strongest element ever known to man is the pubic hair of a woman. When a man gets it stuck between his teeth, he can be led any-where." (The late Roy Bean, Attorney at Law and an admitted Sybaritic Barbarian)

"You can always tell a level-headed person from the eastern part of Texas. He or she is the one that has snuff dripping out of both corners of their mouth."

"If a man and woman marry in Liberty County (Texas) and divorce in Hardin County, are they still brother and sister?"

An old police expression: "Mexicans are like cue balls. The harder you hit them, the more English you get out of them."

Description made of a power blackout on an overcast night: "It's as black as a whore's heart out there."

Overheard at a police Lieutenant's funeral following his suicide. The dead man had been an avowed atheist, and had been somewhat rabid about his hatred of religion. As two gray-headed Sergeants stood beside his coffin, one commented to the other, "Just look at him now, would ya' Tommy—all dressed up and no place to go."

"The fairer sex has never been the gentler, it's the lioness that does the killing, you know."

"My sister calls her new boyfriend her Latin Lover. Hell, a Latin Lover ain't nuthin' but a f**king Meskin."

"There are very few social problems that can't be cured with a 12-gauge shotgun and a load of buckshot."

The following statement was part of an actual Internal Affairs Unit complaint. A patrol officer was alleged to have directed this statement toward a double-wide, battle-axe type woman while making a family disturbance call. "Excuse me ma'am, but who is running things back in Hell while you're here with us?"

"All I ever date is sluts. That stands for *single ladies under twenty-six*. When they pass that benchmark (get beyond age twenty-six) they become slots—*single ladies over twenty-six*."

"Listen up, stupid, if you're looking for sympathy around here, you're gonna find it between the words shit and syphilis in the dictionary."

Description made by a nine-time convicted felon: "I'd say he was about as happy as a queer with two assholes."

With the gay community gaining political clout, and the era of political correctness being ushered in, the street officers were subjected to yearly sensitivity training. Calling members of the "light in the loafers" community names like "queer, fag, shit-packer or pillow biter" became highly frowned upon by the department. The yearly in-service training consisted of some officer reading the regulations, followed by some flaming members of the gay community talking for an hour or so about "their" community. One group of street officers became noted for using creative phrases (but not on paper) such as "members of the indefinite sex, Sodomites, Gomorrah-Chucks, or Quadra-Sexuals." Statements began to be heard out on gay domestic squabbles such as "Hush now, Sweetie, you've had your say. Now it's this Sodomite's turn to tell his side of the story."

"The three most dangerous things in the world are, a Mexican in a pickup, a queer with a sharp tooth, and a Coonass (Cajun) with a high school education."

"The three capital crimes in the state of Louisiana are murder, rape, and pissing in a crawfish hole."

"You could tell by the way that Sumbitch walked into the room that he was as angry as a festered cat's ass."

The following is a quote from the scene of a family disturbance call. An elderly grandmotherly-looking woman with big blue eyes complained about the way her daughter-in-law talked in front of the grandchildren. "Officer, when I say the word 'shit' it's one thing, but when she says it—well, it just sounds so damned common."

Statement of a defense attorney to a client in the hallway of a courthouse: "Let me see if I can get you to grasp the situation from my point of view. Even a bass wouldn't get caught, if he'd just keep his damned mouth shut."

"The first causality out here was truth, followed by the poor bastard who just assumed room temperature." (Description as to how a dope-related murder investigation was going.)

Statement of an Internal Affairs investigator: "I'm like a cat with a problem, too much stuff and too little sand to cover it with."

"Anybody satisfied with what they got likely doesn't deserve any better."

"No matter how lovely, how thoughtful, how poised and beautiful she might be—I promise you that somewhere out there is someone who has already gotten tired of her shit."

"Real policemen ride the night shift and drive patrol cars."

"Golf was invented so that white people would have an excuse to dress up like Negroes."

Homicide supervisor describing one of his investigators: "That Bastard is so illiterate that he doesn't know a semi-colon from a small intestine."

"You can tell a Vietnamese from a Cambodian just by looking at them. The Cambodian's head is rounder. The Vietnamese's head is more narrow. A Cambodian's head will completely fill the rear sight aperture of an M-16 at fifty meters."

In the words of an old Homicide Lieutenant, "The three most over-rated things in the world are, sex to a young man, the Texas Rangers and the F.B.I."

Words of wisdom from a recently-divorced cop: "Before I'd ever get married again I'll go out and become 'buy-sexual.' I may pay to get it, but I damn sure won't marry it. My daddy always said that if it flies, floats or f**ks you ought to rent it—and I think he was right."

The process of picking of a jury panel in capital (death penalty) cases in Texas is a long, drawn-out process. The potential jury members are interviewed individually by both the defense and prosecution and they have to fill out some rather long and detailed questionnaires. These go into life experiences of the prospective juror. Has he or she ever been a crime victim? Are they related to, or friends with, police officers? One blue collar member of a potential jury pool was asked if he could give somebody a death sentence. The man pondered for a second and responded, "I think my boss would let me off so I could drive to Huntsville (the location of Death Row) and take care of it, but I'd have to check." He was naturally struck by the defense team.

There are two brothers in Houston that practice criminal law and they are reported to have two fee schedules. The first is, if you supply the witness to lie for you. The second is, if they have to provide one.

A statement made during a break from the bench by the presiding judge, who had a white trash murder trial in progress: "The only thing we haven't had put into testimony in this case so far is trailer houses and pit bulldogs, and I'm sure that's only a witness away."

"Working around here is like pissing in a pair of dark pants. You get a warm feeling for a short period of time, but nobody really notices."

"The truth's not in 'em—a crook will lie on credit when he could tell the truth for free."

"Pimps were invented so that drug addict whores would be able to wake up in the morning and see something sorrier than they are."

"God gave men superior physical strength, so that it would be more of a fair fight." (The words of an unnamed Homicide investigator just after he walked out of a divorce court proceeding.)

Sign posted in a donut shop in Needville, Texas: Bad Cop, No Donut. –The Management

Handwritten note seen upon a men's bathroom wall in an adult bookstore where a Homicide investigation was being conducted: "My mother made me a homosexual." Written below this in a different hand and in a different colored ink was, "If I give her the yarn will she make me one?"

Statement made by a reformed motorcycle gang member who had found Jesus: "Officer, if he comes around acting like that again, I may have to do something I'll have to repent for later."

"Do that again and you'll need to be sized for a colostomy bag."

"Stupid got shot so many times that he had flow-through ventilation like a 1974 Chevrolet Caprice."

"The most traumatic day of the year in this part of town is Father's Day." (Old patrol officer in the Third Ward sector of Houston.)

Inquiry made by a Homicide investigator at a "cut 'em up-shoot 'em up" kind of scene in and around a trashy north side beer joint, asking the first responding unit at the scene, "Are the participants in this shit storm related to one another?" The uniformed officer shifted his quid of tobacco and responded, "I believe their all dog kin."

"I was in the bathroom at the time" is a phrase Homicide investigators hear quite often when investigating beer joint killings. One detective reported that he surveyed the patrons at a cantina double-shooting death scene and determined that thirty-two people had reportedly been in the one stall unisex bathroom at the time of the shooting. Even all of the band members claimed to have been in there too.

A quote credited to Charles Manson following the Tate mass murder trial: "Not everybody is afraid of a gun—but everybody is afraid of a knife."

"Whenever you get around a good ol' boy type of fella, put your hand over your wallet."

Statement of a street gang member brought into Ben Taub Hospital after being beaten badly and stabbed. Uniformed officers responded to the hospital check. Jesse Torres came in from an unknown location by private auto. He was lying on a gurney awaiting treatment and was asked the standard line by patrol officers to see what happened. His response was classic. "I was roller skating and failed to negotiate a curve."

"It's hard to say just when sainthood is bestowed upon these lower forms of life. It's somewhere between the time they pass on, and the time some ambulance-chasing attorney starts talking to the family about a lawsuit."

"It's my opinion, therefore, it has to be true."

Located in southwest Houston is a neighborhood named Meyerland. Its developers, the Meyer brothers, and many of the original residents, were Jewish. The Jewish influence remains strong to this day. The cops call this sector of the city either The Bagel Belt, or the Promised Land.

"When you're schizophrenic, you're never really alone."

Statement made by a burly male police sergeant during a mandatory sensitivity training class, regarding the gay community: "What do you mean I don't understand your community? Hell lady, I've been a lesbian all of my life."

A stabbing victim's description of her attacker made to uniformed officers: "She a big ol' ugly bitch-gorilla lookin' thang. She gots urnge (orange) lookin' hair and she wearin' a pink dress, you can't miss her."

"Now that Yassar Arafat is no longer alive, you may well be the ugliest man in the world."

"Sarg, I know you and the rest of the administration are behind us in this matter. We've felt you there on several occasions."

"You can do anything right, or you can do anything wrong. If you work at it you could probably fart with class."

Words of wisdom from a training officer who was messing with his rookie: "In this neighborhood (an area inhabited by many gays) you need to think about if you really want to hit someone with your nightstick. You see, around here that action might be looked upon as foreplay. The recipient of your attention may now be expecting to sleep with you."

A message found on the bedside table beside a much-disliked police Lieutenant when he awakened following triple bi-pass surgery: "We have canvassed the squad and have concluded that you are such a horse's ass that, in the event of your death, we will have to hire three paid mourners. That way, at your funeral it will look like someone in this world actually gave a shit about you."

"A mind is a terrible thing."

"Blacks are the only group that have been in this country for over 200 years and have yet to learn how to speak the language."

Quote from a west Texas version of William Shakespeare: "It's a foul wind that blows from the stockyards."

In 1974, a twenty-year veteran of the Houston Police Department Homicide Division gave this lecture to Houston Police Academy cadets: "You will be charged with a multitude of tasks in your police career. The one that is of greatest assistance to the investigation of major crimes such as murder, armed robbery and sexual assaults is animal registration. One of your specific job functions and goals should be to ensure that all street animals have their photos and paw prints on file."

"I ain't afraid of nuthin' with a meat skin asshole."

This is one side of a telephone conversation between a black Homicide investigator and an alleged assault suspect. "Looky here, Roger Wayne. You were supposed to be in my office yesterday afternoon for a statement. I've got enough to file on you with what I've got, but I think there's more to this deal and I want your side of it. File on you with what evidence? From the statements of Latisha and her new boyfriend, that's from what evidence. Now I want a sworn statement from you before I present this case to the District Attorney—you hear me? I want you in my office tomorrow morning at nine a.m., do you hear me? That's nine a.m., white man's time. Do you know what that means? That means on time!"

From a family disturbance-assault arrest situation: The estranged husband is being taken off in handcuffs, and he calls back to his wife, "Your momma wears a Jock!" She answers, "Yours needs to!"

A friend will help you move. A real friend will help you move the body.

An assault suspect justifying his kicking the stuffings out of another idiot: "We were just arguing. Everything would have been just fine if he just hadn't put his dick beaters (hands) on me."

"Oh yeah—well, if a cat has her kittens in the oven, that don't make 'em biscuits. (Translation unavailable.)

The following statement was made by a constable following his conviction on corruption-related crimes: "I'm a victim of racism, sexism and all kinda 'isms."

"If that son-of-a-bitch died tomorrow and was buried in a garbage can, you'd be hard pressed to find pall bearers."

"That woman would carve your heart out with a dull knife and enjoy every minute of it."

"The only cure for a pedophile is a liberal application of small to medium caliber projectiles to the back of his head."

As her ex-con, convicted sex offender son is being handcuffed, a loving mother asks what her son is being arrested for. When she is informed that he is charged with raping a seventy-four-year-old woman she tries to explain his predicament. "He can't help it officer, it's just the dog in him."

A gentleman was brought into the Homicide office for a witness statement following a street murder. He had a pseudo-Africanized middle name and the investigator typing his statement asked for its spelling. The man in question answered, "I'm not really sure, but that's okay, 'cuz I don't use it very often anyway."

Sign written on the back window of a disabled car being towed down the street by a raggedy old pickup truck: *CAR IN TOE.*

From a firearms instructor, who ran a school that taught civilians, police, and military special operations units: "America needs to be a place where the criminals are more afraid of the decent people than the good folks are of them."

Spoken by a Texas prison administrator: "Depending upon which unit you are talking about, somewhere between five and ten percent of our prison guard population should be standing on the other side of the bars."

OVER A BAITED FIELD

Marcus Alexander was eighty-one years old and legally blind. He could see fairly well up close, but beyond fifteen to twenty feet, everything became just shapes and shadows. He had outlived two of his three children and his wife. He lived alone in the same house that he and his wife (Miss Betty) shared for fifty years. To supplement his social security income, Mr. Marcus collected aluminum cans and sold barbecue sandwiches. He fired up his 'que pit every Friday and Saturday and had a regular clientele.

Mr. Marcus had a regular route that he walked early each morning. He gathered and flattened his cans and put them in a large wooden bin that butted up against his back fence. When he filled up the bin his nephew would come over with his pickup truck and make a run to the scrap dealer. At one point, it became obvious to Mr. Alexander that someone had been stealing cans out of his bin. He noted the thefts seemed to be occurring on either Tuesday or Thursday nights. The elderly homeowner decided to lay in wait to try and catch the thief.

The first night (Tuesday) Marcus sat in the dark, on the patio just behind his house. He had his old double-barreled shotgun in his lap, hoping to scare off the thief. At eight thirty, someone jumped the back fence, and a shotgun blast into the air caused the wayward party to go back from where he had come. Two nights later, he sat up late again, and saw two shapes come over the back fence about ten p.m. Mr. Marcus then heard somebody rustling about in his aluminum can stash. This time he decided he "was just gonna dust da' britches of 'dat thief, and teach him a lesson." He cranked off one barrel and heard thrashing sounds from inside the can bin. Then everything got quiet. He never saw or heard any more movement. After waiting a couple of minutes, he went inside and called 911. The responding patrol units found the late Willie Clayton lying dead as a hammer among the flattened aluminum cans. Homicide was called out.

In Texas, theft at night is grounds for killing someone. The killing at hand was a straightforward rehabilitation of a thief, adjudicated by buckshot. Officers Forrest and Michaels made the scene, and the first thing that Forrest noted was that the weapon used was a Damascus steel double-barreled L. C. Smith brand shotgun. The weapon was likely worth more than the old man's house. In the course of the scene investigation it was determined that Mr. Marcus thought he was loading his "twice barrel" with birdshot, and had mistakenly crammed it full of #1 buckshot. Willie caught the full load in the tripe from a distance of thirty-five to forty feet. From there, he simply passed on to his just rewards. From an overview of the scene it was determined that the two objects Mr. Marcus had seen coming over his back fence were a 55-gallon plastic garbage can and the late Willie Clayton. Willie must have learned the Boy Scout's credo of "Be prepared."

The shooter hit it off well with one of the investigators, a Detective Sergeant named George Michaels. Michaels read Mr. Marcus his legal rights and told him that he didn't have to make a statement or it could be used against him at a trial. Marcus listened politely and responded, "I don't care what y'all read to me—I'm gonna tell you the truth anyway." Everybody laughed and said how refreshing it was to meet a man interested in telling the truth. Michaels took the old man's statement on a confession form. He covered all of the bases so that the shooting of Saint Willie was justifiable for a multitude of reasons. The senior citizen-shooter had never been arrested in his life. The dead man, however, was no stranger to the iron house. After the confession was signed and witnessed, Michaels called the night shift chief prosecutor at the intake section of the district attorney's office. After going over the facts, the prosecutor agreed to present the case to a grand jury without any charges being filed. Michaels checked with Forrest to see if he needed to clear up any points with the shooter before he called for a unit and got him a ride home.

Forrest told him, "No, there's no more to be said. It's just a damned shame that we're gonna have to put Uncle Remus in jail."

Michaels went ballistic. "What the hell for? Theft at night is justifiable homicide in Texas and you damned well know it!"

Forrest replied with a completely deadpan facial expression. "Why, for shooting over a baited field, of course."

A general round-house cussing followed, allowing that Forrest was a sorry low life son-of-a-bitch of the worst order. To this, Forrest inquired, "You knew my mom?"

IN THE GHETTO

Phillip Marsh was a slight and swarthy-complexioned slumlord in southwest Houston. He personified all of the bad traits ever attributed to northeast coast or eastern European Jews. His personal holdings in the city of Sodom (Houston) consisted of two run-down apartment complexes. Because he could manage apartment complexes at the highest of possible profit margins, Phillip was always in demand to manage some other slumlord's properties. The neighborhood that these hovels were located in consists of several square miles of nothing but two- and three-story apartment buildings. Scattered throughout these rabbit warrens (that humans are expected to live in) are a few mom-and-pop stores in strip centers. The major east and west roadway in this neighborhood is Gulfton Street, and the neighborhood has long been dubbed "The Gulfton Ghetto."

The Gulfton area was founded in the 1960s boomtown days of Houston. This is where all the Yuppie and Swinger types lived. If you lived in Houston and were getting a divorce, you moved to the Gulfton area. There are complexes that cover four or more city blocks. One even has its own pharmacy and grocery store inside the confines of the complex. Several of the huge complexes had their own nightclubs.

When the oil bust hit, Houston fell upon hard times. The economy at that time was then almost completely based on the oil industry. With the coming of hard times, two things dropped in the apartment industry in Houston: the occupancy rates and the socio-economic class of the renters.

First, the complex owners went after the welfare dollars by seeking out the HUD Section 8 housing money (single mothers with dependent children). The complexes slid further into decay and then the rush of Hispanics hit town. The complex owners found out that the lower-income working class Hispanic would live in their seedy and rundown complexes and would pay weekly in cash for the chance to do so. These folks were glad just to have a roof over their head and the chance to work two jobs six or seven days a week. If the paint on the wall was peeling or the faucet dripped, it was of little consequence to them.

Phillip Marsh managed only complexes that rented to low-income persons, and were inhabited by either blacks or illegal aliens. Marsh's reputation was that he could squeeze more money out of a slum property than anybody in town. An example of his miserly methods can be seen in the fact that the only utility he supplied to his tenants was water. To ensure that the downtrodden masses didn't use too much of his water, Marsh had his building engineer dramatically lower the water pressure to the units. Water-saver showerheads were never required to conserve natural resources on any of the dumps he managed. Marsh kept his complexes full and collected his rent weekly. If tenants didn't pay their rent on Friday, their meager belongings would be in a dumpster early the next week.

His apartment buildings were never as noisy as the others in the area, and they were pretty well devoid of gang thugs. This occurred because he hired heavy-handed off-duty police officers to deal with dope dealer trash and gang trash. Marsh was such a hustler that he even farmed out his cops to other complexes. He then picked up a few extra dollars by pimping them out to complexes he didn't even manage. The usual eviction laws and due process did not apply to Phillip Marsh. Things just happened. In spite of his justifiably bad reputation, Marsh's complexes stayed full. That was because they were quieter and safer places to live.

In Spanish, the word *pinche* (pronounced peen-chay) can mean one of two things. It can refer to someone being miserly, or it can stand for the word f**king, as in "He's a f**king idiot." Both meanings of the word applied to Phillip Marsh. Most all of his Spanish-speaking employees and all of his renters called Marsh "Pinche Filepe" behind his back. They all had a Pinche Filepe story to tell. One of the most common was that you do not ever want to complain to Pinche Felipe if you discovered that your apartment was infested with either rats or roaches. If you do, he will charge you with a pet deposit.

God, in his infinite wisdom, sometimes metes out judgment upon or against the unjust on this side of the grave. In the case of Mister Marsh, the Lord has proved he has a wonderful since of humor as well. Pinche Felipe lived in a fancy neighborhood and drove expensive sports cars the whole time he managed his rathole apartment complexes. When he was outside of the Gulfton Ghetto he wore the fanciest of clothes and socialized with many of Houston's "Beautiful People." Today he has fallen from grace and is a heroin addict. He is scuffling out on the street, looking for his next fix and just trying to stay alive. Gracias Dios.

FAMOUS LAST WORDS

I Ain't No

Officers Clarkson and Harris rode 17A23 on the late side of the evening shift (three p.m. to eleven p.m.) in what is called "The Bottoms" of the Fourth Ward. The Bottoms is also called "Freedman's Town" and the neighborhood consists of small wooden shotgun shacks and very narrow streets. The area is just west of downtown and is trying to transform from slums to Yuppie lofts. The only major landmark in the area is a government housing project called Allen Parkway Village. The street animals live in either shotgun shacks or the housing projects, and the Yuppies live in high-rises. The upscale high-rise apartments have sprung up close enough to the shacks to supply good hunting for the nocturnal feral humans of the area. This area's street vermin are equal opportunity predators. They prey upon their own every bit as much, if not more, than they do on people outside their own community.

The two officers had just driven through "The Projects" for the third time in their shift when they heard a string of shots coming from a street just north of them. They responded and found an eighteen-year-old black male lying in the middle of Robin Street. The front of his T-shirt was stained red. Clarkson called for an ambulance as he rushed up and knelt beside the wounded kid. Clarkson asked the badly injured teenager,

"Who shot you, boy?"

The young man, Roosevelt Lee, raised his head up, looked Clarkson in the eye and exclaimed, "I ain't no boy." He then fell back and died without identifying his killer. His lifelong friends who had been present during the shooting claimed to have seen nothing.

The orientation of the street animal is not that of a normal functional human being. He is a feral human and can be likened to any other domestic animal gone wild. This class of feral animals is exceptionally dangerous. They cannot visually be differentiated from members of the population that are not psychopaths or sociopaths. They look just like a domesticated being and can masquerade as one. One of these animals will show up in court (at trial time) with a Bible and rosary beads. He is a predator that lives for himself, and only for his own gratification. Should his friend get killed, the dead man is no longer of any value to him. His friend's killer may someday front him some money or dope, and thereby has some potential future value. Emily Post would swoon. What's more, it is very hard to convince middle American that these vermin are really out there, particularly at the time of sentencing.

Over the next decade or so, either Harris or Clarkson would occasionally comment to one the other, "I ain't no boy!" To which they would both laugh.

The "Shoot-Me" Syndrome

Each year, every team of investigators gets to make at least one "Shoot me" or a "Shoot me, Motherf**ker" murder scene. These deaths (when found in a family setting) tend to take place after macho-man beats the tar out of his beloved and she runs and grabs some sort of gun. His last words on earth are often, "Well then—just shoot me, bitch!" or "You don't have the balls to shoot me." If the shooter has the presence of mind (or is coached as to what to include in her statement by some helpful detective), ninety-nine times out of 100 she will walk out of the police station that night without any charges. All she has to say is that she was afraid she was going to be badly beaten or killed by her now-room temperature significant other or husband. Better yet, if you simply throw in a busted lip and some torn clothes, you will have the makings of a justifiable homicide in Harris County, Texas. Pass Go, collect $200, and save the cost of a divorce lawyer. What a deal. Sometimes the suspect (the dead man's widow) can even get the state of Texas to pay for the funeral through the Victims of Violent Crimes Fund managed by the Texas State Attorney General's Office. Ain't life grand?

The "Just Shoot Me" syndrome (or phenomenon) has a first cousin who goes by the name of "Shoot me, Motherf**ker." These shooting scenarios occur in both casual as well as family settings. When the Homicide team calls in from the murder scene and talks to the Duty Lieutenant he will ask "What do you have out there?" They will answer him that the dead man was a "shoot me, Motherf**ker," and the Lieutenant will understand completely. Everybody in the squad who will be taking witness and suspect statements, when told those three famous words, will know how the script played out just prior to the bark of a firearm. The soon-to-be-ventilated party does something to prompt another party (the shooter) to pull a firearm and point it at him. Out of bravado or anger, the year's next murder statistic utters either of the two listed magic phrases to show his contempt for the person with the gun. Many times, the Dummy will even advance upon the armed individual as if to disarm him or her. This is the point in the story where friend-boy or Hubby Dearest gets multiple projectiles sent into his chitterlings. As they say in the business, "It was all over but the screamin' and the buryin'."

One of the truly great benefits derived from working a murder squad in a big city is that you regularly get to see justice being meted out upon some really deserving people. The world is generally a better place, and the best part of it all was that you've had the chance to enjoy it all from a front row seat, in color and unedited. Investigators often kick around the notion that the shooters in these cases should possibly be filed upon for aiding and abetting a suicide. Though in all honesty, the dead party, by his macho actions, may have really committed an assisted suicide. The shooter, however, does not know that they may have unwittingly been enlisted into the whole affair as an accomplice.

Society has become more violent over the last two decades, and people are less prone to yell out the "shoot me" in beer joints and at low-life social events. The expression of "Be careful what you ask for in life, because you might just get it" has never been more true. Ask, and you may well receive.

Adios Frenchy

This situation has been recorded not because it is homicide-related, but because it would be criminal not to share it with the rest of humanity.

Albert "Frenchy" Bateaux was a transplant from his native Louisiana to the south Texas Gulf Coast city of Victoria. Despite forty years living west of the Sabine River, he'd never lost his strong "Coonass" (Cajun-French) accent. The last words he ever spoke on this earth pretty well reflected the highest of the priorities in his colorful life. As Frenchy laid on his deathbed, Marie, his dutiful wife, of many years sat quietly beside him. As she held his hand he looked up at her and said, "You know Cher, I've had a pretty good life. I caught me some damned good fish." After making this final declaration, he died.

So Say Duh Fox

A man known locally as "The Fox" was encountered as he lay graveyard dead (a technical term) in front of a northeast Houston beer joint. The Fox wore a large brass belt buckle that bore the inscription: "Don't take life too seriously, you'll never get out of it alive."

Parting Shots of Two Idiots

These are often-quoted last words of a southeast Houston nightclub patron. He was taking up for his girlfriend who had just been insulted by another gentleman. The dearly departed was observed to shove the rude club patron and shout out the phrase that would immortalize him: "Don't you be callin' my bitch a ho." The object of his wrath then put two .38-caliber bullets into the ten-ring centered upon our hero's chest.

The second statement was made by an Acres Homes (northwest Houston) firearms expert, which he made in front of several witnesses.

These words passed his lips just before he sent a .38-caliber wadcutter bullet coursing through his whiskey-addled brain. "You see, you can tell they's blanks—'cause they's all flat on the end."

His Last Two Hits

Marvin Gay, Jr. was a 1960s and early 1970s recording star. He was shot to death by his father in the city of Los Angeles, California. The Homicide Division of the LAPD investigated the case. The morning following the murder, a police pistol range silhouette target with two bullet holes in its torso was found stuck on the wall in the Homicide office. It bore the inscription, "The two latest hits of Marvin Gay, Sr."

JUDICIAL ENGINEERING

In an unnamed Texas county, a special program ran for twelve years in a felony criminal district court. Prior to his appointment to the bench, the honorable jurist of this court was a rather flamboyant prosecutor for over twenty years. By living and working in the same small community for a couple of generations, he got to know both the good area people and also the very dregs of society. Only after he was several years into his retirement (and while under the influence of some very good sour mash whiskey) did he disclose the terms of his private societal improvement program. He dubbed his program "Judicial Engineering." When defendants he knew to be "just sorry" or dangerous individuals came into his court, they were channeled into the engineering process. In blunt terms, they were legally funneled or railroaded into the Texas prison system. Their trips to prison were always handled according to the law, and governed by the rules of codified procedure.

His court (like most in Texas) did not have a public defender system in place. Local criminal attorneys would hang around the courthouse attempting to get appointments to represent indigent persons. Unofficially, this system is called "feeding at the public trough." To represent these very undesirable persons, our judge would assign one of two local attorneys. On any given day, either of these two lawyers could best be described as either being a jerk or an anal orifice. They provided an adequate enough defense, ensuring that none of their cases could ever be overturned for incompetence on the part of their client's appointed counsel. In other words, they covered all of the bases.

Both of the attorneys in question were so abrasive by their very natures that they badgered and harassed all of the state's witnesses. Jury panels always became quite hostile due to the hateful actions of the defense counsel. The jurors came to loathe the two attorneys so much that they took it out on their clients. All of the defendants known to have been represented by these two were convicted and were generally given maximum sentences. Oddly enough, the lamebrains that were being defended seemed to really like the quality of their representation. They honestly believed their attorneys fought well for them. Their mouthpiece put on a good show, and they went down swinging. Lady Justice may have been blind to the courtroom proceedings but the honorable judge in question sure as Hell wasn't.

MOUSE

Participants on both sides of the criminal justice system are often found to be afflicted by "The Snake Bit Syndrome." One northside Houston crook named Eugene G. Fletcher (alias Mouse) stands out as a true hard luck example. Eugene was one tough character, having both the nerve and ability to do well in many criminal enterprises. He would always do his homework, and would always case every potential robbery or burglary job. Unfortunately for Eugene, despite all of his diligence, his world regularly got transformed into a dung heap. Fate always seemed to hold back and wait for just the right moment to kick the snot out of poor old stupid Eugene. He wasn't afraid of injury, cops or jail. This was good, because he got to see a lot of all three of them. In his free world, life he would rock along for a while, and Eugene would do pretty well for himself, and then the whole world would fall in on him. Eugene had seen some county jail time and a short term in the Louisiana State Penitentiary before he hit his first real major calamity.

Shortly after his first prison hitch our boy developed a taste for Quaaludes. These felony class drugs have never been imported legally into America from Mexico. Mouse found his dope connections were always looking to buy other types of illicit prescription drugs. He would, at times, pull an armed robbery of a pharmacy. While there he would gather up not only the cash but also the most marketable of the drugs that they stocked. Fate dealt Mouse an almost fatal hand on his fifth drug store armed robbery. It befell him one winter evening about eight p.m. while heisting a Walgreen's drug store. This location was a block off the Eastex Freeway and just barely outside Houston's northeastern city limits. Unfortunately for Eugene, two marked Sheriff's Department patrol units chose to meet in the parking lot of the same Walgreen's while he was robbing it. The two deputies were visiting like two old ladies over a back fence when the silent hold-up alarm call dropped.

Eugene "Mouse" Fletcher was exiting the store when he saw the squad cars. He knew from casing the location that there was only one way in or out of the building, and that was the front door. Fletcher took the young female cashier hostage, holding her in front of him with one of his arms around her throat. In his other hand he held a revolver. The cops got behind their squad cars, and they were positioned unknowingly between the pharmacy's front door and Eugene's stolen getaway car. Mouse thought that his only option was to hold the cops at bay and try and make it to his car. He decided to get them to back off by cranking off a few rounds. His logic told him the cops would not return fire because of their concern for the hostage's safety. After he fired his first shot, Eugene's hostage fainted dead away from fright and dropped to the pavement. This left Eugene Fletcher caught out in the open, with his pants down around his ankles and his tail feathers in the wind.

Somehow the surgeons at Ben Taub Hospital were able to patch up all the multiple bullet holes in his rotten carcass. They even had to put a steel plate in his skull to shore up some of the damage. He served eight years of the twelve-year sentence he pled guilty to. To have gone to trial in this case would have been fruitless. Identification or putting him at the scene would never have been a problem for the prosecution.

Mouse was eight months into his parole before he fell in with a dope addict ex-con girlfriend named Glenda Faye Boykin. She was a scrawny, chain-smoking old skank who had an even more extensive criminal history than Eugene's. Mouse's job as a maintenance man at an apartment complex could not come close to supporting their combined drug habits. After a few months of light burglaries, Mouse went back to shopping with the business end of a gun. Unfortunately for him, he chose to hijack the wrong pharmacy. This one was located next door to a meat market owned by a redneck butcher with a Browning A-5 shotgun. Eugene's significant skank (girlfriend) chose to accompany him to ensure he procured her favorite brands of drugs.

Mouse and Glenda were so intent on their mission that they didn't notice one of the drug store's patrons slipped out of the front door. The customer ran next door and asked the business owner to call the police and report the armed robbery in progress. The butcher had his wife call 911. He then caught up the shotgun he kept behind the counter just in case such an occasion ever presented itself. The scattergun in question had no plug in its magazine, and it held half a dozen trap loads containing number eight birdshot. The armed Good Samaritan took up a position behind the front fender of a handy pickup truck and waited for the dope addict duo to appear.

Eugene and Glenda exited the store, clutching grocery bags like two kids on Halloween night. The butcher called out for them to stop, and Mouse responded with a pistol shot that hit the windshield of the pickup. At that point the street dance was officially opened. The shotgun opened up at a distance of about twenty yards, and both crooks were well patterned with birdshot. The butcher first shot one crook and then the next. The birdshot knocked them down and penetrated about one-fourth of an inch beneath the skin.

The crooks got knocked down, and got up just in time to get knocked down again. The female hijacker gave up after the second trap load knocked her down. Eugene had enough gumption to run over to an adjoining property. He was promptly caught by uniformed officers who found him hiding under a car. A positive identification was simple—you just looked at the south side of either suspect. You could also note that maybe three to four ounces of birdshot had patterned nicely from their shoulder blades to the backs of their knees. The he and she bandits were put on trial together and both were sentenced to life imprisonment for being habitual criminals.

Mouse had it in him to be a notorious type criminal, but every time he got on a roll he tripped after stepping on his own tail. The redneck butcher is still cutting and wrapping meat but now he stokes his beloved A-5 shotgun with Remington Express #00 buckshot loads. He also has newspaper clippings from the Alief Advocate newspaper framed on the wall of his business. That way he can, from time to time, relive the grand and glorious day when his dreams really came true.

ONLY A LITTLE

Latrice Evans left her common-law ex-con husband of eight months due to his inability to keep a job and because of his violent mood swings. She felt certain he was using heavy drugs again, though he denied it. She waited for him to go off to a Super Bowl party, and then she had two men with a moving van remove the valuables out of the rent house they'd shared. She left him a few items and a pleasantly worded Dear John letter. The following day, she had the phone and utilities cut off to the house that had once been their love nest. To say that Junior Charles was upset would be an understatement. He had obviously come to relish his kept man status. After throwing a juvenile bitch fit he made threatening phone calls to both his former beloved at work and to her invalid mother.

Three days after Latrice fled their less-than-happy home, Junior caught up with her. Junior was a street predator by nature and knew that people are creatures of habit. He knew that after work Latrice often frequented the self-service gas station at the intersection of Waco and the East Freeway. That is where he laid in wait, and caught up with her. The spurned gentleman announced his presence with the shout of "Hello, bitch!" followed by a flurry of punches. One witness said that Junior's timing would have impressed Mohammed Ali. To Junior's surprise—and ultimate demise—Latrice pulled her trusty and rusty .25 automatic pistol from her purse. Without saying a word, she got the undivided attention of her former Stud Muffin by shooting him one time in the tripe. The jacketed mouse gun bullet clipped a major artery, and the rest is history. Latrice told the first responding police unit that she shot him "just to cool him down a little, and get him offa my case."

As they say in the ghetto, "Junior passed." As they say in Homicide, "He became rehabilitated," even before the paramedics got to him. Latrice told the responding detectives, "It was only a small gun—and I only shot him a little." They were amused and did their best not to laugh in her face. Her statement was taken on a confession form, and her small but adequate artillery piece was tagged in the firearms lab. The black Annie Oakley was allowed to go home that evening and the matter was referred to the Harris County Grand Jury without charges.

In Houston, and throughout most of the state of Texas, murder is a justifiable act when a wife beater gets ventilated, folded, spindled, or mutilated. The unofficial clearance assigned to this matter by its investigators was "urban renewal." Sometimes these types of cases are called *practice cases* by investigators. These types of investigations keep you in practice so you don't get rusty while you are waiting for a real murder to come along, one involving a real human being. When all parties in a non-justifiable trash killing are lower forms of life, it becomes a win-win situation. One dirt bag goes into the ground and the other goes to jail.

HE NEVER STOOD A CHANCE

Leeland Bishop Sauls, also known as Beebop, was born on Houston's northeast side. He was what Houston cops commonly call a Northside Turd. His folks were both hard-working and dependable people. Leeland, however, was pure-D, card-carrying white trash. White trash is a southern term that has nothing to do with one's economic level. There are decent folks that are poor, but there is nothing on earth lower than white trash. White trash are said to be like chickens; they are filthy in their habits and lifestyle. "Only white trash and chickens will screw their own young and crap in close proximity to where they eat."

In this story, our hero's junior high school principal said that Leeland should be made into a Planned Parenthood poster child: "Be careful that you don't produce something like this." His first parole officer held that Leeland could have been an organ donor at any point in his life, because he was brain dead as far as anyone could tell. Each city has its pet term for its sorry low-life types. In Atlanta, Georgia, they are called *maggots*. The Los Angeles Police call them *assholes*. New York City Police call their unwashed masses *scum bags* (condoms). In Houston they are just plain *turds*.

Leeland was nondescript in appearance and his academic achievements were less than remarkable. The only thing he could do in life to distinguish himself was to screw up. There, he had always excelled. Leeland began to smoke grass in the sixth grade and he quit school in the ninth grade. One of his favorite lines was that he spent the best three years of his life in the fifth grade. He referred to the year he spent in the ninth grade as his senior year.

His first felony charge came when he reached his age of majority in Texas, age seventeen. He got two years' probation his first time out of the box as an adult. The terms of that agreement with the great state of Texas were violated before six months were completed. He then became a ward of the state for one year. Leeland's parents were blue-collar working stiffs who described themselves as "beer-drinking Baptists." They maintained a home and always had a room for their wayward son. This lower form of life's father maintained that Leeland's whole criminal career probably netted him less than a few thousand dollars in cash and cost him untold years of his life. Leeland just loved downers. He wanted to operate at 33 1/3 rpms while the rest of the world was traveling at 45 rpms. Leeland would stay out of prison a short time and then fall in with the beer joint crowd. From there he would return quickly to the drug scene. He would begin stealing from any and every one he ever knew, and his immediate family suffered the worst of it. His grandmother claimed Leeland would steal the wet out of water if he could just figure out where to sell it.

Leeland finally came to the end of his rope (both literally and figuratively) one rainy fall afternoon. He had been out of prison for three months this time, and had begun using a synthetic morphine product. He again began to steal from everyone he knew and from many persons that he did not. This drug must have brought something into his pathetic life he had never known before—remorse. For the first time in his life he felt bad about his life-long sponging off of and stealing from his family members. On the last day of his life, Leeland committed his only known civic-minded act—he hung himself. Unfortunately for his parents of twenty-eight years, he did not have the decency to go off somewhere and do the deed. Instead, our scholar chose to hang himself in his aging parents' closet. Not only did they have to discover his sorry remains, but now they were doomed to reflect on his stretched neck and distorted features every time they went into their closet.

Leeland knew he was a gutless individual and that he might back out on his plan if given the chance. He used a method often employed in prison to hang himself. He made a noose and then tied himself off to the clothes bar in his parents' closet. In prison, the soon-to-be-dearly-departed tie their belt or a fabricated rope to the cell bars. During the next bed check their cadavers are found "just hanging around." Leeland knew that when he knelt down, pressure would be placed on his carotid arteries. Very quickly that pressure would squeeze them shut and he would pass out. After passing out, the weight of his body would continue to increase the pressure. Ultimately the lack of blood flow to his brain brought the soon-to-be-sainted Leeland to room temperature. The resourceful thing that our genius did, however, was to bind his hands. In doing so, his passing was duly noted by the Homicide Division. Thereby his final words became known throughout police channels all along the Texas Gulf Coast.

At the time of his death, Leeland was wearing white Converse brand high-top tennis shoes, called "Chuck Taylors" on the street. He removed the lacing from one shoe and tied a slip knot in each end. One loop he attached to one wrist and then he tied his hangman's noose to the clothes rod in his folk's closet. Once the noose was in place, Leeland reached down and affixed the open slip knot to the other wrist. He did so in a manner so that one hand was in front of him and the other behind him, and the string was under one leg. His hands were now bound and he could not reach up and release the knot. Nor could he use his hands to push himself up and save his life if he changed his mind. His parents arrived home after work and found the lifeless remains of their misguided child. The first units to arrive on the scene found a white male hanging by the neck and saw that his hands were tied. They did what they were supposed to do. They called Homicide and the medical examiner's office. They also sealed off the scene and held it until the cavalry arrived.

Detectives Forrest and Neal were working the four p.m. to midnight shift and were assigned the scene investigation. They drove in the rain through the rush hour traffic to less-than-scenic northeast Houston.

They met with the patrol officers who first made the scene. The detectives noted the family and friends huddled up under a carport. The blue suits advised that the family told them upon arrival that the complainant was an ex-con drug addict. The family theorized that Leeland had ripped off some drug dealer who hunted him down and settled the score. Dopers and their families know that if you rip off a dope dealer he has to try and hunt you down to either brutally beat or kill you. If he doesn't, every other junky in town will try and rip him off too. There's nothing personal about it, it's strictly business. Drug killings are called OSHA cases. For a dope user or dealer, getting killed is simply an occupational safety hazard.

Forrest worked in the Texas prison system prior to coming onto the police department, and had seen similar hangings. He noted the unlaced tennis shoe on the dead man's foot and that the shoe was still in place. There was a stack of newspapers in the closet beside the body and right up against it. The stack was close to eighteen inches tall. It would have been knocked over had there been a struggle between the dearly departed and some person trying to kill him. What clinched the investigation is the following suicide note found on his parents' bed. Though his name is unknown to most of mankind, his epitaph will live on for many years in police channels.

Dear Mom and Dad,

I know this is gonna be hard to take—but its best for everyone. I just pull y'all down and hurt the ones closest to me. This way I won't be a burden. I've always let you down and I've always been a failure. I just don't fit in or belong anywhere. I think one of the problems is that I am just Butt Ugly. Even in prison nobody called me by my last name—they just called me Ugly. Also, I've never found a woman who wanted to be mine. I must have the smallest penis in the world—because every woman I've ever been with has to me so. Beleave me—it is gonna be better without me around.

Cockless and ugly, I never stood a chance,

Lee

Forrest and Neal whooped and laughed at the late Leeland's words. They then went out into the front yard and spoke to the mourners. The family of the late Saint Lee was informed that he ended his own life due to his drug use and depression over the heartache and shame he'd brought upon his family. The investigators kept a straight face and a somber demeanor the whole time they spoke to the Sauls family.

Neither detective broke out laughing because they knew better than to look at one another. The crime scene unit that made the scene with the detectives was given a direct order to make several photocopies of the above suicide note prior to tagging it into the property room.

The whole division delighted in Leeland's last words, which were posted on the bulletin board for all to see. Requests for fax copies came in from not only other divisions, but also from several far away agencies. The senior evening shift Lieutenant claimed his headstone would someday proudly bear the now infamous words first penned by the late Leeland Bishop Sauls: "Cockless and ugly, I never stood a chance."

LITTLE RODNEY

Rodney Williams (pronounced Rotney Willums) was best known in the projects as "Lil Rotney." He was the product of the genetic and social cesspool on Houston's northeast side known as Kelly Courts. "Kelly Coats" is a run-down, old red brick government housing project located in northeast Houston. As horrible a place as it is, Kelly Courts is never likely to pull down the property values in the rest of the neighborhood. One old street cop who did a tour in Vietnam during the 1969 Tet Offensive explained it like this, "To clean out Kelly Courts you're gonna have to drop two rows of napalm. The first will get the two-legged rodents. The second strike will be for the roaches." A garden spot of humanity, it ain't.

During his first nineteen years on earth, Lil Rotney had several brushes with the law. He had seen the inside of the Harris County Jail three times since his 17th birthday. He'd also visited the City of Houston Jail a couple of more times than that. Young residents of Kelly Courts learned early on how to spot both marked and unmarked police cars. In the 'hood, cars with black wall tires and garbage can lids for hubcaps driven by guys in cheap suits are cop cars. Rodney, however, had never heard of an arson investigator. In the great state of Texas, arson investigators are certified as peace officers. They investigate arson-related crimes, draw up warrants, arrest crooks and put them in prison.

One day, Rodney was walking down Jensen Drive when three guys pulled up alongside him in an unmarked police car. They jumped out and pointed guns at him, providing him with the official Houston Police Department execution of a felony warrant greeting of "Freeze, Motherf**ker." Young Rodney was "cuffed and stuffed" into the back seat of the unmarked city car. The captive was next treated to a ride into downtown Houston at the taxpayers' expense. When he inquired as to the reason for his detention he was told to shut up and that everything would be explained to him when they got to "The Office."

When Rodney's captors pulled into the Fire Command building, he became concerned. While being escorted into the building, Rodney inquired, "What we doin' here? This ain't no poe-lease station." Once inside, he was informed by an investigator named Faulks that he was in the Arson Bureau. Rodney exclaimed "Arsenic, arsenic. I doesn't know nothin' about no arsenic." He went on to ask, "Just what is arsenic anyway, and how much time can you get for it?"

The answer came back, "Arson is the intentional setting of a fire—and you can get anywhere between two and twenty years for it."

This really piqued Rodney's interest and he further inquired, "How come da' difference in da' number of years?" His captors explained (lied) that it all depended if it was a new or old house that got burned up. Little Rodney literally beamed as he proudly exclaimed, "Oh man, that was the oldest mother-f**king house you ever did see."

Life is hard. It's even harder when you're stupid.

Rodney Williams would later be identified and charged in several murders and armed robberies. He ultimately pled guilty, receiving five life sentences, rather than face the chance of getting the death penalty for robbery-homicide. Rodney had been running with a little group of thugs that were feeding off of their own violence. They started out with assaults and strong-arm robberies, and moved up to armed robberies. If a group of this sort is not jailed pretty quickly, they become frenzied in trying to outdo one another in violence and bravado.

A bit of street-corner psychology can help in understanding how the *urban predator* acts. Once a group of young street animals begins committing violent armed robberies they will start shooting and killing people. Their crimes continue to escalate and become needlessly more violent as they attempt to outdo one another. The term that relates best to this sort of behavior is "pack frenzy." This phrase is generally used to describe animal behavior. There again, street vermin give animals with fur, claws or feathers a bad name. A blue tick hound by himself is a laid back and very easygoing animal. He would normally have to speed up in order to slow down. Alone, he is generally not aggressive toward other animals. Put three blue tick hounds together (a pack) and they will run down and shred a bobcat, a very substantial foe. Little Rodney by himself could not win a fair fistfight with a healthy fourteen-year-old. He and his friends, however, could gut shoot you and watch you bleed to death in the gutter with a seemingly detached interest.

RECOIL

The Psychological Services Unit of the Houston Police Department assists with the mental health needs of its officers. They mostly deal with problems involving the officers' family or marital problems. They are also regularly "pimped" for input by the Hostage Negotiations Team. Homicide and Sex Crimes investigators, at times, make inquiries for insight into the thought processes of the differing flavors of whackos they are hunting or trying to get confessions from. Another of the mandated functions of this unit is that when an officer is involved in a shooting he or she must be interviewed by a departmental psychologist. The goal of this interview is to determine if an officer is suffering from what has come to be called Post-Traumatic Stress Disorder.

Michael James (also known as M.J.) was a street-level narcotics officer. He had been an Army Ranger and was a combat veteran. During his military service he had been severely wounded by hostile gunfire and his recovery and rehabilitation took a couple of years. Since joining the police department, Michael had been involved in two previous shootings, both of which had been fatalities. One had been on duty and the other was while he was in an off-duty capacity. Michael was devoted to his wife and son, as well as to .45 Colt automatic pistols and Remington pump shotguns. Michael was a bright and articulate man with a master's degree in business administration.

He'd tried a life in the "square world" but found he sorely missed a vocation that came equipped with an adrenaline high. He found police work to be a good fit. There was no gray in this man's orientation. The bad guys took on the role of the enemy. He accepted the use of minor league crooks as informants to catch major league criminals. He justified this program as using a rat as bait for a larger predator. He also considered bait to always be expendable.

After dispatching his third armed criminal, Michael was one of the very first officers to be ordered to have his routine interview with the Psychological Services Director, a Dr. Fred Rogers. Michael first had to fill out a personal information packet so that the department's psychologist might better understand his subject. The conversation between the two men was exceptionally short and went as follows:

Dr. Rogers: "I see that you have a master's degree and are an army combat veteran. It also says here that you have been in two prior shootings. Were either of those shootings fatalities?"

M.J.: "Both of them were."

Dr. Rogers: "Tell me, what did you feel immediately after you shot that man the other night?"

M.J.: "Nothing but the recoil."

Dr. Rogers: "Get out of my office."

M.J.: "I'd be glad to, sir."

WHO, ME?

"Who me?" or "You talkin' uh me?" are two statements often heard by street police officers working ghetto and barrio districts. You can draw down on a robbery suspect with your shotgun—yelling at him to put his hands up—and get the "Who me?" response very often. This response comes to just about any sort of inquiry, even something as simple as, "I need to speak with you for a minute."

A classic example of the utterance in question came from a convenience store burglar who sought to ply his trade just east of downtown Houston. He had sledge hammered his way through a cinderblock wall only to trip the motion detector on the silent alarm system. When the cops arrived, the suspect sought refuge in the attic above a drop-in acoustical ceiling. An area K-9 unit checked by and the dog alerted on the attic area. The officers checked it and illuminated Homey with their flashlights as he clung to a metal beam. When officers shouted, "Hey you! Come down from there!" he replied with the standard, "Who me?" response. One of the arresting officers retorted, "Not you Bubba; we're talking to the guy standing behind you." The somewhat mentally challenged criminal pondered this for a moment before turning and looking over his shoulder.

STAND UP GUYS

The following statement was made by a gentleman who had survived to age sixty while rubbing shoulders with some of the roughest characters along the Texas Gulf Coast. On pretty much a daily basis, he dealt with organized crime and labor union thugs, as well as longshoremen in ship channel bars. The man had been a prizefighter and a labor union leader, among other things. He was schooled in the use of both a knife and a gun and was still not opposed to using either one. As they say, the man had been over the mountain and had seen the elephant.

"This younger group coming up ain't much. When the Feds come in and bust up an operation, it's not a question of if somebody in that group is gonna roll over and turn state's evidence against you. Now it's just a question of who's gonna do it first. You want to know why your taxes are so damned high? It's 'cuz there's so damned many people on the Federal Witness Protection Program. There are so many rats out there that they gotta jack up everybody's taxes just to support the bums. I tell ya' there just ain't no more stand-up guys in this world."

STREET TERMS

Mistified

Verb. Term used by crime scene units and Homicide investigators to describe the aftermath of what a shotgun or high-powered rifle does to a human head at close range. "I'd say he was plumb mistified by the whole situation—all over the south wall and ceiling of the living room." This condition is, at times, also referred to as being scatter-brained.

Able Mary Fox-Trot

Alpha letter call signs often used over police radio channels. Common acronym is A.M.F., and the direct translation is "Adios, mother F**ker."

Poe-Lease

Ebonics pronunciation of the word "Police" in black neighborhoods. Often, a knock on the door in a ghetto area will be answered with a call from inside of, "Who dare?" If officers answer, "Police!" they are likely to hear "Who?" Again, officers call out "Police, open up!" and you again get the "Who?" response. If, instead, officers respond with the phrase "It's the Poe-Lease!" the inhabitants will yell back "Be right which ya', Officer."

Street Verb Conjugation

Conjugation of the verb *to be*: I be—You be—We be.

Alsatian Acupuncture

Police slang. Canine police officer's term for the biting of a suspect by a German shepherd police dog. "He attempted to flee on foot, and in the course of being arrested he sustained Alsatian Acupuncture to both legs and a forearm."

Louisiana Search Warrant

One Law goes to the front door. The other Law, he goes to the behind door. The Law up front of the house, he knocks on the door. The Law that stands at the behind door, he yells "Come in." The Law at the front door, he kicks the door down.

Operation Sparkle

Operation Sparkle kicks in when a social, government, or political event is about to take place. Since street people might offend theatergoers or some politico's contributor, event organizers often don't want them hanging around the "high rent district." The street people, then, are either arrested or rousted. We can't have them offending the beautiful people. Uniformed troops get the word and they hassle the street people, running them into some other area for a time.

Operation Sparkle occurs in most every large city in their high-dollar or theater districts. It is not a written command and it takes place after the troops get the word in roll call. The rabble gets their short- term marching orders. Many times, paddy wagons pick up an unusual number of suspects for littering, or lesser and unimportant violations. When the street people see what is going on, they drift to friendlier climates. Supervisors never come out and tell officers directly to hassle and jail the vagrants. If they did, the ACLU (American Communist Liberation Unit) types might decide police were acting in a conspiracy to violate the civil rights of the unwashed and downtrodden. In small town America, the local police sometimes simply pick up the undesirable folks and transport them either to the city limits or the county line. It's a matter of effectiveness versus efficiency.

Juke

Verb. Pronounced as in the word "jukebox." Local slang term heard in Houston, meaning *to stab somebody.* "He walked up to the man and juked him without so much as saying a word."

A Mexican B.A.R.

Street police term used for a cheap .22-caliber revolver. Term dates back to the mid-1960s to the mid-1970s and relates to those types of handguns once dubbed "Saturday Night Specials."

IBM

In the southern part of Texas, the initials IBM neither designate a computer company's name nor does it refer to an Intercontinental Ballistic Missile. IBM relates to a very short Hispanic, an *Itty, Bitty Mexican.*

Charp Guns

The culture of combat has changed very much over the past thirty years. Far fewer combatants now will use a knife on one another. It seems to be far too "up close and personal." There has been an influx of recent immigrants into this country from war-torn countries where violence is common. Hispanics now would rather carry a handgun than a knife. It's *muy* macho to have a 9mm or .38 Super multi-shooter handgun. The construction worker type will drop a week's pay or more on a "Charp" looking handgun. Charp (sharp) looking guns are often nickel-plated and have some parts that have been gold plated. These guns are at times described by policemen as "looking like a pimp's front bumper." If it's macho to have it, it's even more macho to shoot it off into the air outside the beer joint as you're leaving on Saturday night—just to show everybody that it shoots as good as it looks.

Load 'em on Sunday, Shoot'em all week

Term describing a high-capacity semi-automatic pistol, or a gun with a high capacity magazine. "He had one of them load 'em on Sunday, shoot 'em all week kinda guns."

Paramour Law

An old Texas law that came off the books about 1972. Prior to that date, it was justifiable homicide if you shot a man that you caught having sexual relations with your wife. Many people still mistakenly think this action is still legal. Others think you should have legally been able to shoot your spouse. In an ideal world, who knows?

Hip Pocket Move

There was a time in the fair city of Houston that to justify killing a Hispanic or Black, all you had to do was claim that he was reaching for his hip pocket. This was in a time when fistfights settled problems and only real low-lifes carried a knife or gun. This was a defense used by both police and citizens alike. The Blacks and Hispanics would tell you right up front that they shot an individual because he reached for his hip pocket and they feared he was going for a knife. The expression was "Everybody knows that all (fill in the blank with "Blacks" or "Mexicans") carry knives." Many did, and some could come out of their hip pockets with one rapidly and monogram someone with great dexterity. You still encounter some old time crooks trying to justify killing someone by using this as a defense.

To Mark Someone

Verb meaning *to mark* (pronounced "mock"). A practice in the black community where someone (very often women attacking other women) will slash another person on the face. Black people tend to scar badly and the goal behind the slashing is to leave an angry raised scar. Weapons of choice are many times box cutters, though regular knives and straight razors are also often used. The practice is used to show your displeasure with someone, so that they will remember their indiscretion every time they look into a mirror. Another method used by blacks to mark one another is to throw lye or boiling water on one another. The lye would bleach out the skin and burn, where boiling water just scalds. The victim of any of these methods can vouch for his attacker's displeasure. "He caught her with another man, so he mocked her." It's the gift that keeps on giving, just like herpes.

Haint

Noun (pronounced *haynt*). Term from the Deep South—particularly East Texas—used by both Blacks and Whites. It is used to describe a very ugly person that would most likely be seen in a haunted house or graveyard setting. "She was a hainty looking ol' thang, but she sure could cook."

Stinker

Term used for a dead body investigation where the body has been there too long. Uniformed units will try and get you out there, and they don't want to stand around too long. Investigators have to stand around with the crime scene unit to try and determine if foul play was involved, and if so, what needs to be documented, photographed and collected. The problem with these investigations is that the smell permeates your clothes and hair. If you're unlucky, the body fluids will soak into your shoes, requiring you to throw them away. For this reason, many investigators keep rubber boots in the trunks of their cars. It was from one such scene that the media caught a statement from one Homicide investigator that came back to haunt him. He thought the cameras and recorders were off when he made the offhand comment, "You know it's been a bad day when you get home and the dog rolls on you."

High Rate—Cause A of Death

In the ghetto, this occurs when the dearly departed was reported to have cursed or "disrespected" his killer. The slight made toward someone's character in these cases takes place just prior to that person having the hell shot out of him. The unofficial cause of death can then be attributed to "A high rate of mother-f**king in a no-mother-f**king zone." In the barrio, the same situation is called a high rate of macho in a no-macho zone.

Boss

A term used by convicts in the Texas prison system, as well as in many other states in the Deep South. The cons will either address a guard as "Boss" or possibly "Boss Johnson." Some old-time crooks will address either prison guards or police officers as "Captain," which comes out as "Cap'm." The convicts almost delight at calling the guards Boss: "Good morning, Boss" or "How you doin' Boss?" They use these phrases almost like they're going out of their way to speak to them. What the cons won't tell you is that in their world, the term "Boss" actually stands for "Sorry son-of-a-Bitch" spelled backwards. Examples of which might be "I'll be right with you, Boss" or "Shakin' that bush, Boss." The prisoner can get in trouble or lose privileges for cursing at the prison guards, but a little Bossin' never got anyone in trouble.

Punk

Term used on the street in the black community identifying a man as being a homosexual. There is a problem often times when white middle class Americans talk with young blacks and use this term. One employer was assaulted because he did not speak the language. He was trying to get an employee to be less abrasive. He told his new hiree to calm down, because he had been acting like some kind of street punk. The soon-to-be-ex-employee did not translate the statement that he was acting like a street tough, but rather some prancing queen. Homey told the police he thumped the man for disrespecting his manhood.

A Pimp Stick

A device used by pimps to keep their working girls (prostitutes) in line. They take a coat hanger and straighten it out. The hanger part is left on one end. Pimps use the hook end to whip the offending prostitute if she gets mouthy or breaks the rules. The rules are generally holding back money, not hustling her assets hard enough, or trying to run off.

Question Marking

Term used to describe the beating of a whore with a pimp stick. That is because the process leaves welts in the shape of a question mark. The process does not permanently disfigure the merchandise if you don't break the skin during the proper application of the tool. That way, her future street value is not diminished. When your other whores see the week or so of misery the beaten party goes through, it helps keep them in line also.

Mexican Foreplay

Patrol officers working in the barrio routinely call Saturday night wife-beating "Mexican foreplay." The head of the house comes home drunk after an evening at the beer joint. He gets yelled at by his wife and he slaps her around. Then Sancho wants to fool around before falling asleep. In the ghetto this practice is sometimes called either "bitch-slapping" or "Jap-slapping."

Felony Stupid

Often times the cause for arrest at disturbance scenes where one of the parties talks himself into going to jail. As he's being hustled off in handcuffs he'll invariably cry out, "Why am I going to jail?" The answer may vary from "felonious stupidity," "Violation of City Code Statute P.O.T.P." (Pissing Off the Police), or sometimes something as bizarre as "Sodomy on a Chicken." This always sounds funny at the time, but when it is written down in a letter of complaint, or during courtroom testimony, it somehow loses some of its humor.

Drive-By Slapping

In the gay part of Houston (known as Montrose), gay blades regularly drive up and bitch-slap their significant (or insignificant) others and then drive off. The local police term for such an act is called a "drive-by slapping."

The Bitch-Slapping Squad

Unofficial name for the Family Violence Unit of the Houston Police Department. This unit is also sometimes called the "Slut-Slapping Squad." The determination as to which term is put into use depends on what led up to the alleged assault.

Insurance Pain

Police term regarding a type of injury, generally sustained in a motor vehicle accident. Sort of like getting your feelings hurt and you see dollar signs. These folks will get into an auto accident and call their lawyer first, and then they will call for an ambulance.

The King's Meat

Term used in black churches identifying some drop-dead gorgeous female member of the congregation. She will be the mistress of, or the private stock of, the head preacher. One of the deacons may be seen admiring the virtues of this member of the opposite sex and will be told, "Yeah I know she's pretty, Brother, but stay away from that. That's the King's meat." There have been many beatings and more than one killing involving somebody "messing with the King's meat."

The Gladiator Floor

The floor of the Harris County Jail where the inmate population is male and between seventeen to twenty-four years of age. These are the problem children in any incarceration setting. They are kept together and the number of deputies on that floor is about fifty percent higher than on other floors. In the words of an old head deputy, "The whole orientation of this group is to either fight or f**k. If they could just figure a way to do both at the same time, they'd think they'd evolved into the perfect life-form."

Cell Block Bitches

In many cellblocks there are persons that act as the female counterpart in a prison relationship. Some relationships are monogamous, while some guys share or pimp their bitches out to other slugs in the population. The male convicts are not allowed to wear makeup but they can get powdered drink packets from the commissary. The wannabe females will put Kool-Aid on their lips as a replacement for lipstick. When arresting a young ex-con on the street, if the cops want to mess with him they'll tell him, "I bet the other guys really make a big fuss over you when you put Kool-Aid on your lips." Strong denials as to being anybody's punk invariably follow.

Catching Fits

Epilepsy is very common in the prison and criminal populations in America. This condition is often the result of someone sustaining a head injury. This group as a whole is prone to violent behavior and lifestyles. The term "catching fits" is heard on the street to describe a full-blown epileptic seizure. "Y'all come quick—Junior's catchin' fits again."

Add-A-Dick-To-Me

Street slang term used by cops. The story goes that this is a highly sought-after sex change operation whereby a lesbian woman can change her ways and claim male gender status. "It would be a dream come true if she could both afford and could get someone to perform an add-a-dick-to-me."

Rut and Heat Attacks or Killings

Street cop slang term used for lust or supposed love-induced animalistic street fights or attacks which occur due to carnal interests on the part of the participants. The parties in the affray will be of the same sex and the motive for their fight will usually be a person of the opposite sex. Sometimes these love triangles are unofficially codified as two bucks fighting over a hot doe, or two bitches in heat fighting over a street dog.

Mistaken Identity Injury or Death

These situations occur all too infrequently. They usually happen when urban predators or bullies misjudge their prey and are themselves either injured or killed. The injured party mistakes the other party for a person who does not have a gun or a knife, or the *cajones* to use it. Unfortunately, in some jurisdictions the authorities actively hunt down and wrongly prosecute the real heroes of the day. Thankfully, other than in Dallas County, justice generally still reigns in Texas.

Author's Note: In several instances throughout this book I make disparaging comments about Dallas. I would like to say at this point that I have nothing but respect and empathy for the officers that work in any city in Dallas County, Texas. I do, however, loathe the hellish political climate that they are forced to work in, and what passes for a criminal justice system there.

DIESEL THERAPY

There exists an abusive treatment program method, known as *diesel therapy*, used by our federal prison system to break specific persons while they are in custody. These persons do not have to be gang members, problem inmates, or violent offenders. They just have to have fallen from grace with someone who has the power to make their life miserable. There is a great distinction between power and authority. Those subjected to diesel therapy often come out broken men, having been forced to live under harsh and substandard conditions.

The Federal government has prisons scattered all over this nation. The transport and delivery system used to move the inmate population is handled by private contractors. These companies use buses with barred windows and cages that go on long, meandering drives across America. The inmates being shuttled spend their days shackled hand and foot, sitting in cages inside what was once a school bus. They are fed twice daily. The first meal is breakfast and the other is a baloney-type sandwich and water. When the day is over, the bus stops at a pre-determined county jail. There, the prisoners are locked down for X number of dollars a night. The inmates are housed for the night, fed breakfast and given a sack lunch for their second meal. Their bus ride may take a couple of days, or may be as long as several weeks.

If you happen to be a person the system wants to abuse, and who has no political clout, you could be made to live within the transport program. You get transferred from prison to prison on a regular basis. You live on the road, shackled hand and foot. You eat two substandard meals a day and never get any rest. Your life has no stability. You may get to stay in a federal facility for a couple of days before your next transfer comes in. Mostly you sleep and eat in a county jail that is the low bid provider for the civilian transport contractor. "I'm from the government, and I'm here to help you."

This is the program I reported on earlier, where the East Texas Sheriff named Humpy died following eighteen months of treatment. Those who put him into the "diesel therapy program" had the power to do so. They were not, however, ever *authorized* to do so. You will likely never see the term diesel therapy written down again. The program officially does not exist and never has.

MEDIA PERFORMANCES

Particularly in the case of police officer-involved shootings, the media seems to work diligently at finding alleged "witnesses" who will make either outlandish or controversial statements. One must keep in mind that the media companies are in the business to either sell papers or television commercials. Above all else, making a profit (not reporting the truth) is the bottom line. If they can get a man on the street who identifies himself only as "Bamma" or "Jimmy J" and claims he saw an officer shoot someone without justification—now that creates viewer or reader interest. The headline "Police Shoot Armed Felon" is nowhere near as provocative as "Witness Claims Friend Murdered by Police." After getting "Bamma" on the six and ten o'clock news, the TV and print reporters never have to worry about the story again. Homicide detectives investigating the case will now become forced to hunt down "the witness" who just got his fifteen seconds of fame before he crawled back under some rock.

Sometimes politicians in impoverished neighborhoods will parade such tripe before the cameras—seemingly trying to get free airtime. They don't seem too interested in the written word media, presumably because few of their constituents can, or even bother to, read. The vast majority of these politico's claims are stilted at best and outright lies at their worst. Their orientation seems to be "You can't let the truth get in your way—

and please make sure you spell my name correctly."

When a witness's allegations are discredited or proven to be outright lies, the liars are unfortunately hardly ever taken before a grand jury to repeat their lies. If they were, they could be indicted for *aggravated perjury*—a crime for which probation is not possible in Texas. A possible reason for this is that district attorneys are first and foremost politicians, and they do not want to alienate themselves from any potential voting block.

When Homicide investigators locate the latest TV stars of the day, these witnesses must be interviewed and affidavits must be taken from them. These truth-challenged individuals will stand and boldly tell you that they overheard normal toned conversations from 300 feet away. Some will say they "saw it all" from places outside any possible field of vision. Actual eyewitnesses are hard enough to get the truth out of. Couple this with a lowered intellect and your problems seem to increase exponentially. This sort of mental midget will tell you what other people said they saw—just as if they saw it that way themselves. Impressing upon them to "tell me only what you saw with your own eyes—not what someone else said they saw" is difficult.

Perhaps the only way to get close to the truth is to tell your subject, "Everyone sees something different in every incident—tell me only what you saw with your own eyes—that way I can put all of the pieces of the puzzle together. Other people may have missed something that only you saw." Witnesses will tell you that they saw guns fired when they were simply pointed at them. This includes police officers who have just been involved in shootings, and who, in all honesty, could pass a polygraph test regarding being shot at. What we perceive has occurred and what actually happened in life are often two very different animals.

The following set of circumstances produced the following two sworn witness statements. One police officer and two civilians were shot in this exchange. Both civilians were Hispanic and the incident took place in an almost exclusively black neighborhood. Officer John Kranz and his brand new rookie partner were cruising a parking lot frequented by illicit vendors of a synthetic Morphine product called "D's." Kranz spotted a

"Mutt and Jeff" (one small, one large) pair of Hispanic males standing beside a compact Dodge car. He'd seen one of the men (the skinny one) outside a dope house earlier in the week.

Officers stopped the men, separated them and began to question them. The rookie demanded identification, but instead of his ID, the crook pulled out a .38 snub-nosed revolver, firing at him one time from point-blank range. The trainee was hit just below the elbow and the bullet lodged in his gun arm, shattering the bone. The impact knocked him down, and he was able to scramble for cover before the pain really set in. Kranz's suspect reached his hand into his right front pants pocket for the folding buck knife he kept there. Upon hearing a gunshot, and seeing his partner fall, Kranz saw "Gordo" with the gun in his hand. Kranz punched Skinny's ticket with a .40-caliber bullet from his Glock pistol. Then he moved on to Gordo. As he ran, Gordo fired three times at Kranz. Kranz hit the running Gordo a total of four times. Unfortunately (for society), Gordo survived his wounds, and lived to once again become a ward of the state of Texas.

See the attached two sworn witness affidavit statement documents to get a more clear understanding of just how everyone sees circumstances from a slightly different perspective.

> **Witness Statement**
>
> State of Texas
> County of Harris
> September 20, XXXX
> Time: 1930 Hrs
>
> Sworn before me, the undersigned authority, this 20th day of September appears Steve Marquis, who swears and affirms that the information contained in this document is true and correct to the best of his knowledge.
>
> My name is Steve Marquis, my Texas driver's license number 00000XXX, and I live at XXXX Nubian Street. I am a black male, 23 years of age, having been born 01-05-xxxx. I am unemployed. My home phone number is 713-XXX-XXXX. An alternate phone number I

can be reached through is 281-XXX-XXXX.

Tonight I was hanging out with some friends at the fish market at Scott and Corder. Three Mexican dudes were standing beside a blue car in a parking lot directly across Scott Street from where we stood. Directly a marked cop car pulled up and two of the Mexicans started shooting at the cop car. The cops jumped out of their car and hid behind the off side of their car, and they were steadily returning fire at the Mexicans. Another uniformed cop car pulled up with cops hanging out of all four windows shooting pistols. I saw two of the Mexicans get shot, and the third one ran off. I heard that the one that ran away went over on the next street and stole some boy's shoes, but I didn't see that part of it.

_____

Signature of person making statement

_____

Notary Public for the State of Texas

Witness Statement

State of Texas
County of Harris
September 20, XXXX
Time: 1915 Hrs

Sworn before me, the undersigned authority, this 20th day of September, appears John Harris, who swears and affirms that the information contained in this document is true and correct to the best of his knowledge.

My name is John Harris. My Texas driver's license number is 00000XXX. I live at XXXX Longmont in Houston, Texas. I am 19 years old, having been born 6-19, XXXX. I work at Peakload at XXXX Walker. My home phone number is 713-XXX-XXXX. An alternate phone number I can be reached through is—none.

Tonight I saw three people get shot. One was a cop and the other two were a couple of Mexicans. I know one of the cops that was involved, Officer Kranz, from the neighborhood. The shooting took

place across Scott Street from where I stood. I saw the Mexicans out there the last night. One of my homeboys was bragging last night that he sold the Mexicans some birth control pills that he had scraped the brand name label off of. He said they thought they were buying "D's." I guess they came back looking for homey tonight, but they ran into the cops instead. The cops pulled up and proceeded to jack up the two Mexicans. Both cops and both Mexicans pulled out guns, and everybody started shooting at one another. The only one that didn't get shot in the deal was Officer Kranz.

_____
Signature of Person making Statement

_____
Notary Public for the State of Texas

SPEAK NO EVIL

Many times statements made by officers come back to haunt them far more often than the actions they take. There are a few (very few) enlightened police agencies that actually teach their line officers what to say during a fight or confrontation. The smart ones teach their officers the correct phrases to yell out during training by striking a heavy training bag with their nightsticks. You don't curse someone or call them names, but rather call out the right phrases. When this is done, complaints and allegations fall off markedly. Crowds don't seem to get as hostile and grand juries don't see civil rights violations as often. If you're yelling "Please stop! Stop Resisting!" while you beat some knuckle dragger into submission with your stick nobody gets offended. The only exception might be the recipient of your attention, but who cares about him anyway?

A case in point is the poor choice of verbiage used by one Houston Police Sergeant who justifiably used a taser gun to light up a wildly out-of-control traffic violator. His actions were never questioned as to his choice of equipment or for his actual use of force. Unfortunately for him, the media reported that just after he'd made Silly dance the funky chicken, our Sergeant said to a nearby officer, "That was better than f**king." It was a slow news night and the uniformed supervisor was the only hot story in town. The print media and all four local television stations carried him as their lead story. They thankfully substituted the word *sex* for the "F" word. The then politically-correct chief of police attempted to fire the man. Fortunately, he was only able to give him a short suspension and transfer him off the street. "Wow, have you ever seen anything like that?" would never have brought the young Sergeant to center stage. It's like your Momma told you, "If you can't say something nice, don't say nuthin' in public or in front of people you can't totally trust."

MEXICAN HIT MAN

Nacho Salazar walked into the Special Crimes Section of the District Attorney's Office wanting to file charges on a man for shooting him. He was first thought to be a possible nut case when he claimed that his shooter was already wanted as an international criminal. Nacho had been shot in the shoulder two weeks before while he was in a nightclub in a little two-mile square town called South Houston.

He told the investigator, Edgar "Stu" Stewart that the local police had made a police report, but didn't seem too interested in chasing down the man who had attempted to kill him. Salazar said that the South Houston cops were "nothing but a bunch of Rednecks" and he didn't think they were too interested in working on what he called "just another Beaner shooting." Stu took the man's information and began an investigation. He verified with the South Houston Police Department that the shooting of this person occurred on the alleged date and time. After speaking with that agency's only detective, Stu agreed with Nacho. They really didn't seem too damned interested in the matter.

After the facts of the case had been verified, Stu began to question the shooting victim at length. The shooter was identified as a de-frocked (disbarred) lawyer named Rudolpho "Rudy" Garza who was now running a gas station in adjoining Galveston County. Rudy was said to have lost his license to practice law following a drug and murder-for-hire conviction in federal court. He had only been out of prison eighteen months at the time that Nacho's shoulder was destroyed by a .45-caliber bullet. The victim knew the suspect, as they had gone to high school together in the town of Donna in the lower Rio Grande Valley. They were, at the time of the shooting, rivals for the affections of the same beer joint lovely (woman). "If that's not enough," Nacho blurted out, "he's also wanted for killing a policeman in Matamoras (Mexico) two months ago." The investigator asked if Nacho could prove up this last bit of information, and Salazar pulled out a Mexican newspaper from his briefcase. He pointed to a composite picture on the front page saying, "That's him right there—and you can read it yourself about him killing that cop." Of course neither Stu nor anyone else in the Special Crimes Unit could read Spanish. It took them thirty minutes to find a jail deputy named Ray Padilla to translate the document and verify its contents. Padilla then called the officers of the Federal Judicial Police in Matamoras, Mexico.

Ray Padilla spoke with the police commandant in charge of the whole state of Tamaulipas, a Jorge Gomez. He verified they held a warrant for the arrest of Rudolpho Garza for the killing of a federal judicial policeman. Rudy Garza and his brother-in-law were fleeing from a drug-related contract killing (they had just committed) just south of Matamoras when they became involved in a head-on automobile collision with the federal policeman's car. The policeman was killed outright and Rudy's brother-in-law sustained a badly broken leg and could not walk. Garza fled the crash site on foot and was thought to have escaped back into Texas. Commandant Gomez said that Rudy's brother-in-law died later the same day from "complications" arising from his injuries. The brother-in-law had, however, lived long enough to give a complete confession, and identified Rudy and described their crime in detail. The commandant asked if Garza was in custody, and Ray advised him that he was not, and that information about the man had only now just come in. The Mexican Police Commander requested that they be kept up-to-date regarding the wanted man's status. A sworn affidavit was taken from Nacho (the shooting victim) and the investigation began. The next day,

Nacho Salazar and a bartender from the South Houston night club made a positive identification of a photo of Rudolpho Garza. Charges were filed and a warrant was issued for his arrest.

Rudy Garza was on parole from the federal prison system when he shot and wounded Nacho Salazar. He was therefore denied bond by the District Attorney's Office. After the warrant was signed and made valid by a Judge, Stu and another detective drove south into Galveston County. They pulled up to Rudy's gas station and walked in. They found their man doing an oil change at the grease rack. He was arrested without incident. It was only after they were headed back into Houston that they mentioned that the Mexican government was interested in his extradition. Garza was at first dumbfounded, and then he begged the detectives to pull over and just shoot him right then and there. They advised him they could not, and they booked him into the Harris County jail.

After returning to the Special Crimes office, Stu had Padilla come over to their offices and call Commandant Gomez. Padilla told him that Mexico could now begin their extradition proceedings. Ray Padilla would speak for a minute to Jorge Gomez and then stop and advise Stu what had been said. He first turned to Stu and said, "He's asking that we bring Garza down and meet him around noon tomorrow halfway across the International Bridge leading to Matamoras. He says that if we can do this favor for him that we can party for a week at his expense." Stu Stewart was taken aback by this request and advised Padilla to inform El Commandante that the Mexican authorities needed to go through the proper diplomatic channels in order that they might extradite the fugitive back into their country. There would be no meeting on the International Bridge. Padilla went back to his telephone conversation and shortly turned to Stu with a shocked expression on his face.

"He just asked me where we had Garza right now and I told him he was in our county jail. He asked if there was any way that they (the Mexican Police) might come and visit with Garza while he was incarcerated. Without thinking, I told him that could easily be arranged. Then he asked me if we had a basement in our jail that they could visit with him in. I told him that there were no basements or soundproof booths in our building."

The state charges against Rudy Garza were ultimately dropped as the complainant failed to show up at the grand jury, even though he'd been contacted twice to do so. The county ultimately turned the defrocked lawyer-turned-hitman loose, as the right paperwork was never filed. Two years later, a photo was sent to the Special Crimes Unit from the Mexican Federal Police. Rudy was center stage. He had about 300 bullet holes in what was left of his naked body. It appears everyone who felt like it was allowed to put a few rounds in him to display their pleasure. It appears justice was finally served.

An interesting aside regarding Mexican contract killings is that the killers are often brought in from outside of the country. When some Mexican nationals in Houston or Dallas have a bad Mexican terrorizing their community, it is not uncommon for them to pool their money and hire a killer who lives inside of Mexico. Conversely, talent imported from north of the border will commit many of the contract killings that occur within Mexico. Their motive is that it is more difficult to trace the parties doing the hiring when the hit man can't be linked to the dead man, and he lives many hundreds of miles away and inside a foreign country.

The killers that come out of Mexico will many times kill their intended victims and then add some spectacular or unusual twist to the episode. An example might be that they may shoot and kill the targeted victim, and then hack up his or her body up with a machete. One hitman shot his victim and then drove a 10D nail into the dead man's forehead. From the nail, he tethered a live scorpion on about a four-inch long piece of string. The hired killers do this sort of thing because they want their clients to feel like they got their money's worth. Who says customer service and job satisfaction are a thing of the past?

MOOSEFACE

For decades now, the intersection of Jensen Drive and Liberty Road has been a site where prostitutes have peddled their wares. The working girls ply their trade in this neighborhood around the clock, rain or shine. Scattered throughout the area are cheap hotels and motels that cater to the down and out and also to homegrown local low-life individuals. The ladies peddling their assets will sometimes rent a room or a "trick pad" in such a motel and conduct their mechanical contracting businesses therein. When facilities are included in the business arrangement, the soiled doves will quote prospective clients a price for services that includes a short-term sub-lease for the room rental. An example of this would be "That will cost you thirty and five," which means thirty for the girl and five for the room.

It was in such a room at the Star Motel on Liberty Road that Felton Howard's lifeless body was discovered. The cleaning crew found his remains just before noon. He was clad only in a t-shirt and his socks. He'd been shot in the chest and was as stiff as a carp. The one thing very much out of character at the murder scene was that his personal effects were still there when the cops arrived. His pants were folded neatly atop the chest of drawers with his wallet, money, and car keys still in the pockets. No murder weapon was found at the scene. A murder occurring at this garden spot that was not accompanied by a robbery or a dope deal was darned well unheard of.

The motel's proprietor, Sabu (Sammy) Patel could only tell the detectives that the room had been rented by a woman who went by the name of Peaches. It was a two-day rental and she had paid in cash. He had no motel rental registration form on her, as he had long ago stopped taking any such information. The only description he could give of the woman was that she was very tall, dark-skinned, homely and wore a large Afro hairdo. Sammy also said that Peaches did not rent from him frequently. When asked if she was a prostitute, he claimed he did not know "because we do not allow that sort of thing around here." A station wagon parked just outside the motel room's front door was found to be registered to the dead man.

The victim was determined to be married and to have lived with his semi-invalid wife only a couple of miles from the murder scene. He'd left the family home about nine p.m. the night before, saying that he was going out to have a couple of beers. He never returned. His wife had no idea what he was doing in a place like that, "bein' a deacon in the church and all." His station wagon was towed to the central fingerprint stall for processing. Unfortunately for the detectives they were forced to obtain a search warrant to process the murder scene for anything beyond photos and removal of the body. If the murder suspect turned out to be Peaches, then the rented motel room would afford her the same constitutional rights to privacy as her own home. Without a warrant, anything collected there would never make it into evidence at a trial. Ultimately neither the processing of the motel room or of Howard's car led to the immediate identification of the suspect.

The break that cleared this particular case was like so many others— the magic phone call. The crime had been profiled on all four of the local television stations, and a plea was made for anyone with information about this crime to call either Homicide or the Crime Stoppers program. What did work was that the scene detectives and the uniformed beat cars stopped and talked to people on the street and passed out business cards. The day after the murder, the detectives went back out and spoke to people standing around on the street and to area business owners. They also got ahold of the beat officers on all three shifts. The uniformed officers were each given a wad of approximately 100 business cards with the detectives' names on them. Also printed on the back of those cards were the words "Crime Stoppers Pays Cash for Information!" and the phone number 713-222-TIPS.

The Blue Suits stopped and talked with working girls, bartenders, and convenience store clerks. If these folks claimed to have no knowledge of the crime they were given a card anyway and asked to pass it on if they heard of someone that might know something. The cops also added a teaser that if somebody passes on information they can make $1,000 just by dropping a dime on the killer. The uniformed officers were also instructed to describe the victim and his vehicle to everybody they spoke to. The cops also inquired if anyone knew a tall black street whore calling herself Peaches. Greed is a wonderful thing, and the Crime Stoppers angle paid off with a tip. The working girl that Patel knew only as Peaches was in fact a "he-she" (a cross-dressing male prostitute) named Berry Archer. The district beat cops did not know him by the name of Peaches, but did know him as Mooseface. Many times the process of going out and talking to people, knocking on doors and passing out business cards is referred to as "making your own luck." It's not glamorous, and it's not high tech—but it works.

Berry Archer was identified one week after Felton Howard's body was found. There were partial fingerprints found in both the motel room and in the dead man's car that were linked to the suspect. The homicide gods further smiled on officers, because Archer had an outstanding warrant for being a parole violator. A photo of Archer in drag was found in the Vice office, and Sammy Patel was able to make a positive identification of Archer as the ugly female he knew only as Peaches. Sammy at first did not want to cooperate, but when he was asked if he knew how many building inspectors there were in the city he became quite civic-minded.

Miss Peaches was snagged by a street cop, and Berry Archer was put back into the system. Archer admitted killing the victim but said it was an accident. The suspect was a scrawny, horse-faced individual with breast implants he claimed he obtained in Mexico. He had not yet been able to afford the re-plumbing job that was required to complete his highly-coveted sex change operation. His confession (though very self-serving) became required reading in Homicide. It also helped to convict him. Confessions are almost always admissible in court. Oftentimes all you want is for the document to put the suspect at the scene and the weapon in their hand. After that, you simply hope and pray that the crook will put down some flagrant lie. When you can prove their alibi to be a pack of lies, juries will hammer them. So it was with this case.

Statement of Person in Custody

State of Texas
County of Harris
July 27, xxxx
Time: 1945 Hrs.

Prior to making this statement, I, Berry Archer, have been advised by Sgt. R.D. Harmon, the person to whom I am making this statement, that:

1. I have the right to remain silent and not make a statement at all, and any statement I make may be used against me at my trail.

2. I have the right to have an attorney present to represent me prior to, and during, any questioning.

3. If I cannot afford an attorney, that one will be appointed for me free of charge.

4. I have the right to terminate this interview at any time.

5. I have read and understand these rights and waive them to make this voluntary statement.

About two weeks ago, I was turning tricks over off Jensen and Liberty. A nice looking older man in a green station wagon came by and we visited some. I asked him if he wanted a date and he said he did. He said that he didn't have a whole lot to spend, and we settled on a price of twenty-five and five. We rode over to the Star Motel and when he went into the bathroom, I got naked and jumped into bed. When the old guy got into the bed I went down on him. He kept

---

feeling around on me, and I tried to move around and keep him away from my privates. He finally reached around and grabbed ahold of my dick. That's when he went completely crazy. He jumped up and started yelling "You ain't got no pussy!" over and over again. I told him, "I thought you knew." He then started yelling that he wanted his money back. I told him that there was no law that said I had to give his money back. The old guy went over to one his boots and pulled out a black gun with brown wooden handles. I jumped up and grabbed him just like a natural man. We fought over the gun, and it accidentally went off, shooting him in the chest. I put my mini-skirt back on and I ran off to my Aunt Jana's house.

I took the gun with me, and I sold it the next day for thirty bucks to a guy on the street that they call of Low-Down. I did not mean to kill the man. I was just trying to get the gun away from him when it accidentally went off.

_____

Signature of Person Making Statement

_____

Witness

See the attached confession for the details and synopsis.

Archer's statement is what sunk him. Tests run on the dead man's T-shirt proved the fatal bullet was fired from a distance of more than three feet. The complainant very likely was killed with his own pistol. His wife would testify that he regularly carried a .38 revolver in his boot. Archer further sunk himself by demanding to appear in court in drag. His attorney kept mixing up his client's gender, and stammered as he referring to Archer first as "he" and then as "she". The jury was kept both awake and entertained that way.

NOT HIM THIS TIME

On Sunday morning July 20, 2003, a *man down* call dropped at 0600 hours. An unknown male was reported down in the median of the roadway in the 10500 block of Martin Luther King Blvd. This could be a drunk passed out, a sick call, or who knows what. Unit 13D20 was dispatched. Officer H.D. "Heavy Duty" Morgan arrived six minutes after being dispatched. Upon arrival, he found a dead black male who appeared to be either in his late teens or early twenties. The man was lying on his side. The dead man's pockets had been turned inside-out and he was cold to the touch. Morgan called an ambulance anyway, covering his assets just in case he was later asked why he had not. Next, Morgan called Homicide from his cell phone.

A cell phone is required equipment when working that particular neighborhood. The local phone booths often smell strongly of urine. What's more, even finding a phone in working order is at best a crap shoot. A detective driving into Houston from suburban Pearland stopped by the location. They also had a crime scene unit on the scene quickly. There was really not much of a scene. It consisted of a dead body lying on a trash-littered median between four lanes of concrete roadway. There was no evidence on or about the body. The victim appeared to have been shot, and he either walked to the location where he was found or his remains had been dumped there. Either scenario was possible.

Regarding his pockets being turned inside-out, this could have been done by whoever killed him, or by a neighborhood opportunist who simply happened upon the remains. "The Lord helps them that helps themselves ya' know."

When the body car (transport van) arrived from the Harris County Medical Examiner's Office, the police were almost finished with their scene investigation. The investigator from the morgue, John Mixon, rode to the scene with the transport driver. John had no more than exchanged his "howdys" with the Homicide guys when an older model Ford slid up. A rather large woman, later identifying herself as Shirley Ann Lawrence, boiled out of the car. She stalked up to the secured area—secured with crime scene tape—wearing a grim expression on her face. It is not uncommon for investigators with an unidentified cadaver to have family members of the dearly departed show up with great fanfare. The "drums in the hood" often communicate far better than the fiber optic network systems of AT&T.

The woman strode up to the crime scene with noted purpose in her manner. When she got to the grassy portion of the median, she threw her hands up over her head and screamed out, "Oh Laud, they done kilt my baby!" She then "fell out." The term "fall out" in the black community is a verb, meaning *to become overcome by emotion and to faint or to swoon*. An example of the past tense usage of this verb would be, "She done fell out."

Unfortunately for the lady in question, she chose to fall out beside a rather large and very active fire ant mound. Her revival was brought about in short order, but not by means of the Holy Spirit. She was interviewed and related that she had been called by friends and was told that her child's freshly-sainted remains had been discovered just as the sun came up. As there was no identification upon the body, Mrs. Lawrence was asked to view the remains to make a positive identification. She walked up to the youth and gazed upon his lifeless and slack-jawed face. She then proclaimed, "That ain't him." Mrs. Lawrence then pulled a cell phone from her purse and made the following statement to some unknown party. "Put the fish back in the freezer and call the folks in East Texas. Tell them that it ain't him this time." She then simply turned and walked back to her car.

THE PARK PLACE RANGERS

The uniformed patrol services for the southeast quadrant of Houston was served for several decades out of a run-down building located at XXXX Park Place Blvd. The Park Place Station's night shift officers from the mid-1960s through the late 1970s were known as the Park Place Rangers (after the Army Airborne Rangers). They referred to themselves as the Rangers, as did the rest of the department. They were often bigger than life and wilder than Hell. The number of cops on the street during that time period was surprisingly small and if you got into a storm—you were expected to take care of it.

Everyone graduated from the police academy with a .357 magnum revolver. The city has never issued weapons and police were allowed to carry any weapon they desired as long as it was .38 caliber or larger. In addition to a sidearm, many cops carried blackjacks and any type of shotgun, carbine, or battle rifle they wanted. On slow nights the troops would go hunt coyotes (with their rifles) in rural areas off Highway 288, just south of the city. If you were a burglar and you were caught, you expected to get a good ass-whipping at the very least. There was no really high-rent district in southeast Houston, and no shortage of low rent people to jack with.

The southeast side of Houston has always been a mixture of rough lower- to middle-income, blue-collar neighborhoods and industrial areas.

During this time period (60s and 70s) the Southeast Station had one of the department's highest numbers of officer-involved shootings. This was a rough, multi-ethnic part of town inhabited by any number of people that were not afraid to fight with, or shoot it out, with the police. Telephone Road was the major north-south roadway, and it was (and still is) infested with dive bars, cheap hotels, drug addicts and whores. Biker gangs were prevalent in Southeast Houston and the Bandidos had a safe house in the Garden Villas subdivision. A disturbance call at that location once brought out several police units, and a wild gunfight ensued. Several hundred rounds of ammunition were fired. The final score was the Park Place Rangers two, Bandidos nothing.

The wild and kick-ass side of the Rangers helped to recruit some good citizens into becoming Houston Officers. One officer named Andy Andrews related that, as a kid, his first exposure to the police came after seeing them repeatedly pull through a drive-in movie around midnight in their patrol cars. The cops would pull up and meet on the back row with some "wild dog" police groupies. They would stand around with some gal hanging on them for a bit, as they listened to their squad car's radio. The cops would openly mix drinks or sip on beers. From time to time, one of the Blue Suits would climb into the back of a custom van with some sweet thing. After seeing the cops around a time or two, Andy began striking up conversations with them. He befriended one cop named Fred who he asked one night what they were going to do when they left the movie. Fred responded with "I don't know, we will just cruise around looking for trouble, and if we get lucky we might get to kill a burglar." The next morning while on his way to work Andrews heard on his pickup radio that Fred and his partner had killed a burglar thirty minutes after they pulled out of the drive-in movie. Two days later, Andy was in the Houston Police Department's recruiting office. He took a substantial cut in pay to get a job where he could carry a gun, drive fast, drink beer, chase women on duty, and maybe get to kill a burglar. Only in America—the land of opportunity.

There were two particular officers riding night shift out of the Park Place Station that seemed to be in competition as to who could kill the most Dirt Bags. The older of the two officers survived the 1968 Tet Offensive in Vietnam. The second joined the department at age nineteen and was tutored by the very best. Both men were uncanny pistol shots and both babied their .44 magnum Smith & Wesson revolvers. You might break your knuckles on someone's head, but you never hit anyone with your pistol. It was said that on any given day both men lived to either shoot dice or to kill a burglar. Keep in mind that under Texas law, it is justifiable homicide for a police officer to kill a burglar at night and the burglar need not be armed. The department's deadly force regulations have since been restricted to situations involving self-defense, or the need to save another person's life.

The Rangers were also alleged to give flying lessons to crooks. This practice supposedly consisted of throwing burglars off of one- or two-story roofs. Rookie officers were supposedly amazed that people could regularly survive falls from a second story roof and seemingly not be too worse for the wear. It didn't really matter if the suspects were handcuffed or not. If he fell on his head and died from a broken neck, nobody really cared. Besides, "Who are you gonna believe, me or the dead guy?" Your report simply stated that after you handcuffed him, the crook stomped on your foot and then broke and ran. It was simply a matter of his bad luck that he fell off the roof in his attempt to make good his escape.

The Park Place Rangers drifted into oblivion after two different throw-down guns turned out to be traceable. Several officers from their ranks were filed on in federal court for civil rights law violations after their statements proved to be bogus. Both of the shootings in question were justifiable, and would have skated through the system if the officers had simply told the truth. "The System" was so distrusted at that particular time in Houston's history that street officers always tried to work around it. Unfortunately, the "us against them" mentality prevailed. At the time all of this was going on, the chief of police was Carol Lynn, and Fred Hofheinz was Houston's mayor. Chief Lynn would go from his police department job to a Texas state prison cell. Mayor Hofheinz would, some years later, be indicted for racketeering in the state of Louisiana.

The two most prolific shooters among the Rangers were never caught up in the two federal civil rights cases. They typically did not involve themselves in shootings when multiple witnesses were present. They were, however, very closely scrutinized and their numerous shootings were investigated by several different grand juries. When either of these two men had been involved in a shooting, only his partner had ever been present. Most times, that partner (according to their statements) had been checking the other side of the building when the shots were fired. If you weren't there when it went down, you can only testify to what you saw when you walked up. "It was all over when I got there."

Park Place Rangers—no strangers to danger.

THE WOLFMAN OF MONTROSE

Claude Ronnie Beck, better known as "Ronnie Beck", was a big ole' strapping country boy from Fordyce, Arkansas. He'd never met a stranger, and though he was an aggressive street cop, he got along well with both criminals and the citizens. He was both tall and broad at the shoulders, and when you met him he struck you as being a truly decent man. It was said of him "If you had a daughter, this was the kind of young man that you would want her to bring home to meet you."

He bore a strong resemblance to the television star Max Baer on The Beverly Hillbillies and was called "Jethro" by his coworkers (after the character played by Max Baer). Ronnie worked the night shift by choice and was aggressive in his hunt for crooks. It did not matter if they were drunk drivers, wife beaters or burglars. He always wore a lop-sided grin and though not a golden boy, was a man that people seemed to both like and remember. What's more, anyone who had an occasion to spend any time around the man had a Ronnie Beck story to tell. Ronnie practiced a type of policing that was both folksy and efficient. He stopped as he went about his appointed rounds and took the time to visit with people. From cooks at all night restaurants, to cab drivers, to bus station attendants— they all knew Ronnie and they all called him by his first name.

Though extremely friendly he was not opposed to a "Good ole' root hog or die" street fight. Being somewhat of an inventor—and on good terms with a machinist—Ronnie fabricated a flashlight out of a piece of cast iron pipe. The goal here was to make a piece of equipment that was "Ronnie Proof." He had dropped and broken a multitude of lights in a couple of years on the night shift. A less powerful man would never have lugged around what was deemed by one partner to be an industrial grade boat anchor. Ronnie Beck, however, tucked his custom flashlight under his arm like it had been fabricated out of aluminum cans. That very flashlight saved his bacon one night while he was answering an assault call in the 6500 block of Cullen.

It was not until he'd stepped from the car that Ronnie determined he'd walked into an assault in progress call rather than an after-the-fact report call. For whatever reason, Ronnie became the focus of all the hostilities the four men involved could muster. A neighbor called in that he had seen a police car pull up—and a crowd of men descended upon the officer "with arms a-flailing." When the first responding unit arrived on the scene he found three black males lying unconscious in the front yard and Ronnie trying to wear out his new flashlight on a fourth gentleman. Ronnie received several solid shots during the fight, but he was the last man standing. One of the officers that helped transport the prisoners from Ronnie's street dance wondered aloud if the neighbor had called out of concern for Ronnie, or the four idiots that had jumped him.

Ronnie, like most Houston officers, worked off-duty police-related jobs. He worked security at a government housing project located just east of downtown called Clayton Homes. Most of the residents at that time were Hispanic. Ronnie noted as he made his rounds that many of the kids looked rather unkempt. He went out and invested in a pair of barber's clippers. Free haircuts to the young male population were now available in the complex security office. One of Ronnie's famous expressions was "Come here Julio, so we can lower your ears. We need to be able to tell you from your sister." It wasn't long before the kids came to Ronnie's Barber Shop with requests like, "My Mom says you need to leave my hair a little longer on the top and block it in the back." The other cops who worked at Clayton Homes with Ronnie knew he never made any money there. Instead, he wound up spending it on the kids.

Every other weekend during the summer, Ronnie would fill the bed of his pickup with kids and take them to a major league baseball game at the Astrodome. On top of his regular job and an extra job two days a week, Ronnie joined the organization Big Brothers and Sisters. One of his heartfelt desires was to help kids that had no adult male role model. He had seen firsthand that many kids with no decent male influence were often on a collision course with disaster.

Going to work for Ronnie was fun. He both loved and assaulted life. He had a soft spot in his heart for kids, down-and-out street people and horseplay. A rubber Wolfman mask and a pair of hairy clawed hands lived in his briefcase. The Wolfman only came out on bright, moonlit nights. When Ronnie was riding a one-man unit, the Wolfman might be seen driving the streets west of downtown in a marked patrol car. There is no way to determine the number of auto accidents caused by people gawking at the monster driving the cop car.

When he was riding with a partner, the Wolfman rode in the back seat of the police car behind the wire cage. Sometimes, around five in the morning (as the illegal aliens were standing at the bus stops, waiting to go to work) a police car would pull up. The Police Werewolf would jump out of the car's back seat, roaring and clawing at the air. The illegals would scatter like quail. The Wolfman would walk around, picking up their sack lunches. Officer Ronnie would be found fifteen minutes later passing out sack lunches to street people in the Mission District.

Sunday mornings would find "Jethro" (Ronnie) in a coat and tie inside the Faith Missionary Baptist Church. There he met and married a young lady named Sheila. After a short honeymoon, he was back on the night shift. Eighteen days after his marriage and nineteen days before his twenty-fourth birthday, Ronnie stopped a suspected hit-and-run driver on the Southwest Freeway. The traffic stop was on the shoulder of the highway, approaching an overpass. As he was walking up on the possible hit-and-run vehicle, a drunk driver operating a motor home struck and killed Ronnie Beck. A wrecker driver known as "Stuttering Danny" saw the killing and chased down the motor home and forced it off the roadway. The vehicle's intoxicated driver was the wealthy owner of a motorhome sales and service company. He was charged with murder by auto. After a jury trial, the defendant was sentenced to one year of supervised probation. The rank and file officers were livid.

Funeral services were held in both Houston, Texas and Fordyce, Arkansas. Ronnie's remains were buried in his hometown as per his wishes. During the Houston services, a bunch of hardened street cops were brought to tears when they saw groups of crying kids from the projects enter the church. The kids came to their friend's funeral carrying bunches of wildflowers that they'd picked from vacant lots and had bundled together.

It was determined that just prior to his death, Claude R. Beck had applied for and had been accepted for a position with the Arkansas State Police. He had found both a vocation and a woman that he loved and he wanted to go home. This story is but a poor attempt to pay tribute to a fine individual who truly lived and enjoyed life.

BIGOTS

There are very few real seething bigots within the ranks of police departments. If they get into that line of work they don't tend to last very long. Many officers have strong feelings and opinions toward any number of groups or sub-groups. Their bias may be of an ethnic nature, toward some religious orientation, or even toward some lesser segment of society such as *bikers* or *dopers*. Likely one of the most creative bigots to grace a police department was a black male cop named Cortez Scott. With concerted effort on his part he was able to keep his hate in check well enough that it did not overwhelm him and pull him down. Cortez hated "black gangster trash" to such a degree that it took on a passion usually reserved for religious zealots or terrorists. To him it was almost a religious calling to jail a "Gangsta."

Officer Scott came to Houston from his beloved northern Louisiana in search of employment. He was raised in the backwoods by a bigger-than-life grandfather who had been in the lumber business. "Daddy Jack" was a man driven by two things—honor and his religious convictions. Cortez would say later in life that his grandfather was the only man he'd ever known that truly lived his religious convictions. This man, the only father figure in Scott's life, had two interests outside of his immediate family, his church and coaching boxing teams. He was a powerful man in his community, who had straightened up more than one wayward youth "by knocking the Devil out of him, and bringing him back to reality." It's hard to get respect from the neighborhood toughs when the word gets around that some fifty-five-year-old kicked your butt when you lipped-off to him. Particularly when your buddies hear that he had come to talk with you about being more respectful toward your mother. The old man was "Much-Man," and in his 20s twice won the title of middleweight boxing champion of the Pacific Fleet.

Cortez worked off-duty security jobs in order to make financial ends meet. He worked at The Summit, a huge sports arena and office complex, located just west of the downtown area. He directed traffic there three weekday afternoons, and on many weekends worked special events. Cortez was an old-timer on the department and had worked The Summit for almost twenty years. Younger officers often teased him by telling people that when Cain slew Abel, Cortez was the first officer on the scene. With his seniority working at The Summit, Cortez could opt out of working certain events there if he wished. Some officers refused to work rock concerts, while others disliked other types of events. Because of his unbridled hatred of gang trash, nobody could understand just why Cortez Scott always seemed to make sure he was available to work every rap concert. To compound the oddity of the situation further, Cortez seemed to actually look forward to the events.

During these events, Officer Scott always chose to work a post nearest the concession stands and the restroom area. This was not looked upon by the cops as the best of possible assignments, but with his seniority on the job he could pretty well call his duty station. The assignment in question was the site of enough disturbances that two cops were always required to be there during any such events. A young Officer named Rick Langford was partnered with Cortez one night. He came back reporting that he'd finally discovered why "Old Cortez" worked the Gangster Rap concerts and always chose to work the worst of all possible posts.

Cortez Scott was finally caught in the act. He was discovered, just prior to a highly-touted rap extravaganza, hosing down the walls above the urinals in the men's bathrooms with a large industrial-sized spray can of chemical mace. Cortez confessed immediately to Langford after being caught. He explained that his actions were motivated by a desire to get back at the group of people that stood against everything that he believed in. These were the vermin who made him embarrassed to be a black man in America. He claimed to have come upon a means by which he might truly "hit them where they live."

Cortez had devised a plan by which he used the bathroom habits of black men against those who he despised so much. When nature calls a black male, he typically will put the palm of one hand about eye level and flat against the wall above the urinal that he stands in front of. In his other hand, Homey will hold his manhood. After taking care of business, Homey would often grab his Johnson to shake it with the hand he'd just held up against the wall. By doing so (after Cortez had chemically treated the wall), Homey would effectively set his own dingus on fire.

The beauty of this program, Cortez explained, was obvious. Even if his victim ran to the sink and ran water upon his injured member, the damage had been done. He claimed to be able to get an accurate count of just how many "gang turds" had their pee-pees blistered by their distinctly unusual gait as they left the men's room.

"Just think of it. If Sweet Thing gets to feeling spunky when they gets home, she'll never believe ole' Romeo when he claims he got his manhood blistered by using a public restroom. What's more, the gang-banger's love life is effectively put on hold for a minimum of five to seven days. Ya' know, there ain't no tellin' just how many bastard children wasn't born simply because of my program."

SNAKE BIT

There are some street officers that trouble seems to actively seek out. Now we're not talking about some crude or crass Bubba-type that goes around hassling people for no good reason and gets punched in the face. The officers alluded to here are simply folks that are sought out by bizarre or tragic events. The phenomenon afflicting these individuals (in police circles) is known as being a "shit magnet." That substance is said to always roll downhill. When said substance reaches the bottom of that hill, these are the guys who are always standing in the way. They, and those unlucky enough to be working with them, will ultimately get splattered, and regularly. These rather remarkable events tend to blow up in front of the *snake-bit* cop every two to four months. If you ride partners with one of these guys you need to be equipped with two things: Disability insurance and the knowledge that you should always keep your powder dry. The adage that best applies to these guys is "He can walk into a Sunday school picnic and it will turn into a bloodbath".

Jimmy Dulaney was such a man. He came to Houston PD after a five-year hitch with the Atlanta, Georgia Police Department. He was involved in several shootings while he worked for both agencies. "Jimmy D" was nice-looking, pleasant and outgoing. Sometimes, however, it seemed that the hounds of Hell dogged the man's heels. His arrest numbers were always high as it seemed that crooks almost stumbled out in front of him trying to get arrested. The problem, however, was that when Jim showed up, folks very often decided they wanted to fight. If he got into a high-speed chase, a fiery crash might be the end result. On his first day on the "solo'" motorcycle squad, Jim tried to stop a speeder. That speeder, unbeknownst to Jim, was an armed robbery suspect who was fleeing a jewelry store robbery. If that was not enough, the "jacker" had a hostage with him. A gun battle ensued and Jim had to lay his shiny new motorcycle down on the pavement for cover. The suspect was wounded and gave up. A year later, motorcycle cop Jim was chasing a speeder, who drove a quarter of a mile down the road before running over and killing Jimmy's partner, Ray Ramos. Ray, at the time of his death, was writing another traffic violator a citation. After a few years, you started to hear "He's one hell of a nice guy, but if you ride with him, you'd better wear bullet-proof underwear." Every station has one or two such officers. Just why they are so afflicted, no one can really say.

Jimmy D left the ranks of the Houston Police Department after he attained what he described as "twenty years and twenty minutes" on the job. He was one day past being eligible to retire when he and several other officers were given a special assignment. They were called out to assist the Vice Squad in taking down an illegal after-hours nightclub. Jim told his "brothers in law" that he had been in enough shit-storms (a police term) lately, and he would like to hang back. He asked to be allowed to man the door of the paddy wagon and simply load prisoners. After the club's front burglar bar doors were pulled off with a wrecker, a crowd of neighborhood knuckleheads gathered around. For some unknown reason, a "crack ho" burst out of the crowd and ran up and attacked Jimmy—biting a hunk out of his chest. He put in his retirement papers the next morning. His simply said "It's like what the tomcat said after he finished making love to the skunk—I've enjoyed about as much of this as I can stand."

THAT'S MY STORY

Sonya (Sunny) Liston Banks died at the hands of her live-in boyfriend, Arick Jefferson. This occurred in a government-subsidized apartment they shared at XXXXX Telephone Road. She was found at three thirty p.m. by her cousin, Mary Ellen Graft. Mary Ellen had seen Arick walking out to his car about three twenty that afternoon, and asked him where Sunny was. He did not answer, but simply looked at her, and with his forefinger drew a line across his throat. She went to Sunny and Arick's apartment and found her cousin near death, lying on her blood-soaked bedroom floor. An ambulance was called but there was little that could be done. She was dead upon arrival at Ben Taub Hospital's emergency room. Homicide was called and patrol held the scene for the detectives.

The murder scene was inside an apartment that was funded by HUD Section 8 housing funds, for single mothers with dependent children. The rules in such housing situations stipulate that neither husbands nor boyfriends are allowed to live on-site. This, however, does not stop between thirty to forty percent of the complex's residents from cohabitation. The dead woman's cousin identified Arick as the prime suspect, and testified that he did not live in the apartment on a full-time basis. Mail in the suspect's name was discovered inside the apartment that had been delivered to that specific address. A search warrant was therefore needed to process the scene.

The scene was processed and a large, bloody, serrated knife and the suspect's bloody clothing were both found inside a laundry hamper. It was obvious that after the victim was attacked with the knife she'd bled profusely. In the course of fighting with and stabbing Sonya, the suspect's pants, shirt and shoes became covered in blood. Before leaving the apartment, he pulled off his clothes and rinsed himself off in the sink. The water collected from the P-trap under the sink later proved that point. Arick went to a relative's house up on the north side of Houston and confessed his sins. That relation gave Arick a couple of beers and called the police. The defendant was arrested and brought into Homicide, where he gave what has been judged to be one of the most creative and far-fetched confessions of all time. The detective that typed his statement was unable to keep from bursting out laughing while attempting to read the confession into testimony at Arick's trial. The prosecutor ultimately wound up having to read it aloud and into the record. The detective testified that what the prosecutor read aloud was the confession he had taken from the defendant.

Arick was given credit for attempting to explain away his sins and present himself in a better light. His confession, however, could not explain away the two gaping slash wounds on Sonya's neck or the multiple slashes on both of her hands. The injuries on her hands are classified as *defensive wounds* in the language of the medical examiner. The defendant held to his story and had a full-blown trial. On the advice of his attorney, he never took the stand in his defense. Sonya's last common-law husband entered and left the courtroom carrying both a Bible and a string of rosary beads. Arick's mother and a preacher testified as to his good character and reputation in the community. Prior to the trial, the district attorney's office offered the defendant thirty years for a guilty plea. The jury awarded him forty-five years so that he might ponder upon just what it was that he had done.

The following is his confession.

Statement of Person in Custody

State of Texas
County of Harris
July 23, XXXX
Time: 2145 Hrs.

Prior to the making of this statement, I, Arick Jefferson, have been advised by Sgt J. Castro, the person to whom I am making this statement, that:

1. I have the right to remain silent and not make any statement at all.

2. I have the right to have an attorney present either prior to, or during, any questioning. If I cannot afford an attorney, one will be appointed for me.

3. I have the right to terminate this interview at any time.

4. I waive these rights and order that I might make this statement.

I have known SONYA BANKS for a little over a year now, and we lived together about eleven months.

Things have been real strained in our relationship for about the past four or five months. It all began with Sunny wanting to stick her finger up my tail whenever we were having sex. She'd poke me and when I'd jump she'd laugh or smile. Sonya has a cousin named Joy that works for a dentist. She got some white powder from Joy that I think she would sprinkle on me when I was sleeping. It made me sleep real deep. I don't know the brand of the medicine, but part of its name had the word "cain" in it. Some mornings I would wake up and my tail would be throbbing. Sunny would just look at me and smile if I complained about my bung hole hurting.

One morning I woke up and found a magic marker stuck up my butt. Another morning I had some milky fluid seeping out of my rear end. I went to a doctor and told him that I thought I had hemorrhoids, and he gave me some medicine for it. I think her goal was to make a punk out of me.

This morning we argued about money and I left out of the apartment. I returned about three this afternoon and she started in on me again. I told her I'd had enough of her shit and was leaving this time for good.

The next thing I knew she'd picked up a big butcher knife and was after me with it. We fought over the knife, and in the struggle we both fell to the floor. She fell onto the knife and it cut her neck real bad. I tried to help her but it was obvious that she was too far gone. I knew that nobody would believe that it was an accident and that I didn't try and hurt her. That's why I changed clothes and left the apartment.

_____
Signature of person making statement

_____
Witness

THANKS FOR THE FELONIES

Austin Bingle and Allan Cryder were riding the 2200 to 0600 shift out of the Central Station on unit 1A23. They had driven a drunk driver home the week before rather than go through all of the paperwork hassle of a D.W.I. charge. The drunken driver turned out to be the manager of a rather exclusive Italian restaurant. They had just gotten back into service from a "gut-pooching contest" at the aforementioned restaurant when a silent burglar alarm dropped at a tool wholesale warehouse located at XXXX Leeland. This call was in a warehouse district just east of downtown. They drove their marked unit the last block without any lights on. Cryder was driving and he checked the front of the building while Bingle checked the back.

As Bingle rounded the corner and approached the back of the building, a twenty-eight-year-old drug and alcohol abuser named Randy Weeks slipped out of a ground floor window and hit the ground running. He was sprinting dead away from Bingle. Weeks had an obvious vested interest in escaping. Bingle knew that neither he nor Cryder stood any chance of catching a burglar wearing felony fliers (tennis shoes). Weeks was rapidly outdistancing him when Bingle pulled out his .44 revolver and cranked off a round into the asphalt (to get Weeks' attention). He knew from past experience that a crook will do one of two things when he hears a gunshot: stop and give up or hit passing gear.

Weeks slammed on the brakes and "assumed the position" (put his hands on a wall) without a word being said. He obviously had been well-schooled by someone else, sometime in his past. The officers waited for the owner to arrive and turned the building over to him. When they got to the Central Station to book their prisoner, Bingle noted blood on his prisoner's right foot and pants leg. Bingle asked of Cryder, "Where the Hell did that blood come from?" Their prisoner answered, "From when you shot me." Weeks had been hit by Bingle's ricocheting bullet. It entered the bottom of his shoe and exited the top of his foot. The crook had to be taken to Ben Taub Hospital by Cryder while Bingle did some creative writing and filed criminal charges.

Charges were filed upon Randy Weeks for Burglary of a Building, and for Aggravated Assault on a Police Officer with a deadly weapon. The charge alleged that Weeks had a cheap revolver in his hand and pointed and fired it at Bingle as he fled. Bingle fired upon him and the rest was history. A throw-down .22-caliber revolver that predated the 1968 Gun Control Registration Act was tagged into evidence. So were four live, and one fired, rounds of .22 short-caliber ammunition. This was alleged to be the weapon pointed at Bingle when he was forced to defend himself. Six weeks after the shooting, Cryder and Bingle were subpoenaed to district court in this matter. After sitting around for a couple of hours, they were released, after being told that the suspect had opted to plead guilty to a ten-year sentence.

Both officers were relieved and went into the back offices of the court to get their court pay vouchers signed. The defendant in the case was seated in the hallway and was handcuffed to a bench. He was waiting to be taken before the judge to enter his plea. As they walked past Weeks, Bingle spoke to him, asking how his wound was healing up. Both officers were shocked when Weeks answered, "I really want to thank you guys for what you did for me." Neither officer understood his statement, and they asked him what he meant by that. He answered that he'd been in and out of county jails and prisons all of his adult life. He'd always been a nobody and had generally been either ignored or kicked around by the other inmates. Randy reported that ever since he'd been filed on for

Aggravated Assault on a Police Officer his peers now treated him with a lot more respect. He had moved up several rungs on the jail house social ladder, and he owed it all to them. In the jailhouse or prison community, he was now a "somebody" for the first time in his life and he owed it all to them.

ONLY IN EAST TEXAS
OR
CORN PONE JUSTICE

Bobby Joe "Rooster" Smith of Huntsville, Texas was a beetle-browed, caveman-looking individual. He came equipped with both a surly disposition and the intellect of a retarded rock. Juanita Hodges, his girlfriend of only a few weeks, decided she wanted out of their less-than-satisfying relationship. Unfortunately for her, Bobby Joe did not take rejection very well. After seething for twenty-four hours, he abducted her from her trailer house, located just outside of town in an unincorporated portion of Walker County, Texas. Prior to his arrest, Bobby Joe confided in a friend that he had "given the bitch a good thrashing."

What Loverboy hadn't bragged about was her murder. He had driven her to a site along State Highway 19 in adjoining Trinity County. There, he was seen by passersby to beat his victim in the head with a shovel. Still seemingly displeased with Juanita, he continued to show his displeasure by driving his pickup truck back and forth across her unconscious body. Apparently the gentleman was not yet satisfied with his work product. He further proceeded to throw Juanita (along with his multi-purpose shovel) into the bed of his pickup. Then he drove to yet a third location, a family deer lease in nearby Madison County. Once there, he dumped what was left of his former lady-love into a low place near the camp house and set her on fire. Now, apparently satisfied with the job he had done, he chose to cover the cadaver with dirt.

In Texas, jurisdiction for the prosecution of a criminal act is determined by the location where a crime was committed. The criminal episode in question spanned three counties. All three of the jurisdictions shared an ability to prosecute. Generally, as it was in this case, prosecution takes place where the body is found or recovered. The prosecutor chosen to represent the state was a veteran with over twenty years of trial experience. His name was Edmund J. Hurst and he came from Walker County, where this case had begun as a kidnapping. He was also the most experienced prosecutor in the area.

There are two phases to a criminal trial. The first concerns itself with only determining either guilt or innocence. The second is the punishment phase and it begins upon an affirmative finding of guilt by either a judge or jury. Bobby Joe had an ego even larger than the size of his bib overalls (pronounced "overhalls" in East Texas). Halfway through the jury selection process, Bobby Joe asked to be able to fire his court-appointed attorney. He further petitioned the court for the right to represent himself. The judge reluctantly allowed his request but kept the appointed counsel at the defense table to advise the defendant upon points of law and procedures.

The case was presented by the state to a homegrown, East Texas jury. In small town Texas, logic generally dictates "If he got indicted, then he's got to be guilty." Keep in mind that in this part of the world, table fare is often referred to as "vittles" and a "thirty-weight soot gravy" generally accompanies each and every meal. Though the defendant was from an adjoining county, Bobby Joe's reputation for being Walker County *white trash* had drifted over into Madison County prior to trial time. The witnesses told what they had both seen and heard. The scene photographs depicting all of the involved locations were admitted into evidence. A state-appointed psychologist testified that Bobby Joe knew right from wrong and was not retarded. The shovel recovered from the bed of Bobby Joe's pickup was admitted and the DNA blood evidence collected from it was linked to the murder victim. The trial itself was only window dressing. The defendant did not help his cause by trying to intimidate and bully witnesses during the course of the whole trial. The jury had been adequately alienated and its members were simply biding their time.

The most memorable part of this trial was the closing arguments. Bobby Joe was so full of himself that he even had a tape recorder running so he could revel in his brilliance at some later date. The man representing the State of Texas closed with the following statement:

Ladies and gentlemen of the jury, I want to thank you for taking the time to see that justice is served here today. You have heard the witnesses and you've seen all the evidence. The photos you have been given attest to what truly a horrible crime has been committed. The defendant has been linked to this crime by both witness identification and by irrefutable blood evidence found in his truck after the murder. Bobby Joe Smith told people what he was going to do and he did it. Now he needs to be held accountable for what he has done. It's time for y'all to step up to the plate and do the right thing. I'm gonna ask you to go in that room (pointing to the jury assembly room) and convict this man. It's the only thing you can do. You can't just let this man go free after he drug that poor girl's body around like a dead armadillo on a string. I know the quality of folks y'all are. I just want to thank you for your time and being here to do your civic duty.

The jury filed out of the courtroom after being given their instructions by the presiding judge. They marched back into the courtroom a scant fifteen minutes later. They had picked their foreman and found the defendant guilty. Three of them had even taken the time to use the facilities. Edmund Hurst knew more than just a little about theatrics. He would often tell a young and budding prosecutor "Kid, you've always got to play to your crowd."

Justice was served in this case, in as much as Bobby Joe never got to live out his sentence at the tax payer's expense. He died in prison from a case of mistaken identity. He thought the little guy he had just begun slapping around was somebody who didn't have a shank (a homemade prison knife). Edmund Hurst went on to become a state district court judge. He became somewhat of a local celebrity and acquired a taste for far better whiskey than he previously could possibly have ever afforded.

NOTHING BUT THE TRUTH

There is an old adage in police work that goes "Tell them the truth and scare them to death." This generally refers to actions taken by a subordinate when he answers questions put to him by a supervisor. The following are two such situations.

A statement was made to a grand jury reviewing a police-officer-involved fatal shooting. A uniformed officer on a family disturbance call had been forced to shoot and kill a mentally disturbed man. The mental case had been cradling his infant nephew in one arm and held an upraised knife in his other hand. The young officer in question was trying to talk the whacko into putting both the knife and kid down. Without warning, Crazy stabbed the child in the face. The cop was standing a mere eight to ten feet away when the stabbing took place. The officer shot the suspect eleven times with a 9mm pistol. There were the typical allegations of excessive force made by *poverty pimp politicians* like, "Why didn't he just shoot him in the shoulder?" Fortunately, the knife stuck in the kid's jawbone, and he survived with little more than a scar and a story to tell. The grand jury foreman asked the young officer why he shot the dearly departed so many times.

The officer's response, in a slow drawl, was "Well, you see the man had a knife in his hand, held in an ice pick-like manner. When he attacked the child I had a clear shot and I took it. He never turned loose of the knife until he hit the ground. It's like this, every time I shot the man he jerked and moved, and every time he moved I shot him." The grand jury was at first startled by the frankness of his response. Ultimately, they wrote the officer a letter of commendation and all the members of the jury signed it.

Robert (Bobby) Falco was another officer who adhered to the aforementioned logic. He was a field training officer, meaning he trained rookie police officers. His task was to teach them the practical application of what they had been taught in the police academy. He took pride in his job and didn't care much for lazy or incompetent people.

Falco was assigned a black female rookie named Brenda Starky. Brenda had two years of college and spoke and wrote her reports in Black English. It was Bobby's opinion that his job did not include teaching speech and grammar. He figured that by now she was probably too old to housebreak anyway. He therefore opted to try and teach her the basics of the job and to show her what needed to appear in her offense reports. She was aggressive on crime and thought that the word *mother* was only a prefix. Falco looked upon this rookie just like he did the rest of the world. Everything was placed on this earth for his entertainment. They got along well enough and laughed and cut up through the portion of the training program they were assigned to ride together.

Falco used the "tell them the truth" mode regarding a police car involved auto accident. His female rookie and he had been driving through a residential area when she began talking about another female officer they had just seen earlier at the city jail. The women had gone through the academy together and her friend was now dating yet another rookie policeman.

Their conversation went as follows:

Brenda: "I don't know what she see in him. I don't like nuttin' 'bout him. Besides, he stink."

Falco: "He stinks?"

Brenda: "Yeah, he smell just like old pee."

Falco: "Nasty old ammonia piss?"

Brenda: "You know him?"

Bobby Falco was laughing so hard that his eyes blurred and he hit a parked car. The District Sergeant and an Accident Unit were called out to the wreck site. Falco knew that he was going to be found to be dead wrong by the Accident Review Board, no matter what. Rather than make up some story, he told them the truth. After the Sergeant regained his composure, he responded "That's all well and good Bob, but now we have to figure out what the hell we're gonna put down on paper."

THE GULLAH

The Gullah Motel (pronounced Gulla) sat in the 4200 block of Lyons Avenue in a less-than-scenic part of northeast Houston. Again, you would be hard-pressed to find a more picturesque part of northeast Houston. This establishment was far more than just a two-story hot-sheet joint or rolling cathouse. The Gullah was a drug-infested Septic Tank where an unbelievable amount of narcotics-related activity took place. Dope deals from one-gram bags to kilo transactions happened there all the time. The term Septic Tank is used by street cops to describe such a place because "turds float into and out of there all day and night." The amount of drugs that were either sold or used at that location was almost beyond one's comprehension.

An insight into the quantities of drugs consumed there might best be gained from taking note of the huge number of used syringes that littered the area. The alleyway behind the motel was literally paved with used syringes, in some places up a quarter of an inch in depth. Similarly, when you walked on the asphalt parking lots on either side of the building, at least every other step crunched from the crushing of some junkie's used rig.

The manager of this fine establishment was a chubby, middle-aged Asian that the street cops nicknamed Whoa Fat. He was so called after the Asian crime boss on the television series Hawaii 5-O. Whoa Fat was a shrewd and enterprising businessman who is thought to be responsible for far more deaths than any known American serial killer in history. He began his hotel enterprise by renting rooms either by the hour, day, or week. He then began picking up extra pocket money by selling cigarettes, either by the pack or one at a time. His next high-profit item was small pieces of brass screen to put in the bowl of the glass crack pipes known as *straight shooters*. Whoa Fat's best profit-per-item for several years, however, came from his syringe sales. The dirty little secret that his syringe-buying customers did not know was that he sold used syringes.

Daily, this cottage industry capitalist would walk the complex, picking up the best-looking syringes and syringe caps off of the ground. He would then take them to the bathroom in his office. There, the syringes were taken apart, rinsed with tap water and then reassembled. The rigs were then sold out of a wicker basket from the front registration desk. The AIDS virus is capable of remaining live and viable for seventy-two hours outside of the human body. Whoa Fat's recycling program very likely killed or contributed to disease-related deaths of untold persons for over a five-year period.

The motel was a constant source of problems for the police and area residents. Trash came from all over southeast Texas and Louisiana to do business at the Gullah. Police cars were in and out of the area all day long with shootings, overdoses and the everyday problems that occur when large numbers of dopers congregate. Ambulance crews would not come onto the property after dark without a police escort. Unfortunately, you could round up fifty drug dealers from the neighborhood, and their positions were filled almost before the booking process was completed.

The Gullah remained in operation for many years until it was seized and demolished by a federal drug task force following scores of criminal indictments. It took the federal government's resources, with the wiretap laws and conspiracy statutes, to bring the operation down. The United States Conspiracy to Commit statute was instituted under the administration of the great civil libertarian Abraham Lincoln. This law does away with many of your constitutionally-guaranteed civil rights. If you are in the same state at the time of an alleged offense (and not in jail or an intensive care ward) you are almost assured to be convicted. The statute in question is a wonderful tool for law enforcement, unless you happen to be the focus of their investigation.

ON TOP OF OLD SMOKEY

Illegal gambling operations, because of the very nature of their business, have two potential threats: cops or robbers. Robbery suspects like to hijack high-rolling dice or gambling operations. Every year in Houston, and on many occasions, people are shot and sometimes killed during robberies of illegal gambling houses. Cash is what the robbers are after. Their victims very often fail to report the crime, because they were involved in an illegal activity at the time of the offense. For this reason, the game operators will often post a lookout to call in if they spot police or possible "jackers" headed toward the game.

Lookouts don't tend to be persons of the highest caliber, but if they can be relied upon to stand beside a pay phone and dial a number, they're hired. The lookout is supplied with a roll of quarters, and somebody checks on him every thirty to forty minutes to give him a break or get him a beer. Gaming operations are set up in locations where there is parking for clients and away from prying eyes. The players are generally known to one another, and a new player can gain entry if accompanied by somebody who is already known to "The House." The gambling house makes its money by the cutting of each pot to the tune of ten percent. The potential for making money by running such a place is great, if you are willing to risk a felony arrest or being shot by some junky stickup man looking for his next fix.

One of the oldest high-stakes dice games in Houston is run at the warehouse of Bell's Tree Service on Houston's north side. Bell's warehouse is located on a dead-end street. There is a phone booth at a gas station one block north of the shop that has a commanding view of the whole area. This is the site where Bill Bell had placed a "spotter" for many years. From this vantage point, the lookout could call the warehouse's back phone line and the game could be shut down before cops or potential "jackers" can even pull up in front of the building. The regular Friday and Saturday night lookout used to be a smart-mouthed old character called Smoky. He truly delighted in mocking the cops if they pulled up, because he had already called the gamers. Smoky was jailed occasionally for something minor like littering or public intoxication, but that was about as close to Bell's operation as the cops got. The gamblers, at the end of the night, would get together and bail Smoky out. Then they'd all then go off and have breakfast. Going to jail occasionally is just "da cost of doin' bidness" in many chosen vocations and lifestyles.

A veteran Vice cop named "Little Frank" Wilson was infuriated to no end by the way Bell ran his operation, seemingly with impunity. He didn't have any use for Bill Bell or his arrogant flunky. Little Frank studied the setup and noted that the phone booth was directly across the street from a 24-hour pharmacy. The pharmacy counter was at the rear of the store and was raised about two to three feet above the floor. From where the pharmacist stood, you could look out the front windows and see the phone booth in question—about 100 feet away and across the street. A plan came to Little Frank one Saturday night as he lay in bed next to his fat wife. He got up and drove past the intersection and noted Smoky sitting on a barstool he'd set right beside the pay phone. Little Frank drove two blocks down the street and used the phone at a convenience store to call the pharmacy.

"Prescription desk, may I help you?"

"Yeah, is that you standing up at the counter in the back of the store?"

"Why yes it is."

"Good, now listen up good, Motherf**ker and nobody has to get hurt. Look out the front window of the store from where you're standing.

That's me across the street in the black leather coat and hat. I came into your store earlier today and put a bomb in there. You've got five minutes to put all the money in a sack and have someone bring it over here to me and I'll let you live. Now get the lead out of your ass."

The pharmacist called 911 instead. In short order, a couple of squad cars slid up to the phone booth and Smoky greeted them with a caustic "What the hell do you bitches want tonight?" He was astounded when they pulled guns on him, ordered him to the ground, and then kicked his butt. Smoky was still in the county jail the following Friday night.

Another low-life gentleman, who went by the street name of "Frog", was hired to replace the incarcerated Smoky. The new lookout made it into his second weekend before he was alleged to have called the pharmacy across the street and to tell the manager, "Looky here, Motherf**ker, do as you're told and nobody gets hurt." Frog (proclaiming his innocence all the way) hit the Iron House for *robbery by threat*, just like his predecessor. Since then, Bill Bell hasn't been able to get anyone to work as his lookout. The police have even busted his game a couple of times.

Crime continues to pay pretty well, but these days it's increasingly hard to get good help.

THE REAL LAW

Southwest Patrol Channel Dispatcher, 1735 Hours:

Fifteen Edward Thirty, *meet the Brazoria County Unit to serve a felony warrant. That unit will meet you in the convenience store parking lot at the intersection of Almeda and Reed Road. Brazoria County advises their unit will be in a white unmarked car. Advise as to the exact location of the warrant's execution before running it.*

When Officers Langford and Crawford pulled into the parking lot, a huge Texas Ranger named Jack Smith stepped out of a white Ford, and just kept unfolding out of it. He stood at least six feet four inches tall before he was topped off with a white cowboy hat and was shod in western boots. His Ranger's badge was pinned above the left breast pocket of his western-style dress shirt. Also gracing his left side was a nickel-plated, heavily-engraved .44 magnum Smith & Wesson revolver, carried in a hand-tooled leather cross-draw holster. Smith advised the two uniformed officers that he had felony theft arrest warrants for a father and his two sons that lived on a nearby street. The Houston unit advised their dispatcher of the location as they pulled up in front of it (in case the suspects were monitoring the police radios channels).

The house at XXXX Almeda School Road was a small brick building with burglar bars on all of its windows and doors. Crawford went to the back of the house while Langford and the Ranger went to the front door. Their knocks were answered by a portly and rather hostile woman named Velveeta Nixon. She claimed neither of her sons, nor her husband, were at home. She also defiantly refused to unlock the burglar bar door. Her mind changed rather rapidly when Ranger Smith made the following statement in a rather businesslike manner.

"Woman, I am executing a felony warrant upon this address today, whether you like it or not. If I am required to force entry into this residence, I can promise you that no one will be able to live here for at least three days."

The lady of the house unlocked the burglar bar door and allowed the lawmen into the house without further protests. The three suspects were found hiding in a back room. The wanted subjects named in the warrants were arrested without incident and were transported to the Brazoria County jail.

THE SANCTIFIED MAN

There exists in the very low income black neighborhoods a certain class of charlatan that will call himself "The Sanctified Man." These gentlemen are combination con-man and evangelists who travel around speaking to the multitudes. They preach "The Word" and are said to be exceedingly good at passing the plate. The manner by which they put the touch on the flocks for their supposed worldwide ministries is said to truly be an art form unto itself.

These scholars attempt to pass themselves off as being Jesus Christ, having returned to earth. They are the second coming. I have personally met two of these gentlemen in the past thirty-two years. Both men had feet of clay, or had just stepped in something far worse. According to departmental records there are several of these vermin out there, spreading the word and attempting to fleece people. The following is an attempt to document the two occasions that I have encountered this sub-species of rodent.

The first Sanctified Man I encountered was in northeast Houston. He was trying to give "religion by injection" to a female member of his flock when her husband came home. The husband, in his confession, admitted he'd earlier told the sanctified brother-man to stay away from his beloved wife. The con-man/preacher-man chose to ignore the warning of premature earthly departure and continued to see the lady. The enraged husband came home early from work and caught the two lovers in the act. Both the wife and her lover were shot with an inexpensive .22-caliber revolver.

The responding ambulance crew pronounced the female shooting victim dead at the scene. When I walked up to the house, the Sanctified Man was being wheeled out of the house on a gurney. The man of the house was handcuffed and standing placidly in the front yard beside a uniformed police officer. As the Sanctified Man was being loaded into the meat wagon (ambulance) he called out to the forlorn husband, "You see, I told you I'm the Sanctified Man. I'm Jesus Christ and I can't be killed." One of the paramedics was obviously not impressed by the dialog. He turned to his partner and flatly stated, "Well he may not have killed the jackass, but he sure as hell made him holier than thou."

An interesting aside in this case was that the husband thought he was justified in this shooting. His intent was to kill his wife's suitor, not his spouse. He did not know that the Texas Penal Code (no pun intended) had been amended two years earlier and the Paramour Law had been removed. That law made it a justifiable homicide to kill a man that you caught in the act of having carnal knowledge with your wife. The shooter claimed he was attempting to kill the Sanctified Man and that his wife's killing was an unfortunate accident. He was subsequently charged with, and later convicted of, murder. Another apparent oddity in dealing with these charlatans is that it appears to be a big deal in the lower quarters for a woman to get bred by these rodents. There is truly no accounting for taste.

The second of these scholars that I met was under arrest for driving while intoxicated. He was handcuffed and placed in the back seat of a patrol car. We were headed downtown to take a Breathalyzer test when he began his sales pitch, trying to get out of going to jail. I lied to him by saying that I did not understand his statements about being the Sanctified Man, or why I should turn him "aloose." When asked just what the Sanctified Man was, he responded that he was Jesus Christ—just having returned to earth. To which both of his captors responded in unison "Yeah, sure." The Sanctified Man replied, "You give me fifteen minutes alone with your wife, and she'll tell you I'm Jesus Christ." The officer in the front passenger's seat was a newlywed and took immediate offense to this statement and yelled out, "Look out for the dog."

According to the prisoner injury report, a very large dog ran across the Southwest Freeway in front of the patrol car. The driver was forced to slam on the brakes to avoid hitting the loose animal. The prisoner sustained minor cuts and abrasions to his nose and lips when his face hit the wire mesh screen that separated the officers and prisoners. The Sanctified Man got to see the city jail that night and drunken driving charges were filed against him. It is unknown just what, if anything, he had to say when he appeared before Pontius Pilate the next morning in the county courthouse.

SO MANY WOMEN, TOO LITTLE CASH

Any unit clear and close to make a Shooting-Ambulance call in 17 Adam 20's beat—XXXX Jack Street in front of the Normandy Apartments.

Officers Anderson and Baker were a few blocks away from the shooting scene when the general broadcast came across the Central Patrol channel. They pulled up to see the ambulance crew from Station 79 loading a shooting victim named Billy Tyrone Knox. The man on the gurney had a single gunshot wound to the inside of his upper left thigh, not far from his manhood.

Billy was alert, readily identified himself and gave his home address and phone number. When asked what happened, the supposed victim became both vague and evasive. Baker took notes as Knox shifted into what Anderson so eloquently described as "the lying piece of shit mode."

"I was just standing in the parking lot minding my own bidness when a dude I ain't never seen befo' just walked up and shot me, fo' no reason." Further, he was unable to give any sort of accurate description of his alleged assailant. The ambulance crew directed the blue suits to the exact spot that they'd picked up the obviously truth-challenged shooting victim. The officers picked up a blood trail in front of Apartment 3 and followed it to its source—the front door of Apartment 17 in the same complex.

A matronly woman wearing a housecoat, identifying herself as Doris Bernhardt, answered their knock at the door. She greeted the cops with "Come on in, Officers. I've been expecting you." Ms. Bernhardt admitted shooting "Billy T" but claimed she did so only after he had threatened her and attempted to hit her with a hammer. She said that Knox was married and that she was his "part-time lover." He came over to her home that evening demanding to borrow money because he had lost his paycheck in a dice game. When he was met with refusal, he exploded and chased her around her apartment while threatening her with a hammer. Doris said that as she ran through her bedroom she snatched up her .22 revolver from her bedside table. Her intent was to shoot him in the cajones "to put an end to all this craziness." She missed, though, and hit him in the upper leg. The cops recorded her side of the event and then collected her pistol and the hammer that lover-boy left behind on the floor. Their next stop was Ben Taub Hospital emergency room.

Billy denied ever brandishing a hammer or even threatening "Lovie." He explained that his injury was his own fault—for having so many women in his life.

"You see Officer, I gots me a livin' woman (wife), a lovin' woman (Doris) and a girlfriend. I lost my paycheck in a game earlier dis evening so I went and tried to borrow me some money offa Lovie. My ol' lady is flying in tomorrow evening from California and I wanted to take her out to dinner. I still had me some open time dis evening, so I wanted to take my girlfriend out somewheres. Doris and me, we argued—an' dat's how I got hurt."

The officers took down the information, tagged the evidence they'd collected in the property room and completed their report. Anderson lamented that he really wished Doris's aim had been a little more true. Baker responded with, "There might yet be some justice in this case. There's always hope that Ben Taub Hospital may kill this silly bastard for us with a secondary infection. Him and his honey-dipped dick! Then the world would truly be a better place." Anderson laughed and replied, "Yeah but if he does die, one of the goofy bitches in his life will probably want to have his pecker bronzed and use it for a door stop—or maybe even as a gear shift knob."

THEOLOGY OF THE TRIGGER
OR
JUST SOME KILLER QUOTES

This is a collection of quotes from a group of modern-day killers of men. None of them was just a one-time killer. Some enjoyed what they did and liked the reputation that went with it. Others of them appeared to just like living on an adrenaline high.

"Just take that extra half-second to pick up on your front sight. At the very least, learn to just look over the top of your weapon. At the distances we're talking about, that's all you're gonna need. Put your front sight in the middle of his torso, and don't stop shooting 'til he's down and is no longer a threat."

"When you do your target practice, work on your concentration. Think the words *front-sight-squeeze*; *front-sight-squeeze*; *front-sight-squeeze*. After you shoot your weapon dry, always reload. Never let your weapon stay empty, or even part-way empty. Reload before you re-holster your weapon. When you're under pressure you will always revert back to your training."

"The only reason to shoot a handgun with one hand is if the other one is broken or is otherwise occupied."

"It's the damnedest thing when you're involved in a shooting—it's like you're detached from your senses. The world is now about three feet wide. You see the muzzle flash, but the blast from your pistol is distant and muffled. Afterwards your ears don't even ring. Fire the same weapon at the pistol range without earplugs or muffs and your ears will ring for two days."

"The worst part about shooting some idiot is having to go before a grand jury. You go before this panel of citizens. You put your left hand on a Bible and raise your right hand. Next you have to read this statement out loud. Therein you acknowledge that you understand that if you lie under oath that you will go to prison forever and have a three-hundred-pound muscle-bound roommate that wants to be your proctologist."

"You can't miss your way out of trouble. Speed is fine—but accuracy is final."

"Carry only the best quality ammunition and be sure to carry enough gun. Don't carry too much gun. You've got to be able to recover from the recoil for rapid follow-up shots. Bullet placement is more important than bullet diameter. A good 9mm, .40-aliber or .357 that you can shoot very well is better than a .45 or .44 magnum that you can't."

"Combat hip shooting should be left to Matt Dillon and Roy Rogers. The only exception is if you are holding a suspect at an arm's length—then you're not likely to miss him completely. The same goes for the shotgun. Don't use pistol grips on a scattergun. They only look cool. Put the butt stock on your shoulder and your face solidly against the gun. Some people think you can't miss with a shotgun—they're wrong."

"If you want to see what it's like to be in a shooting situation—first sprint for one hundred yards. Then show the world just how fast and accurately you can engage your targets."

"Homicide and Internal Affairs will want to walk through or reconstruct your shooting scene with you. Hell, it will be a day or two before some of the things that happened will come back to you. Give them the basics of what happened, but don't get long-winded. A lot of what occurred there you never saw or heard. Don't be afraid to say, "I was really scared and just knew I was gonna die," or "I'm just not sure of everything that was going on in all of the excitement."

"Street animals are dangerous and can take one hell of a lot of killing.

Just 'cuz he's shot doesn't mean he's no longer dangerous. He doesn't think like Middle America. It probably won't be the first time he's had to fight for his life. Don't sell him short and don't let your guard down."

"We don't use force equal to what we come up against. What's more, we don't fight fair. If he acts like he wants to use his fist—you use your stick. If he has a knife and is within twenty-one feet of you—you use your gun—he can close that distance in a hurry." (Spoken by an officer who had been badly cut up by a suspect.)

"Only carry factory ammunition. If you're involved in a shooting with handloads, then some ambulance-chasing lawyer will have a field day with you. 'Oh I see, you couldn't find deadly enough ammunition, so you had to go out and make your own!'"

"Anything worth shooting once is worth shooting twice. If you're justified in firing your weapon one time, you'll be justified in firing it a second time. Ammo is cheap, but police funerals are not."

WAYLON

Waylon J. Pilsner
Lawman and Lawyer

When You Just Don't Know
Who The F*ck Else to Call

512-XXX-XXXX

Waylon Pilsner was the son of a wealthy north side Houston scrap iron dealer. His father was a huge country and western music fan who named his only child Waylon Jennings Pilsner. The naming process was contrary to Jewish tradition and both sets of grandparents had been appalled. Young Pilsner graduated near the top of his class from Harvard Law School and took a position with the Cook County (Chicago) Illinois District Attorney's Office. Within two years, Waylon had worked himself into a position as an Organized Crime Special Prosecutor. His sole purpose was to go after "Wise Guys" and career criminals.

Momma and Poppa Pilsner just knew that once their baby boy got his courtroom trail experience, he was sure to become one of America's premier criminal defense attorneys. What his folks didn't realize was just how Waylon felt about prosecution. He had once confided in a friend that "The best I can explain it, for me, sending a crook to prison is a sort of a pseudo-sexual out-of-body religious experience."

After two years of prosecuting heavy hitters and major league crooks in Yankee land, Waylon floored his family with the news that he was becoming a Texas State Trooper. He had been accepted into, and would soon be entering, the Texas Department of Public Safety's State Police Academy. Poppa Pilsner tried to put his son back on track by telling him "Boy, finding a Jew lawyer in a state trooper's uniform is like finding a hope chest in a cat house. It's pretty well unheard of."

Waylon was not to be deterred. Full speed ahead, and damn the torpedoes. Trooper Pilsner patrolled the dusty south Texas highways between Laredo and San Antonio. He had an uncanny knack for discovering huge amounts of both drugs and cash. He knew the law and took his suspects' confessions in either English or Spanish. Waylon had become well-known throughout the state because he was not afraid to share his information with other agencies and narcotics task forces. In three years, he had worked his way into the Criminal Intelligence Division. His first assignment was to the Corpus Christi office. Upon reporting to duty he was handed a box of one thousand official State of Texas business cards with his name upon them. He chose to have the above cards printed and used them almost exclusively. A few of the issued and official business cards he kept on hand for old ladies and weenies.

Jaime (Jimmy) O'Banion was half Mexican and half Irish. He was, however, *all* bad. His reputation bordered on being almost legendary. Though he had several arrests under his belt, he had never been convicted of anything worse than a traffic citation. Jimmy was clean cut in his appearance and was every bit as competent a thug as he was a ruthless one. Large-scale thefts, running drugs and kidnapping were strictly business. He strove always to take only calculated risks and to plan and execute each operation with a military precision. Jim always rejected deals with sketchy information or ones that would require rushing blindly into. He refused to become involved in enterprises without first taking the time to do some research and to study the situation. Drunks or dopers could never be trusted or depended upon. They were, therefore, shunned as partners in any venture. He had learned the value of planning, discipline and organization in the Marine Corps.

Jimmy O'Banion was also a member in good standing in the knife-and-gun club. Violence was no stranger in his life. He had been on both sides of cuttings and shootings. Jimmy was credited with the statement "Violence is like anal sex, it's far better to give than to receive." On those few occasions that Jimmy wound up in a hospital, he would always smile and would tell the nice policeman the same thing: "I have no idea who could do something like this to me, officer. But don't worry about it. I'll take care of it when I get out of here."

The night before Waylon Pilsner's transfer into the Criminal Intelligence Division, Jimmy O'Banion lived through yet another shooting scrape. Jimmy had been dropped off at Corpus Christi's Saint Elizabeth Hospital's emergency room by two unknown men. They were said to have just carried him in and left without saying a word. Waylon had heard a lot about the infamous Jimmy O'Banion, but had never met him. After surgery and a couple of hours for the anesthesia to wear off, Jimmy's doctors reported that he was expected to make a complete recovery. He was now up to being interviewed. As the new boy on the block, Waylon was assigned to interview one of the Texas Gulf Coast's criminal "man among men."

Waylon, at this point in his life, was thirty-seven years old, five feet eight inches tall, hatchet-faced and skinny. He had a hawk bill for a nose and wore wire-rimmed glasses. Couple all these factors with his receding hairline, and Waylon looked like anything but a cop. Knowing Jimmy's reputation, Waylon decided to try and run a scam on him. Before entering the subject's hospital room, our lawman borrowed (stole) a white lab technician's coat and wrapped a stethoscope around his neck. Before walking up to Jimmy's bedside, Waylon turned on the miniature tape recorder that he'd hidden in the side pocket of his borrowed jacket.

"Good morning Jimmy. I'm here to talk with you about your condition."

Jimmy replied, with much bravado, "Don't worry yourself, Doc, I bounce back real quick. I'll be well and out of here in no time."

For effect, Waylon stood there for a full thirty seconds before speaking. "Jimmy I've studied your medical history and in the past you've always been lucky and pulled through. Son, I'm sorry, but this time your injuries are so severe that there is no way you are going to make it. The best we will be able to do for you is to try and make you as comfortable as possible up until the end. Is there anything that you would like to get off your chest before you meet your maker?"

Having been told of his impending death, Jimmy keyed on Waylon as his Father Confessor. He named names, dates and locations. He told who did what to whom and who paid for it to happen. After spilling his guts and detailing his rather colorful criminal career, Jimmy did something he had never done before. He went into shock and died right there in front of Waylon.

Waylon was delighted. A dying declaration is an exception to The Exclusionary Rule of law that excludes hearsay evidence. The tape recording contained all the required details. Jimmy had been told he was going to die and that there was no chance of his recovery. Jimmy had held nothing back and went into great detail regarding a wide variety of horrid deeds. What's more, he had even had the decency to fulfill the most important of the elements of the dying declaration. He'd gone ahead and died.

Ultimately, the tape recordings never made it into evidence in either a state or federal courtroom. Grand juries in neither venue agreed with Waylon's opinion that the declarations alone would convict the named suspects. The tape did, however, give up some fabulous intelligence. Throughout the rest of Waylon's law enforcement career, he was known by his contemporaries as "Doc Pilsner."

WHAT DOES THAT SAY ABOUT ME?

In the course of investigating major crimes, you occasionally run up on suspects that are good functional psychopaths. This adversary is intelligent (either in IQ or street-wise) and very likely knows about both police procedure and how the legal system works. He likely will have had a brush or two with the criminal justice system and will have studied it. If this is the type predator you are dealing with, such as a serial killer or rapist, he may even hang out in police bars to see if he can get insight into your investigations. This variety of criminal likes what he does—and the stimulus that sets off his horrid actions or his drives will not register in a normal thinking person's mind. He keeps information bottled up inside him because he knows nobody will accept or be able to relate to him. Neither will they understand his depraved orientation. He truly would like to have a friend, but he also knows that the exposure of his true inner self would either revolt or scare off even the most callous of individuals.

There are the rare investigators that can talk to, and disarm, these twisted persons, and get them to open up. These are persons that the psycho feels a kinship with. Finally—he has met someone who seems to understand his point of view and with whom he can relate. Such a man was Homicide's Rick Landers, a natural interrogator. He interrogates a suspect by first visiting with him for an extended period.

Then, Detective-Sergeant Landers may order out for a pizza and break bread with the suspect. Only after the minimum of one to two hours visiting about everything but police work, will he consider touching on the suspect's alleged crime. He will only enter into the suspect's criminal acts after he has complemented him. "Jack, you seem to be a decent enough fellow, a guy that got dealt some bad hands. Tell me how you got drawn into this situation." The Sickos feel they've found someone who can finally understand life through their mindset and to whom they can talk. Even after they have fully confessed and are charged with multiple horrible crimes, they often hold no ill will toward Landers, still wanting to communicate with him.

Landers was often able to get full-blown confessions from this type of suspect. One such suspect detailed his love of knives, and how he slashed several people to fulfill a deep-seated need to cut flesh. Another freak, a thirty-five-year-old white male named Preston Houck, detailed that he loved to pound women in the head with a hammer. He'd been arrested while attacking an apartment manager at a complex where he'd once worked. It was determined he quit the job unexpectedly one year before the assault. Houck confided in Landers that he only liked hammers with hickory handles. He admitted that he'd once had an old Stanley brand hammer with a plastic composite shaft break on him during an attack. "I'll never use a Stanley product again. It ruined all my fun that day." This gentleman had been in prison as a young adult and he would discuss his exploits only in generalities. He was a good, intelligent psychopath—a cunning and dangerous combination.

Houck would not identify the cities any of his crimes took place in, or names of his victims. He readily admitted that he always studied his victims for any extended period before ever attacking them. Because Rick Landers spent two hours "just visiting" with Houck, he knew he'd been an apartment maintenance man for several years. Houck also mentioned several cities across the country as they talked. A check with the homicide divisions in those cities found several hammer killings that were uncleared. All the killings occurred in apartment complexes.

Bloody fingerprints linked Preston Houck immediately to two of the killings. Houck was found to have been employed at each of the complexes, but he quit each job six to twelve months before each murder. He was eventually put to death in the state of Louisiana for the murder and rape of an apartment manager in Lake Charles. Before his death sentence was carried out, Houck sent word he wanted to see Landers. A week before he was executed, Houck gave Landers a detailed account of all of his killings throughout the country. He knew that Landers was close to retirement and thought maybe Landers could supplement his old-age pension with a book, or through giving lecture tours. Houck also directed Landers to the locations where he had stored all of the trophies he collected from each of his killing sites. He'd collected something from each victim that he could hold in his hands while he relived their murders at a later time. Houck asked but one thing of the aging detective—that he come to his execution as his personal witness and representative.

Landers once made the following comment regarding his ability to extract confessions from some of the worst of psychopaths, the intelligent ones:

"I quit marrying after the third disaster. I can't find a woman who wants to put up with me for any extended period of time. There again, some very sick people, some with the most evil and twisted minds on earth, relate very well to me. It seems they want to open up and confide in me. Hell, they continue to write me even after I've put 'em on death row. There is something about me that somehow causes some of the worst people on earth to relate to me. I'm really not sure what that says about me as a person."

BILLY

Billy Coleman was a quiet and nondescript man who generally stayed to himself and did not stand out from his coworkers. He was a combat veteran who volunteered for the draft at the age of eighteen and served twelve months of combat duty in the Central Highlands of South Vietnam. He had no problems serving his country when called upon, doing as his father and grandfather both had. He chose to be drafted into the Army for two years of service. This was because enlisting would have required him to do a three- or four-year hitch. Bill simply did not want to spend that much time away from his home and family. Upon being mustered out of the service, he went directly into the Houston Police Academy, never missing a paycheck.

Having a steady job with a solid means of support, he married his high school sweetheart. He was both a religious and family-oriented man, though he also understood that at times the only way to handle some idiots was to knock the sin out of them. Billy's quiet manner was sometimes mistakenly looked upon as a sign of weakness by street animals. Billy became known for a short statement that he made just prior to his shooting of an armed suspect. The man in question was very likely committing Suicide by Cop, or Copicide. Whether it was bravado, or a suicide wish on the suspect's part, the end result was still the same.

Billy and his partner answered a family disturbance call on the shallow north side of Houston in a neighborhood called The Heights. The man of the house, Donnie Blanchard, was reportedly drunk and threatening other family members with a knife. His distraught wife answered the door, letting the officers inside. When the officers located the suspect, he was sitting on a couch in the den, holding a hunting knife in his right hand. Billy walked into the room and calmly spoke to the man. He called the drunk by name and told him for the safety of everybody present that he needed to put the knife down. Donnie's snarling response was, "And what if I don't?" That question drew the very calm and very matter-of-fact reply of, "Well I guess you gotta be doin' something when the good Lord calls you."

Donnie showed his bravado by standing up with the knife still in his hand. He sat back down with two Remington 125-grain jacketed hollow point bullets in his sternum. You could have covered both of the entry wounds with your fist.

That night, Billy made good on the first rule of police work—make sure that you go home at the end of your shift. He went home that night, hugged his wife, looked in on his sleeping child, and went to sleep. The grand jury foreman asked Billy Coleman if there was any other action he could have taken that day. He replied, "No, I regret I that I had to kill the man, and Donnie and I will ultimately be judged someday for our actions.

And thus they shall come to judge the quick and the dead.

STATION GUNS

The Houston Police Department has never issued guns to its line officers. Their officers are required to purchase the weapons and ammunition that they carry both on- and off-duty. Up until the year 2000, Houston's cops could carry any type of handgun they desired as a duty weapon, as long as it was a minimum of .38 or 9mm caliber. Anything in a larger caliber was fine. The weapons are now standardized between one of four brands of .40-caliber duty weapons that new officers are required to carry. As before, all cadets in the academy are still required to buy their own weapons. The older officers' weapons were grandfathered in. The police range has to maintain a multitude of different calibers of bullets for the duty weapons used at qualification time. Similarly, officers that wish to carry a shotgun or carbine must supply their own weapon from a list of brands and models specifically approved by the agency.

Up until approximately twenty years ago, there was no record as to what type of firearm (handgun or long gun) that any officer carried as a duty weapon. He supplied his weapon, his own holster and equipment. The attitude that existed then was, "my weapon, my equipment, my business." The department claims the reason they don't issue duty weapons is because officers will take better care of something that they are required to purchase themselves. This is but another example of what is lovingly called "Departmental Bovine Fecal Matter" (or something similar) by the troops.

Prior to the registering of duty weapons with the department, there existed a group of weapons that were known as station guns. These were sawed-off shotguns with pistol grips that sported barrels that were usually in the neighborhood of ten to fourteen inches long. Many were chrome- or nickel-plated, and some even had gold-plated hammers and triggers. Most of these weapons were double-barreled guns and many were so old they had the rabbit-ear style hammers. They were evil looking weapons that caused many a crook to mark his laundry when it was shoved in his face. They were strictly "up close and personal" weapons that one old-timer described as "being ideal for shooting in closets and elevators." These weapons were illegal to own if they were not licensed through the Bureau of Alcohol, Tobacco and Firearms, which none of them ever were. The weapons in question could never be sold outside of the police department. If you got rid of one, you needed to sell it to someone inside the station house, hence the term "Station Guns" was coined.

HOMICIDE NOMENCLATURE

A Homicide scene's initial investigative status is often designated by the victim's actions or scene conditions determined from an on-scene uniformed officer's overview. These are passed along to the next up investigators when they call in for the assignment. Then the terms are written on the blackboard just inside the Homicide Division's front doors. The blackboard is used so the different shifts will know what's going on. This way, the deskman also doesn't have to tell twenty-five different people what kind of a scene is working from the previous night.

The following acronyms are often used:

1. NDY = Not Dead Yet
2. DRT = Dead Right There, sometimes pronounced "Dead Rat There"
3. GFH = Got Feelings Hurt

The investigators will call in after being paged by either the deskman or duty lieutenant. They will be told, "You've got a double shooting in the parking lot at XXXX Clarewood. There's one DRT and one NDY that's able to talk. The NDY is headed to LBJ Hospital by Ambulance. A Crime Scene Unit is headed your way from downtown and I'll notify the Medical Examiner's Office." The blackboard will read with the date, time, location, incident number and investigators. Also present will be a short statement of facts like: *Poss. Gang Driveby-1 DRT, 2 NDY.*

More Unofficial Titles for Homicide Scene Types:

These investigative classifications are used in conversations between investigators to classify the case by means of the victim's attributes, orientation or lifestyle.

Urban Renewal. Took some neighborhood trash off the street, thus removing a canker sore from the butt of society.

Predator Control. When an armed robber, burglar or rapist is killed.

Birth Control. When the dearly departed should have been drowned at birth.

D.S.A.F. Killings. Stands for "Did Society a Favor", saves the taxpayer's money. The world is now a better place.

OSHA Killing. Drug dealer or user is killed. In that vocation, getting killed is simply an occupational safety hazard.

N.H.I. No Human Involvement, meaning all concerned parties (suspect and victim) were lower forms of life. The Los Angeles Police Department once routinely rubber-stamped some murder case file folders NHI where it was applicable. It was sort of a "Who cares?" kind of classification.

Trash Killing. Self-explanatory.

Misdemeanor murder. Same as number 7.

Fagicide. Murder of a homosexual.

Copicide or Suicide by Cop. Getting a cop to kill you; more common that most people think.

IN REMEMBRANCE

Donna Wilson's life came to an end inside a crack house in Houston's Third Ward, after a .22-caliber bullet coursed through her drug-numbed brain. It was never actually determined if her wound was self-inflicted, or if some other drug addict murdered her. The bullet wound was what medical examiners call either *close contact* or *loose contact* in nature. The entry was to her right temple area. The bullet passed through her brain and embedded itself into the far side of her skull. Nobody encountered at the scene or during any of the follow-up investigations would admit to having been in the house at the time of the shooting. Neither would admit to seeing Donna being carried out of the place. Her still-flouncing remains were unceremoniously dumped on the ground beside a vacant house two doors down from the dope house. Determination that she was still alive when deposited in the dirt was made from the scrape marks she left on the ground. These scrapes were left from where she lay kicking and thrashing as she bled out her life's blood.

Technology is a wonderful thing—when it works *for* you. When it doesn't, you are left holding the dirty end of the stick. Unfortunately, atomic-absorption tests don't work on .22-caliber firearms. That caliber just doesn't leave behind the needed trace elements (lead or primer compound) on someone's hands to determine if they fired a weapon. Therefore, the testing of her Donna's hands to see if she'd fired a weapon came back inconclusive. It was easy enough to determine where the shooting had taken place, however. You needed only to follow the trail—sort of like in the Hansel and Gretel story. However, in this case, it was blood left behind, not breadcrumbs. She'd been shot while in the bathroom of an upstairs duplex apartment. She was standing upright (determined from height of the blood spray found on the bathroom wall) when the injury occurred. The victim was then carried headfirst down the stairs by some unknown crack house dirtbags. Spurting arterial blood spray continued along the stairwell wall and down to the street.

The dead woman went unidentified for about thirty minutes following the arrival of the first police cars. Then several family members showed up in a caravan of vehicles. They advised the scene detectives that the dearly departed was a crack-addict prostitute who came from a suicide-prone family. Two of her siblings had killed themselves following bouts with drug use and depression. The victim's boyfriend, Nelson Ricketts, was pointed out from among the crowd of onlookers. He was interviewed and arrested on an outstanding theft warrant. A search of the ex-convict boyfriend subsequent to his arrest produced a quantity of jewelry identified as belonging to the dead woman. Nelson claimed his late girlfriend had, earlier in the day, given it to him to hold for safety's sake. There was no blood noted on the jewelry, but the pieces could easily have been rinsed off.

This sort of predatory behavior is very typical in the world of dopers. The drug users on the street are the two-legged jackals and hyenas of the human race. They will prey on the weak among the decent people. When one of their own overdoses or is killed, the scavengers pick their body clean of any valuables. They will go as far as to steal the false teeth out of a cadaver's mouth, just to see if there are any gold teeth that can be sold for scrap at the local pawn shop.

What was left of this victim's personal effects were turned over to one of her sisters, a woman called Big Tammy. This sibling rummaged through the purse she had just been given and pulled out a large jar of Vaseline brand petroleum jelly. She held it up to about eye level, and looked at the officer she was speaking with. Big Tammy then proudly proclaimed, "I'm gonna keep this in remembrance of my sister Donna—until I use it all up."

SWEET WALLY BROWN

Wallace Duane Brown was the product of a northeast Houston septic tank of a neighborhood called Settegast Place. The locals who either choose to live, or are forced to live, in this urban dump call their neighborhood "City Gas." Wally was a ruthless pimp by vocation and was both clean-cut and flashy in his appearance. Mrs. Brown's son prospered at his trade, and was known on both sides of the law as "Sweet Wally Brown."

This man bought and sold women and young girls of all colors and nationalities. Wally's stable was full of racehorses—or as he described them—"they's all U.S. Grade A Prime Ho's-ain't no poke (pork) chops to be found here." Cash was king. If you had a desire for something on or off the menu, all things were possible and available for a price. Like many gentlemen of his caliber, Wally felt the need to be known by a trademark. This he attempted to accomplish by dropping fifty thousand dollars into the restoring and customizing of a 1976 Cadillac Eldorado Brougham. To him, the car became the symbol of both his manhood and power—with its gold-plated Rolls Royce grill and its elephant skin-covered roof. Whenever he drove his "Rado" to a nightclub, Wally would have one or two of his thugs safeguard it in the parking lot. It was both for security and status that he did so.

Twenty-three-year-old Jack Payton and forty-year-old W.W. (Wee

Willie) Brown rode the power shift (seven p.m. to three a.m.) out of the Northeast Station. Payton and Brown worked well together, and appeared to be complete opposites in every way possible. Payton was a five foot nine Anglo, and slim in build. Brown was ebony black, stood six foot three, and weighed in excess of three hundred pounds. Payton was a tough little snuff-dipping east Texas cracker that had barely gotten out of high school. Brown was college-educated and had been an English teacher before coming onto the police department. Brown left the public school teaching trade in utter disgust. He felt most of his wards had been beyond housebreaking, much less teaching anything to. When he walked away from his teaching job, Brown felt he'd been freed from bondage— and his mother cried.

Brown regularly jailed "bottom feeders" (lower forms of life) that he'd met during the few years he taught in the public school system. In one Internal Affairs complain, he was alleged to have punched out a gang leader after blurting out, "Lester, I whipped your scrawny little ass when you were in the eighth grade and I'm gonna do it again." Brown was outgoing and talkative, while Payton was quiet and hard-eyed. The other black officers out at the Northeast Station claimed that Brown was afraid of only one thing on the face of this earth: his wife Velma. "When she says 'frog', he jumps."

Both of these officers knew Sweet Wally by both his face and bad reputation. They had written up several reports alleging wrongdoing on his part. They had never, however, been able to hang anything more on him than a traffic ticket. One Saturday night about midnight, Payton and Brown spotted Sweet Wally's beloved "Rado" parked in the middle of an otherwise empty grocery store parking lot. They found its infamous owner passed out behind the steering wheel. Brown had Payton help him slide the unconscious pimp into the front passenger's seat. Brown then told Payton, "Just follow me, kid." Payton jumped into their patrol car and did as his three hundred-pound mentor had told him. Brown put the Cadillac in low gear and drove outbound on the Eastex Freeway at speeds up to seventy miles per hour. They exited at Duezen Park, on the western shore of Lake Houston. Wee Willie cruised the park's heavily-wooded side roads with the car's transmission howling until he found just the right spot. At an approximate speed of twenty-five miles per hour, Brown drove the Cadillac between two large pine trees that were about twelve inches narrower than the width of the car. Sweet Wally ricocheted off the dashboard and came to rest on the car's passenger side floorboards, still unconscious.

Brown left the engine running and crawled out of the open driver's window. After exiting the car, the oversized cop walked to the front of car and fired two rounds into the radiator with the .25-caliber Colt automatic that he carried in his left front pants pocket. This insured for Brown that the Caddy's engine would soon burn out. Brown then piled into the passenger seat of the waiting patrol car. The two men returned to duty, with no more said about what just happened.

Just another uneventful day at the office.

BITCH SLAPPERS AND SPOILED CHILDREN

This section deals with the two most common types of male idiots you encounter so regularly in police work. They are the street animal and the abusive spouse or boyfriend. Their typologies frequently overlap and the chief characteristic they share is that they are both self-centered children. These gentlemen have but two words in their vocabulary: "I" and "me". There is only one constant in his life, no matter what his age, skin color or socio-economic status. The Spoiled Problem Child Adult Male is typically taken care of by women. These women tend to be the Mommas, wives, girlfriends or aunts of this man. He will run the streets siring untold numbers of bastard children, in between his robbing, raping and stealing forays. However, you can rest assured that when he gets into trouble or is in need of anything, he will run to a woman for help. You must always keep in mind just who this guy really is. He is Peter Pan, the little boy who never grew up.

The mothers of these men are not battered or threatened nearly as often as the other women in their lives. The significant others in his life, though, can be put in a category designated as "The Most Likely to be Abused." The ladies being abused by these scholars, unfortunately, repeatedly keep taking them back for more. The women who claim him as "my baby's daddy" seem to be the ones who catch the most abuse from these bottom-feeders. The girlfriends and former girlfriends (sans love children) run them a close second. When one of these Stud Ducks wants anything, from money to attention, he is liable to get hostile and mete out abuse toward his current or former beloved. The dominance he is asserting by his use of physical abuse is often followed by the taking of, or damaging of, the woman's property. The taking of car keys or the actual cars is a popular bullying tactic. The flattening of tires and breaking of car and/or house windows seems to be another favorite pastime of this class of Cretin.

In the light of day, putting up with this type of behavior seems unthinkable for any thinking person to tolerate. The sad thing, however, is that for many women, being abused is better than being alone. "Yeah, he slaps me and the kids around, but it's me that he always comes home to. Besides, sometimes he can really be such a sweet and loving guy."

A sub-group of women that stay with these losers are sometimes dubbed "The Savers." They are out to save the misguided soul from himself, or to fix him. They look upon these vermin as birds with broken wings in need of being healed. The homosexual community reports that there is a group of women who are out to save homosexual men from their chosen lifestyle. They call these ladies "The Fag Hags." It is the heartfelt belief of these ladies (the saver types) that the right woman can turn a pile of dung into Prince Charming. Nowhere in the fairy tales, however, did it say that Prince Charming was a junkie and a Bitch Slapper before Snow White straightened him out with love, understanding and affection.

Probably the most common misconception about abused females is that they actively seek out a man of this variety. The other is that she is from a lower income group and is of limited intelligence and education. In fact, the opposite may well be true. He is a predator who actively seeks out a woman who will put up with his abusive ways. She likely will have been raised being abused by a parent, or seeing her mother physically abused by her father or stepfather. In the courtship process between the Predator and Prey (abuser and abused) he will punch or slap her during the course of an argument. His first blows will not usually be to her face, but will most likely be directed to a shoulder. His next move is to attempt to woo her back. He will be the most charming son-of-a-bitch in the world. Once he has her back with him, she's hooked like a fish on a string. From here on, the assaults will become more frequent and the severity of the injuries inflicted will increase.

The good citizens of Houston, Harris County, Texas have long held that if a woman kills her wife-beating husband or abusive boyfriend it is a justifiable act. If he is shot or stabbed while he is in the very act of beating the tar out of her, nobody really cares. This program covers the good citizenry whether he is beating her or upon her children. All that must be claimed by the killer is that she was in fear of death or serious bodily injury from the late Bitch Slapper. However, a grand jury must, by law, review the event. If the facts support her account of what happened, she will be No-Billed, meaning that the killing will be ruled to have been justifiable in nature and she will not be prosecuted.

Crystal Huggins killed her third wife-beating, common-law husband in 1998. At the time of his demise she still had her jaw wired together from a beating that occurred just three weeks before. Prior to being monogrammed with a butcher knife, cadaver number three had beaten her unconscious for coming home drunk from her sister's house. When Crystal awoke on the kitchen floor, she began looking for her three kids. She determined that they were not in the house. On her way out of the back door she picked up a butcher knife. Her soon-to-be late common-law, Beau Goody, saw her as she exited the house and began to throw bricks at her. She fled around the corner of the house in an attempt to avoid him. He ran around the other side of the house and cut her off. The last mistake he made this life was when he caught up with his beloved in the front yard.

The investigation ran its course and the case was sent to the grand jury section of the district attorney's office without charges being filed. When the stabber's statement was taken in Homicide it was noted that she had twice before killed abusive husbands. Beau Goody reportedly knew that she had killed two previous husbands, and he still chose to be abusive. It was the concerted opinion of all of the involved investigators that the dearly departed should have been prosecuted posthumously for Felonious Stupidity.

BUT HER NOSE STILL HURT

Mary Ellen Corder, age 48, lived at XXXX Live Oak with her boyfriend of six months. His actual name was Ernest Cardiac Johnson. His birth took place in Houston's Jefferson Davis Hospital, one of the charity hospitals in the city. A kindly intern helped Ernest's single mother with the naming process. Names such as Placenta, Lavoris, and Labido often come about following the assistance of a nurse or intern with a sense of humor. The local police and fire department called Jefferson Davis Hospital's maternity wing "The Hatchery" because it was the site of untold numbers of welfare births. Though Mr. Johnson seemed not to be handicapped by his given name, his IQ could best be described as being below bath water temperature. In West Texas, they would say "The man is as dumb as dog dirt."

On or about the first day of spring, Ernest awoke to find his dearly beloved lying beside him in bed. She was both cold to the touch, and as stiff as a carp. He called her momma and the preacher. After several choruses of "Oh Lauds" and "Oh Jesuses" someone had the presence of mind to call the police. The first unit on the scene noted Mary Ellen to be a light-complexioned black female with two black eyes and a swollen and somewhat distorted nose. He latched onto Ernest and secured the scene. The next thing he did was to call Homicide.

Sergeants Haskell and Jenkins were assigned by the duty lieutenant to make the scene. The two Detective-Sergeants were olds hands at the game. They were called "Heckle and Jeckle" by their co-workers. This was a Saturday morning case assignment, just south and east of downtown. Their scene was in a low-income area called "The Bottoms" of the Third Ward. The officers that work there call the neighborhood "The Turd Ward." Upon arrival it was immediately determined that the dearly departed and her boyfriend were professional alcoholics. Their rented shotgun-shack house was what is commonly referred to in local police circles as a wino nest. Jenkins commented that the house appeared to have been decorated by Ernest and Julio Gallo. A shotgun house is one that "You can shoot a shotgun through the front door of, and out the back door of, without hitting anything in between."

Ernest claimed that his beloved had been punched in the nose the previous morning by her former common-law husband. He was reportedly an ex-con named "Bootsy" Widner. Ernest had not been present at the assault, but had been told about it by the freshly-sainted Mary Ellen. She told him it took place in front of Ivory's Grocery Store at the corner of Live Oak and Calumet. Mary Ellen went there every morning about ten a.m. to get her "wake-up medicine," which consisted of a Goode's Headache Powder and a 40-ounce Schlitz Malt Liquor Bull. Ernest continued by saying that she also complained of getting a bump on the back of her head from the fracas. Reportedly when she got "doe popped," she fell back and hit her head on the curbstone. Ernest went on to say that Mary Ellen had been taking some pain pills due to a large amount of discomfort from her possible broken nose.

Jenkins went to Ivory's, and the assault story was verified, with no evidence indicating foul play on the part of the current boyfriend. Ernest was brought into the Homicide Division for a witness statement. Mary Ellen was shipped off to the County Morgue for an autopsy, a procedure sometimes called "slicing and dicing."

In matters of this sort, an autopsy will tells it all, and will further indicate if a full-blown investigation is actually needed. Haskell took the statement from the last shack job of Saint Mary Ellen. He had typed enough of them to know he could get away with some creative writing in this case. It turns out, Mr. Ernest had left his glasses at home during all the excitement, so Haskell's main objective now was to see if Jenkins could keep a straight face when he read the affidavit back to Ernest (since he couldn't see to read it himself) prior to his signing it before a notary public.

The medical examiner's office determined that Saint Mary Ellen passed on due to the combination of alcohol and painkillers. The death was ultimately ruled an accidental overdose.

Please read the two-page affidavit that follows for a better appreciation of the lighter side of death scene investigation.

The State of Texas

County of Harris
Incident No. XXXXXXX
Date: July 24, 2001

Before me, the undersigned authority, on July 24, 2001, at 12:30 p.m., personally appeared ERNEST CARDIAC JOHNSON. Upon his oath he deposes and states:

My name is ERNEST CARDIAC JOHNSON. I am 49 years old, and I live at XXX Live Oak. My phone number is 713-XXX-XXXX. I am unemployed. My driver's license number is XXXXXXXX. My social security number is XXX-XX-XXXX. I was born 06-17-52.

I have known MARY ELLEN CORDER from the neighborhood for many years. We have only been close (boyfriend and girlfriend) since the first of this year. That was when we moved in together. Our relationship was based on the church, the Bible and sex.

Mary Ellen liked her malt liquor a lot. The bull was a major league part of her life. Yesterday morning she left the house, as she always did, about ten o'clock. She would go up to Ivory's Store and get her a 40-oz. bull and either a Goode's or B.C. headache powder. When she got back yesterday her eyes were all swoll up and her nose looked like it had been busted. She said her ex-old man "Bootsy" had punched her in the face. She also said that when he hit her, she fell and hit the back of her head on the curbstone, causing her to see all kinds of stars and checkers.

I put ice on her face and Mary started taking some pain pills she

got from a friend named "Little Eva". Yesterday evening she got to drinking a bunch of them bulls and taking the pills for pain. She got to feeling better and we went to bed. Before going to sleep we had sex. Her sex was okay, but her nose still hurt.

This morning I woke up and found Mary Ellen dead beside me. The police came out and asked me to come to the police station for this statement about what took place in the 24-hour period before she died.

I left my eyeglasses at home, so Sergeant Jenkins has read this statement aloud to me, prior to my signing it.

_____

Ernest Cardiac Johnson

Sworn to before me, the undersigned notary public, this 24th day of July, 2001.

_____

Notary Public in and for the State of Texas

SPIC AND SPANN

Johnny Ray Spann and Aurturo Vasquez rode the late night shift in the less-than-genteel southeast quadrant of Houston. Neither man had anything to prove, to themselves or to each other. They came to work for a paycheck and to have a good time. Both men were somewhat jaded toward the world and agreed that idiots were placed upon this earth for them to laugh at. John and Arthur were said to be like nuns; they were always together and never alone. They were openly called "Spic and Spann" by their coworkers and supervisors alike.

Spic and Spann were not out to save the world, or to set it on fire either. Arthur was a first-generation American, whose parents had been illegal aliens before the amnesty programs came along. Johnny Ray had been raised near the Port of Houston and he well understood the ways of the knife-and-gun club. Both men served in the Army prior to joining the police department. They answered their radio calls, ran their calls, and took care of what they ran up on. They did not, however, hunt trouble. Their bi-line was "We're only out for justice, that's pronounced just us."

If you wanted to fight or resist arrest, so be it. If there was a chance one of them was going to get hurt, you were going to get shot. Both men had studied the deadly force statutes of the State of Texas, and neither needed legal counsel to write a statement following an officer-involved shooting. Both had been there, done that, and been cleared by a grand jury to prove it. More than one dirt-bag got the opportunity to blow hot air out of an extra hole following a confrontation with these two.

Burglar alarm calls are so common in police work that cops often complain they feel like unpaid employees of alarm companies. What's more, officers run so many alarm calls that they never expect them to be any good. An alarm that Arthur and Johnny Ray had run a hundred times was at Ed's Machine Shop on Long Drive. One early morning in the dead of winter, they responded yet another time to Ed's. No forced entry was found, but there was an open vent window a full eight feet off the ground. These windows are used for ventilation, either for heat dissipation or to air out a place when welding or fluxing.

Arthur had to climb on top of the roof of the patrol car in order to look inside of the business. Most likely the window had been left open. Anyway, there was no ladder a crook could have used to get inside the shop. For some reason, Arthur could not let it alone and just clear the call with a "No sign of forced entry." He told Johnny Ray that he was going to climb inside, and after checking the place, he would let himself out through the overhead bay doors that would lock behind him. Spann was to drive around the other side of the building and pick him up. Being as agile as a spider monkey, Arthur lowered himself into the building.

With a flashlight in one hand and a .45 automatic in the other, Arthur began to search the interior of the shop. He found the Coke machine's front door was standing wide open. When Arthur pushed it to a closed position, he discovered nineteen-year-old Melvin Calfee standing behind it, with a crowbar raised up over his head. One blast from his Colt government model, and Melvin crumpled to the floor. Johnny Ray, who was parked outside, heard what sounded like mortar fire coming from the inside of the metal building. He went nuts yelling for Arthur, who was somewhat deafened and shell-shocked from the muzzle blast at close quarters. When he wandered over to the bay doors and opened them, he told Johnny Ray, "I got one." To which Spann replied, "One what?" The answer was, "Come on in and see for yourself."

Melvin lay on the floor with blood pooling around his head while the two Blue Suits laughed and carried on. Arthur was telling Johnny Ray how the whole thing went down when Paul Johnson (their back up unit) walked in. Paul walked around the shop and saw a pair of tennis shoe toes poking out from behind a shower curtain near the bathroom area. Johnson called out "Hey, I think I've found another crook. What'cha want me to do with him?" Arthur thought Paul was kidding about there being a second suspect, so he called back to him "Kill him, we don't want any live witnesses."

At the time of his arrest, Thadius Jefferson (the second burglar) had been so frightened that he urinated upon himself. With the second burglar sacked up, all parties concerned were shocked when the dead man on the floor began to moan and move around. He was handcuffed, and an ambulance called. When he was examined by the paramedics it was determined that the only injury suffered by Melvin Calfee was a split chin. When Arthur fired upon the skinny burglar, his bullet only went through the cloth of his oversized baseball jersey. The *fright factor* caused Melvin to pass out, and in doing so, he busted his chin on the concrete floor. At the end of the shift, Johnny Ray tried to console his partner. "Hell Arthur, don't worry about missing a burglar at point-blank range. People will forget about it in twenty or thirty years."

FROM WHENCE I CAME

My family has told me that I needed to put something in this book about who and what I am. That way, you might know what manner of social outcast or misfit I truly am. My paternal ancestors came to Texas when it was still part of Mexico's northern frontier. They swore allegiance to the Mexican government and lied when they claimed to be Catholics. They were granted a large land holding along the banks of the Brazos River.

The reason Mexico let the Anglos settle on their northern range was that they hoped the "Norte Americanos" would act as a buffer against the Comanche Indians. These Indians have been described as being the world's best-ever light cavalry. The High Plains raiding parties attacked yearly, from August through September, terrorizing the whole northern half of the land of Mañana. If you will notice, in this time of year there are very bright and full moons. The Indians chose this as their raiding time so they could travel both day and night. They stole horses along the way to use as both transportation and food as they swept through the area. The Mexicans call the bright full moons "The Comanche Moon." The Indians called it the "Mexican Moon." The Mexicans hoped that the Indians would steal all they needed from the Gringos and not bother to continue down south on their forays. They hoped this would keep the raiders north of the Rio Grande.

My tribe first fought the Comanches, and later moved on to fight the Mexican army and helped to make Texas into an independent nation. One ancestor was captured and taken as a prisoner of war at Goliad, then murdered at La Bahia. Another led an operation to save the Anglo women and children from the advancing Mexican army. That operation came to became known in Texas history as The Runaway Scrape. It has been said we were short on flight and long on fight.

The members of my tribe still tend to have rough ways, and often speak their minds before thinking. Firearms training is taught early in life in our clan. When I married my wife, I told her that the very least she would get out of our relationship was an appreciation of fine firearms. She accepted my hedonistic ways and has given me a fine son to pass this mindset on to. She further has taken to some of the rough-and-tumble members of the tribe, particularly a couple of aging scoundrels.

A family tradition that spans four generations (as far as I can document) is worth sharing. I can trace it back as far as my grandfather. He fled to Houston, a fugitive from justice, a little before World War One. His was a wanted man because he shot and wounded a city marshal in the town of Hempstead, Texas. The shooting took place outside a saloon in a part of that town that was then called Six Shooter Junction. Though he prospered in Houston, my grandfather never returned to the Austin and Waller County area. The man worked hard, drank hard, always packed a pistol, and was no part of a social animal.

When forced to go to church socials and funerals he very often took a hypodermic syringe with him. This he hid off in a sports coat pocket. During and after these affairs, the men would generally stand around under trees at the edges of these events. There, the men would smoke and visit. There were always dogs running loose, for in those days there were no leash laws. Granddad would step off into the privy and fill his syringe with his own urine. He would then carry it in the right outside pocket of his sports coat. He would walk along with his hand inside his pocket holding onto the syringe. When he came upon a deserving party, the hypodermic needle was poked through the cloth of his jacket pocket. He would then lightly spray urine on the pants legs or hem lines of his victims. The people he did this to were members of one of two groups. The first he dubbed either "Brother or Sister Better-than-You." These were folks he described as wearing their religion on their sleeve. The second group consisted of loud-mouthed blowhards who were always trying to impress someone with just how important they really were. The loose dogs walking through the crowds would sniff the "mobile scent posts" (pants legs) and then stop to add their own liquid messages. Granddad particularly delighted at seeing pious or holier-than-thou people lose religion in front of preachers and their womenfolk as they yelled, cursed, and kicked at dogs. Such are my roots.

ABOUT THE AUTHOR

Sgt. Brian Foster is a retired Houston Police Department homicide detective, and lives in Texas with his wife and dogs. Brian can be reached through his website, **www.homicidalhumor.com**.

FROM THE AUTHOR

There are now seven generations of Fosters that have made their homes in Texas. They first came here when Texas was part of northern Mexico and the Mexicans wanted a group of Anglos to serve as a buffer against raiding Comanches from the high plains. By lying and claiming to be Catholic, the early Fosters were able to secure a land grant in what is now part of Austin and Washington counties, along the Brazos River. My ancestors participated in the revolution of the Texians against the Mexican army, and one family member was captured as a prisoner of war, along with James Walker Fannin, following the Battle of Goliad. That Foster ancestor was murdered by a firing squad at the mission of La Bahia. The murdered man's father, already in his seventies, orchestrated part of the Runaway Scrape (as it came to be known) from Austin

County, directing the escape of woman and children from the advancing Mexican army.

My great-grandfather was asked to resign from the office of sheriff of Austin County after he shot and killed three men in front of the county courthouse for "back-talking" him. His actions were deemed too outlandish for an elected official. He was not, however, indicted for murder because the three men he killed that day were all trash and the world was a better place without them. His son, my grandfather, fled to Houston as a fugitive from justice following a shooting near the Washington and Waller county line. He went on to become a wealthy man, but never returned to Austin County, Texas.

I spent twenty-three of the thirty-four years I worked in law enforcement in the Houston Police Department's Homicide Division. I preferred to work the physical parts of the murder cases I was assigned to, and personally averaged twenty-five to thirty-eight actual murder scenes per year. That does not include the cases I assisted in by taking witness statements, confessions, or in executing warrants.

Those who work in a homicide division are exposed to the most human side of life. We see into the private lives of others and must detach ourselves from any emotional feelings to consider everything as evidence. Internalizing what you see day in and day out can consume you. Even someone's child lying dead in the corner must be viewed as evidence for us to properly do our jobs—and stay sane.

I was taught to try and find something humorous in the scenes I worked. I collected odd statements, confessions, and suicide notes that I ran across during my appointed rounds. Some of these melded with other cases, and blarney has been the basis for some of my stories.

I hope you've enjoyed my stories.

Sgt. Brian Foster

Printed in Great Britain
by Amazon